8/07

⁓

Why is it so hard for me to let go of the past? she wondered. Nick was back and already she couldn't get him out of her head. Since the day he had just shown up at her office, she had been reliving their fun times together in his old dilapidated apartment. Then the awful night that had changed her life forever would sneak into her thoughts, and a sharp pain in her heart would bring her back to reality, but her desire for him would not go away.

Lindy began to focus on her breathing—inhaling and exhaling. She tried hard to relax and keep distractions at bay, but her thoughts of Nick kept intruding. Finally, she felt her body and mind relax. A small red sphere appeared before her eyes. Lindy watched as it grew larger and larger, and then everything went black.

⁓

IT'S NOT OVER YET

J.J. MICHAEL

Genesis Press, Inc.

Indigo Love Stories

An imprint of Genesis Press, Inc.
Publishing Company

Genesis Press, Inc.
P.O. Box 101
Columbus, MS 39703

All characters in this book have no existence outside the imagination of the author and have no relation whatsoever to anyone bearing the same name or names. They are not even distantly inspired by any individual known or unknown to the author and all incidents are pure invention.

ISBN-13: 978-1-58571-245-8
ISBN-10: 1-58571-245-0
Manufactured in the United States of America

First Edition

Visit us at www.genesis-press.com
or call at 1-888-Indigo-1

DEDICATION

To my son
Antoine Michael Jones Aparicio
and
children with disabilities

ACKNOWLEDGMENTS

I give thanks to the Creator, my spiritual guides and my teachers. I would like to acknowledge the powerful feminine energy that is now restoring harmony, balance and love to the universe. Therefore, this book is dedicated to all the women who have traveled the road less traveled with me through the dark nights of my soul as well as through the wonderful, blissful times of my life: my mother, Gloria Jones, grandmothers: Ellen Johnson and Berma Jones; my sister, Charlene Jones; my daughter, Michelle Rai Sweeny (Zeta); and my precious granddaughters, SeDona Chiane Sweeny and Siyah Dior-Ari Sweeny. Also my friends: Catherine Lenix-Hooker, Katherine Wood, Leticia Peoples, Sharyn Leigh, Vernetta Graham, and Brenda V. Johnson. And the new sparks of light in my life: Anita Ballard Jones, Keely Porter, Ruth Owens, Arlene Sandifer, Janis Kearney, Mercedes Eugenia, Catrina Davis, Rachel Ballen, Jeanette Carson, and Narcisa Thomas. Special acknowledgments go to my literary agent, Chamein Canton; and to Carla Dean, Doris funny Innis, Tee C. Royal and the RAWSISTAZ, Shunda Leigh, Genesis-Press and my clients and fans for their continued support.

ACKNOWLEDGMENTS

PROLOGUE

Dr. Lindy Lee inserted her key into the back door lock of the Church of Melchizedek. She didn't want to interact with the long line of people trying to enter. She would have had to push her way through, and she was much too tired for that tonight. It had been a difficult week. Church was always crowded the first Friday of the month because of the healing sessions. One Friday evening, the fire marshals had shown up and had threatened to close the church down for having exceeded the maximum occupancy and for blocking the exits. Deep down, Lindy believed someone had called and reported them. Thankfully, the church had received only a warning citation.

However, this hadn't stopped people from coming. They waited outside of the church in hot, humid weather, as well as in the cold and rain. Sometimes the line started forming as early as Thursday evening. People showed up in wheelchairs, on stretchers, leaning against someone or something, hopping on one leg, or crawling to get inside the church. They came from everywhere; they were of all faiths, genders, races and social classes.

Making her way down the long corridor of the old basement, which reeked of mildew, Lindy thought about how the Friday night healing sessions had attracted a lot of unwanted attention from the media. Although Rev. Betty Goldstein barred cameras and TV crews from the sanctuary the first Friday healing sessions were covered by multiple news outlets—local, national, and international—accounting for a steady stream of reports on the miraculous healings being performed by a mysterious presence called the Elder Healer at a small Georgetown church in the nation's capital.

Lindy climbed the short flight of stairs leading to another hallway. A left turn led to the church offices; a right turn led to the area next to the pulpit. Lindy turned right, opened the door a crack, and peered briefly at the crowd. The ushers had put chairs along the sides of the pews and were now busy making sure the exit doors were not blocked.

Moments later Lindy returned to the basement. She heard the chant *AUM MANI PADME HUM* coming from the room that had been set aside for the Elder Healer. There were only two keys to the room. The Elder Healer had one, and the Awakeners had access to the other. Both Reverend Betty and Lindy had been allowed in the room once. That had been in the beginning, when the Awakeners were setting up the room according to the instructions of the Elder Healer. A four-foot white pedestal with a base trimmed in gold was the only object in the room. In the center of the pedestal was a gold chalice embellished with precious stones forming the letter M on one side and the Sanskrit symbol for OM on the other side. She and Betty had stood mesmerized, unable to take their eyes away from the piece.

Lindy wanted so badly to linger in the basement so she could get a glimpse of the Healer when she came out of the room. But to do so, she would have to violate the Elder Healer's request that no one be allowed in the basement area after a certain time during the Friday night healing sessions.

Not far from where Lindy now stood another pair of eyes was also watching the room. Grace Perry, an ambitious reporter for the *Washington Star*, had waited patiently outside in that nasty alley until Lindy had entered through the back door. A few minutes later, Pops, the janitor, had signaled for her to come in, instructing her to hide behind the stairs. One of its wooden planks had a small crack, through which she would be able to see the Healer when she emerged from the room. Grace made sure her camera was ready as she listened to the chanting coming from the room. She was jolted when Lindy returned from upstairs and tiptoed to the Elder Healer's door, pressing her ear to it. When the chanting stopped, Lindy quickly moved away from the door and ran back up the stairs.

Seconds later, the door opened and a hooded figure exited the room. Grace pushed the shutter button on her camera and everything went white, blinding her. Panicking, she dropped the camera and closed her eyes. When she opened them, the basement looked hazy. Shaken, Grace groped her way around to the front of the steps and sat down. Her vision slowly returned. She could hear the chanting coming from the sanctuary. The healing service had started. Still dazed and too nervous to move, she blinked her eyes rapidly and everything came back into focus as if nothing had happened.

Grace walked slowly back to where she had dropped her camera. She picked it up, and checked for damage. Finding none, she pushed the shutter button once again, and the camera flashed as usual. *What in the hell happened?* she asked herself. *This is 1978, not 1878, when people thought to be witches were burned at the stake.*

Steadying herself, she walked over to the room and tried the doorknob. It was locked. *Secrets. Who was this Elder Healer?* Even though the Elder Healer never spoke to anyone during the healings, because of the high-pitched voice when chanting, everyone referred to her as a woman. A*nd what was she hiding behind the locked door?* Grace swore to herself that she would get inside that room.

This had the smell of a Pulitzer Prize. If she could get this exclusive, she would be on her way to the big time. Who would have thought Grace Perry would have gotten this far in her career—a potential prize-winning reporter for the *Washington Star?* For a few more dollars or a bottle of scotch, Pops would be her eyes and ears in the church.

That's what they get for hiring a drunk! Once a drunk, always a drunk. The goody-two-shoes of life were always trying to help someone, only to get screwed themselves.

Grace smiled, suddenly feeling better.

CHAPTER ONE

Rev. Betty Goldstein couldn't wait to get her hands on the *Washington Star*, which was delivered daily to her home in Georgetown. This particular morning, she took the local news section of the paper and left the remaining sections for her husband, Harvey. The paper tucked under her arm, Reverend Betty walked the several short blocks to the church. She wanted to read it in the privacy of her office just in case she needed to scream or let out some choice words. Being in the church would be a reminder to be respectful and not do anything she would regret later.

Betty, as she preferred to be called, let herself into the church and went straight to her office, not even calling out to let Pops, the janitor, know she had arrived. The aroma of coffee coming from his office and the sound of the radio told her he was somewhere in the building.

Her office was small, but richly decorated. She had come a long way from the big, plush office with its wonderful windows she once had on Connecticut Avenue. Mornings, her office would be bathed in sunlight, and whenever she needed a break, she could look out at the passing people and flow of traffic. Not that she had taken a step down. It was just that her office had only one small window facing north, and she didn't get that brilliant sunlight. She had brought with her the African statues, a marble lamp, and her law books; not that she needed them, but they were reminders from another lifetime.

Betty went to her desk and spread the paper out. Dr. Lindy Lee, her friend and almost daughter, stared back at her. The black and white photo was a good likeness of Lindy. She looked startled, but this did not detract from her beauty. Betty sat down to assess the potential impact of the story, which she already knew wasn't going to be good for her or the church.

She was now the minister of one of D.C.'s largest New Thought and Metaphysical churches. Betty had attended the Unity School in Missouri and had become an ordained Unity minister. After a few years, she realized that although she loved Unity, she felt too restricted by its philosophies. Later, she moved to the I Am Activities, but she still did not find what she was looking for. Finally, the Awakeners resurfaced in her life and directed her to the Order of Melchizedek. She then became an interfaith minister by becoming ordained in the Order of Melchizedek, and with the help of the Awakeners, she founded the Church of Melchizedek.

The church had begun with a handful of members, but now had a large membership. Being nondenominational, its doors were open to all. The congregation was all-inclusive, crossing all racial, gender, class, and sexual orientation lines. The church offered what most traditional churches offered: Sunday services, Sunday school for children, a youth program, and a small choir. Betty was the senior minister and delivered the sermon most Sundays. They often had guest speakers to expose the congregation to diverse philosophical and metaphysical ideas.

The Church of Melchizedek looked and conducted business like any other church except the message given by the minister would be considered highly unorthodox, if not sacrilegious, by the fundamentalists and traditional Christians. They believed they were souls having a human experience and that Jesus, Buddha, Krishna, and Muhammad were all great prophets. The minister talked about adhering to the Hermetic Laws and preached that God didn't need one's money, so there was no need to tithe to the church. One could support the operation of the church based on one's ability to adhere to the Law of Giving and Receiving. Therefore, money was not collected during service at Melchizedek; instead, baskets were placed at the rear of the church. Not a Sunday went by that the baskets were not full by the end of the service.

The Church of Melchizedek had become a force to be reckoned with in the political, social, and economic spheres of D. C. Political leaders made sure during election time to stop there first. The church flourished while other churches in the city struggled to stay afloat. Thus, the church had gained many adversaries over the years.

The healing session on the first Friday night of each month was the most popular church activity. Miracle healings, performed by the Elder Healer, reportedly happened during these sessions. It was said people had been healed of cancers, blindness, physical deformities, mental illnesses, rare diseases, and birth defects.

The Elder Healer would enter the dimly lit church chanting strange words and would go immediately to the pulpit. The scent of lilies would be very strong, and many said they even smelled olives. Most thought the healer looked like a Gregorian monk in her long white robe with a hood that covered her face. As hard as they tried, not one person who had been healed could describe the Elder Healer, and they could remember nothing of the healing. When they pulled themselves together afterwards, they would be so overcome with joy that the physical appearance of the Elder Healer didn't matter.

Betty had been approached many times by the media for permission to interview the mysterious healer, but she had denied all requests. She wouldn't disclose anything about the Elder Healer, except that she received no pay for her services and wished to remain anonymous. Her refusal to permit interviews only heightened the media's interest.

The *Washington Star* reporter, Grace Perry, would not take no for an answer. She was ruthless and was determined to get her story. Betty couldn't go anywhere without her showing up. Finally, against the counsel of the Awakeners, Betty agreed to an interview the day after the last healing session.

The reporter reminded her of someone she couldn't quite place. Perhaps it was Grace Perry's mannerisms. In any event, what Betty saw she didn't like. Besides trying to uncover the identity of the Elder Healer, the reporter kept asking questions about Lindy. *Why was she so interested in Lindy?* Betty wondered.

"Reverend Goldstein, what role does Dr. Lindy Lee play in all this?"

"I don't quite understand your question. Dr. Lee is a member of the church board."

"As a medical doctor, how does she feel about these miracle healings?"

"I suggest you ask her that. But I can say that as a board member, she has voiced her support of the healing sessions."

Ignoring Betty's resistance, Grace continued her line of questioning. "She has a young son who is crippled and mentally slow, right?"

"He has disabilities," Betty snapped. *For this woman to be a reporter, she sure is ignorant, if the language she is using is any indication.*

"People are coming from all over the country to be healed, and yet a board member of the church has not let the Elder Healer perform a miracle for her child. Why not, Reverend Betty?"

The question was loaded. "As I stated before, I am not the one to answer for Dr. Lee," Betty said, making no effort to mask her impatience.

"Can you at least tell the public a little more about the Elder Healer?"

"She is a gifted healer and doesn't accept any monetary funds for her services."

"Is the Elder Healer a physician?"

Betty knew she had to be careful answering such a question.

"She is trained in what she does."

"Can you be a little more specific in giving information about the medical school she attended? After all, she is dealing with the lives of people."

"Ms. Perry, the healing work she does is done out of love. And as you know, her work has been exceptional, if not miraculous."

"Some say it is temporary and that it's just a matter of time before people will find their old aches and pains returning."

"That remains to be seen. Time will tell," Betty said.

"Are you aware of the incident involving Dr. Lee when she was in medical school? It seems as if the Elder Healer is doing the same kind

---

of 'playing doctor' that Dr. Lee allegedly did before getting her medical degree." Grace had returned to questioning her about Lindy.

"I have no idea what you're talking about," Betty responded.

The reporter kept drilling her for information about the Elder Healer and Lindy. The church had weathered many attacks on their religious beliefs, but this one was especially vicious. Grace Perry was going for the kill.

Betty had seen signs of this coming, but Grace threw her for yet another loop when she asked, "Who are the Awakeners?"

How did she know about them? Betty wondered. She had to have talked to someone on the inside. Or had her office been bugged? Betty decided she wouldn't put it past some of their adversaries in D. C. to conspire with the reporter.

The church had its board, but the Awakeners, a group of highly evolved spiritual beings, were her silent partners. Betty had relied on them through the years. Only a few people knew of their existence and their involvement with the church.

Betty became involved with them right out of law school. The Awakeners had found her. She was in the law library studying for the bar when she looked up and saw a pair of intense blue eyes staring at her. Betty smiled at the man, and he motioned for her to follow him. She hesitated, but something in his eyes reassured her that she would be safe.

His name was Mark. She followed him to the library's canteen, where they had coffee, and he proceeded to tell her about her life and the psychic visions she kept secret. Betty couldn't believe what she was hearing. How could he know her deepest thoughts? Mark explained that he was psychic and could read other people's minds. He invited her to a meeting the following Friday evening. She went, but more out of curiosity than anything else. She had always dabbled in parapsychology, but never had anyone to confide in about her intuitive gifts. She had seen a spirit, but at the time she had dismissed it as a hallucination caused by the illegal and prescription drugs she had taken.

The meeting changed her life forever. She had never met such a loving group that was so knowledgeable about the sacred wisdom. She was the only black female, but it didn't matter. The group didn't believe in the separation of the races by color. In one of the first classes she took, she was taught to think in terms of souls rather than races, that souls had no color. They became her spiritual family. She had been raised a Baptist, converted to Islam when she was head over heels in love with Ali, and finally married a Jew. Now twenty years later, a hungry reporter was out to get her, Lindy, the Awakeners, and the Elder Healer.

Without batting an eye, Betty calmly responded, "Awakeners? I don't know who you are talking about." From there, the interview didn't get any better, and Betty was grateful when Grace Perry finally left her office.

When she read the headline over the article, *Are They Devil Worshipers or Healers?*, she wanted to scream. The article totally distorted and defiled the truth of who they were. It left the unmistakable impression that they were a cult, but not just any cult. They were satanic. It had always amazed her how reporters could twist the facts to fit their agendas. She could live with it, though. But she was disturbed by the focus on Lindy and how she was nearly kicked out of medical school for practicing so-called unsafe medical procedures. Further, the article stated that Lindy, a church board member, had not let the Elder Healer heal her son, insinuating that Lindy didn't trust the Elder Healer.

Betty had faced worse when she was a civil rights attorney, but Lindy didn't like any publicity, especially the kind that could be damaging to her medical career. She was on the staff of Howard University Hospital. That painful incident in medical school had made Lindy decide not to acknowledge her healing gifts. Now this report was resurrecting it. And Grace Perry wasn't going away; she promised a series of articles to follow.

Betty went down to Pop's office and poured herself a cup of coffee, which she preferred black. Back in her office, she got a bag of cream puffs from the cabinet and began munching on them.

In hindsight, Betty wished she had listened to the Awakeners. They had advised her against giving the interview, but she had ignored them. She had been doing that a lot lately. She had lied about their existence to Grace Perry because they, like Lindy, did not want any kind of media attention. How could she have been so wrong about everything? Betty had gambled that going public would clear up any misunderstanding about the healing sessions and the church's philosophies.

The sound of Michael's walker brought Betty back to the present. The young boy stood in the doorway, smiling. She was only keeping him for a couple of hours today. His babysitter had dropped him off and would be back to get him later. Betty put the article down as she got up to hug the child. She had one more thing to do before she spent some time with him: she had to call his mother before she heard about the article from someone else. Betty had planned to tell Lindy that she had granted the interview to get Grace Perry off her back. But that was only part of the reason. She had a new adviser, Dr. Stanley Higgs, and she had followed her heart and not her head.

Had he seen the paper yet? Of course not, because he would have called me by now.

At the beginning of their relationship, Stan and Betty talked every day and met as often as they could. They acted as though they would never get another piece in life. Each time was better than the last time; they could not get enough of each other. He was funny and strong, yet gentle, and he loved her as much as she loved him—or at least that's what she thought.

Betty had met Dr. Stanley Higgs a year ago at a Howard University Hospital function. He was with his wife, and she was with her husband. The two couples had sat at the same dinner table, with Dr. Higgs seated next to Betty. They almost immediately become engaged in the hottest topic of discussion in Chocolate City: the political climate in the District and the upcoming mayoral election. He asked her what she thought of the up and coming new candidate, Marion Barry.

"Do you think Barry has a chance to win?"

"He will win," she said without hesitation.

"You must be a Barry supporter. You said that with such assurance."

The Awakeners had told her that Barry was going to win, and their predictions were always right. They also said later in life Barry would experience many challenges in his personal life and political career, but she couldn't tell him how she knew the outcome of the election before it happened.

"You're right about the assurance part. I am looking at his strong backing in many high places. That's always a good barometer. Besides, the city wants a change."

"Like the changing of the guards?" he asked, turning to look into her eyes.

Their eyes locked and beads of sweat appeared on the bridge of Betty's nose and between her breasts. The heat she felt was most intense between her legs. Betty found herself fantasizing that he had knocked everything off the table and was taking her right there.

He touched her arm.

"Are you okay? You look a little dazed. Here, drink some water," he said, handing her the glass.

Betty drank the water slowly, willing the fire in her body to die down. She had no control over these emotional and physical responses, which usually occurred at night. She had gone to see her doctor about them and he had told her something about perimenopause. *Was this a hot flash?* She was only in her forties and too young, she thought, to be having hot flashes. Besides, she had never heard of a hot flash making you want to have sex. Betty chalked it up to just being horny.

Sex with Harvey, her husband, lasted five minutes—if he could get it up. Harvey treated her like a daughter and basically let her do what she wanted to do. He supported her through college and law school, and she had grown into a strong and independent woman. In the early years, their marriage was based on them being a power couple. She was the civil rights attorney and he was a professor at Howard University. It was his dream for them to be movers and shakers in D.C., not hers.

The man with the piercing gaze sitting next to her just made matters worse. He epitomized everything that she now wanted in a husband—a mature, successful black man. Betty finally excused herself and went to the restroom, where she remained until she had regained her composure. On her way back to the table, she took a good look at him. He was as good-looking as Billy Dee Williams, with smooth chocolate-brown skin and salt-and-pepper hair. As folks say, "He had the good stuff." He had thick eyebrows and a small, neatly trimmed mustache. His lips were sensuously full, and Betty noticed he had a little gap between his two upper-front teeth, which she found sexy. When she reached the table, he quickly rose and held her chair for her.

The next day, he was in the congregation, that powerful gaze fixed on her. Hypnotized by his eyes, her only thought was of them getting together. He later told her that he had been seduced by her tantalizing voice.

He invited her to have brunch with him that Sunday afternoon at Hogates on the Waterfront. She agreed, but felt a little leery about the place. After church, D.C. folks went to the Southwest Waterfront for brunch at either the Flagship or Hogates restaurants. She worried they might be seen together, but he acted as if it was the most natural thing for them to do. They stayed there for hours. Then they took a walk along the short pathway that ran along the back of the restaurants. She didn't want it to end, and neither did he.

They agreed to meet for lunch at the Hyatt Hotel near Union Station at the end of the week. He called several times during the week, and each time she promised herself that the next time she spoke to him she would tell him about her misgivings about their relationship. However, as soon as she heard his voice on the other end, the doubts and fears disappeared. It was when she didn't hear from him that she felt lost. *Is this what they call love at first sight?* she wondered.

The day before they were to meet, Betty went shopping at her favorite store, Garfinckel's, for lingerie and perfume. Then she spent the afternoon getting her hair done. After years of wearing an Angela Davis-like afro, she had gotten a perm. Her hair was thick and naturally wavy; the perm had tamed it, making it straight and more manageable. Her straightened hair with its auburn highlights was beautiful, but she missed her 'fro' and vowed she would one day go back to it.

The night before the big date, Betty had a hard time sleeping. She tossed back and forth, her mind going over and over the events of the last week. What was she getting herself into? She couldn't discuss this with the Awakeners, and Lindy, who still held on to her traditional values, was definitely out of the question. Lindy and Paul had a perfect marriage, although he traveled a lot. *It must make homecomings a hell of a time.*

Staring at the TV, but not really watching it, Betty thought of how glad she was that she and her husband had separate bedrooms. They shared a household, but lived separate lives. He still smoked his joints. He wouldn't give up smoking marijuana, claiming it was for medicinal purposes. They had drifted apart, and she barely knew him anymore. The one thing they did share was their love for Michael, their godson. The Professor doted on the boy. There was nothing he wouldn't do for him.

As she was drifting off to sleep, Betty's last thought was of Stan and their rendezvous in room 312 the next day. Thinking about him made her hot all over, and Betty knew what to expect. Once she walked through the hotel door, there would be no turning back—not that she would want to. She would beg him for it if she had to. *Could this be the strong, independent woman others saw?* she thought as her eyes closed and she finally slept.

IT'S NOT OVER YET

The Hyatt Hotel was beautiful, with its glass elevator overlooking an atrium. Standing in the elevator, Betty looked down at the lower level area where a baby grand piano was placed on a pedestal in a pond. Exotic plants surrounded it, and trees were adorned with small white bulbs. When Betty stepped off the elevator, she couldn't believe that she was shaking slightly as she walked the short distance to room 312. Not having had sex with a strong black man for such a long time had reduced her to a trembling child. She promised herself that she would get it together.

He opened the door as soon as she knocked, grinning broadly and dressed casually in a blue polo shirt and dark navy pants; he looked as excited as she was. *What a hunk,* she thought.

Stan stepped aside to let her in, then handed her a red rose and a glass of champagne. A waiter stood near the table, ready to serve them. Stan had taken the liberty to order for both of them. They had lobster and filet mignon, asparagus tips covered with a rich cream sauce, and small red potatoes.

Time passed quickly, and Betty realized she hadn't even noticed when the waiter left. Light and easy jazz played softly in the background. When he asked her to dance, she melted into his arms as he held her tightly around the waist. Betty felt as though she was floating. She had read about romantic encounters, and had seen them in the movies, but never had she experienced anything like this.

His lips gently caressed her neck. When Betty lifted her face, he kissed her three short times their lips barely touching. Wanting more, she pulled his face down to hers. His tongue parted her lips, and she thought she was going to explode. They undressed hurriedly and tumbled onto the bed. She pulled back pausing for a moment and looked at his already protruding manhood before placing both her hands around it. She had not been around anything that big since she was in her twenties. Betty wanted to scream for pure joy. She prayed he knew what to do with all he had been blessed with. Hours later, as she lay in his arms, a smile broke out on her face, remembering how they had kept making love. They couldn't get enough of each other. *It's more than the sex,* she thought. It was as if their souls had become one. She was never going to let him go. Neither was his wife, but she didn't know that at the time.

As their relationship grew, she began to depend more and more on his judgment. He helped her with the operation of the church and with personal matters. The only things she didn't tell him about were the Awakeners and Lindy's abilities. Thinking there's a scientific or logical explanation for everything that happens psychically in the world, he didn't believe in the paranormal. Stan had pushed her to do the interview, thinking she had nothing to hide. He didn't know the whole story. The article could destroy her life with him.

CHAPTER TWO

Dr. Lindy Lee looked at the two distraught people sitting across from her. They were in shock, and had every reason to be. Their only child, who was six years old, had just been diagnosed with a very rare form of cancer. The parents looked at her with pleading eyes. Couldn't she do something to help their son? She already knew there was nothing medically she could do to help; therefore, she was referring the family to Children's Hospital.

She had discussed the child's case with the elder Awakeners, Ruth and Mark. Ruth had told her that the young boy had fulfilled his contract for this go-round in life, and his impending death was part of a divine plan to work with the father from the other side. He would help the father to establish an organization that would raise money for others with this rare disease. Before his birth and that of his father, they had made a pact to pay a karmic debt. Of course, the pact had been forgotten once they entered the physical world. Lindy couldn't tell the parents what the Awakeners had shared with her. All she could do for now was to be there for them.

As Lindy was preparing to see her fourth patient of the day, her assistant told her she had an urgent telephone call. She returned the patient's medical chart to its slot on the door and quickly returned to her office. An urgent call could mean that something had happened to Michael. His school was closed for the day, and the babysitter had dropped him off at the church to spend a few hours with his godmother, Betty. Usually Lindy knew when he didn't feel well, no matter where he was or where she was, because they communicated telepathically. Michael's speech therapist, echoing all the other therapists and doctors they had seen, had told Lindy that Michael would never talk, and that he would never walk or lead a normal life.

He had a severe case of neurofibromatosis, or NF, a genetic disorder marked by the formation of tumors all over the body. The condition affected his motor skills, speech, and cognitive development. To make matters worse, Michael was hydrocephalic. A few days after birth, a ventricular shunt had to be inserted into his head to drain off excess fluid. Lindy hated it when some people referred to Michael and other children with hydrocephalus as water babies, because a buildup of cerebrospinal fluid in their skulls made them have large heads.

The Awakeners had urged Lindy to use her healing abilities to help him, but she had always refused. She would not have been able to live with herself if something had gone wrong. She didn't understand how the psychic healings worked, and she had been conditioned by her medical studies to only trust scientific proof, it was the one conflict she had with the healings performed by the Elder Healer.

Michael had proved his doctors wrong, however. At eleven, he was walking with the aid of a walker. He could even say a few words, but he preferred sign language or telepathy.

When Lindy picked up the phone, her heart was racing.

"Betty, is Michael okay?"

"Yes, he's fine. He just left my office to hang out with Pops. He is helping, or more like getting in the way, as Pops cleans the building. He's enjoying all the attention he is getting from everyone here. I called about something else, though."

"What is it?" Lindy asked with an edge to her voice. She did not like to keep her patients waiting.

"The article came out today, and it's not good."

"I didn't think it would be."

"Grace Perry targeted that incident with your professor in medical school. I don't know what repercussions this might have for you at the hospital."

"We will talk about this later. Give Michael a kiss," Lindy said, cutting her off.

Only one person could be behind this vicious attack, Lindy thought while placing the phone on its base, *my mother Margaret. This is her doing. She just won't give up. Why after all these years does she still have it in for me? She has done well in life.*

Margaret had married Rev. Alan Pierce, her grandfather's assistant minister, who was now the senior minister of Mt. Olive Baptist Church, one of the biggest black churches in the city. Lindy was sure her mother was still running the church. When her grandfather had taken ill, Lindy had tried to make amends, but they had rebuffed her. They hadn't attended her graduation from medical school, marriage to Paul, or adoption party for Michael. They had returned all her invitations.

After she had seen her last morning patient, Lindy went to the gift shop and bought the paper. She hated reading it because it was filled with what was not right in the world. It reinforced the negative aspects of life and kept human consciousness focused on a broken world. She only read it if she had no other choice, this being one of those times.

The article was as bad as Betty had described it. Grace Perry, or someone, had it in for the church, the Elder Healer, and her. Again she reflected on her mother's hostility toward her. Perhaps her mother was in cahoots with the reporter.

After returning to her office, Lindy tried calling Betty back to apologize for being so short with her, but her private line was busy. She owed everything to Betty, who had saved her life after what Nick, her college boyfriend, had done to her.

Lindy pulled out the Howard magazine from her desk drawer and looked at the cover picture of Nick Lewis staring back at her. She opened the magazine and read that he was returning to D.C. from Paris, where he had lived for the last eleven years. His famous exhibit, "The Children of Africa," was to be at the National Museum of African Art, and was scheduled to go on tour to fifteen

U.S. cities before returning to Europe. The exhibit consisted of photographic images of the lives of children of all ages from different African tribes. The museum and Howard University were jointly planning an opening-night reception for the exhibit and to honor Nick, who had become a celebrated fashion photographer, from what she read. His work had appeared in top magazines such as *Vogue, Life, Mademoiselle, Ebony, Time,* and *Sports Illustrated.* He seemed to be doing extraordinarily well, but Lindy wondered why he had changed from painting to photography.

Closing the magazine, she stared at the picture again. He looked so good. His hair was cut close to his head, and he had a beard and mustache that made him look older. She felt that old pain in her heart. As much as she tried to forget, forgive, and move on with her life, the longing for him never ceased. She loved Paul, but she still desired Nick, even though he had hurt her badly. She had not seen Nick since she walked away from him eleven years ago.

Nick had deceived her. He had promised to take her to Paris with him. The night before they were to leave, she had finally broken away from her family and the church and had gone to find Nick. Instead, she had found a strange girl bleeding badly in Nick's bed; she was aborting his baby. Without hesitation, Lindy had put her hands on the girl's stomach, and the bleeding had stopped by the time the paramedics arrived.

She had used the healing gift taught to her by her spiritual guide, Mary Magdalene. Tears sprang to Lindy's eyes when she thought of Mary. *Was Mary a figment of my imagination?* Mary had taught her how to heal, as well as telling her about Jesus and revealing her own relationship with Him. Sometimes Lindy could smell the lilies she associated with Mary's presence. After her grandfather banned her from the church, Lindy had gone looking for Mary at the Meridian Hill Park. She had sat on the bench until dusk waiting for her to show, but Mary never came. Eleven years later, she was still waiting. *Was she really crazy, as her grandfather and mother believed her to be?*

Right after that terrible incident with Nick, Betty and the Awakeners had helped her to leave the city for a retreat in West Virginia. They also helped her to pay medical-school tuition. When she started working at Howard University Hospital, she tried to repay them, but they refused to take any money from her.

Lindy realized she hadn't done too badly in life. She and Paul weren't rich, but they lived comfortably in a nicely renovated house on Capitol Hill. Paul was an assistant to Swami Pranayama, a famous guru in India, and traveled with him all over the world. His job required him to live most of his time in India, but he would return home every couple of months for six weeks or longer. He had been gone for nearly six months this time, the longest he had been away from them. Lindy missed him terribly, and so did Michael.

Lindy thought of Paul as more than her husband; he was her best friend. He had always been there when she needed him. They had met when she had just finished undergraduate school at Howard and he was on his way to India. They had been initiated into the Awakeners at the same time. Paul worked for a short time as a clerk in Betty's law office, and it was she who had brought them to the group.

The three of them had spent many nights going over the information Mary had given her about their past lives together. They had planned to write a book based on these revelations, but Lindy's medical-school studies had put everything on hold. Then Betty went off to seminary and Paul to India. The unfinished book was somewhere among the many books in the library of their home; lately, Lindy had been thinking about it. If she could only carve out some time to do some of the things she dreamed about, but it seemed almost impossible as the medical practice and Michael consumed her every waking moment.

Michael needed constant care and assistance. Even though her little guy had come a long way, he still had a way to go to catch up to the children in his age group.

Lindy looked at the photographs of Michael displayed prominently on her desk. Although his forehead protruded, he was still cute. His deep coffee-brown skin was flawless, and he had big beautiful light-brown eyes that stood out against his complexion. He had been abandoned at birth, so his parents were unknown.

Michael was placed at D.C. General Hospital with the other throwaways, as they were called. They were children no one wanted. The nurses called him the miracle baby because the doctors had given him only a few weeks or months to live, but he had held on against all odds. Because of the NF and the lack of love and nurturing, his growth had been slow.

Lindy was doing her internship when one of the doctors asked some of the interns to accompany her to D.C. General Hospital to care for children with disabilities. Lindy volunteered to go without hesitation, as she intended to eventually include disabled children as part of her practice. She was shocked by the conditions in which the children were living. The place was clean and the doctors and nurses were doing their best, but they lacked sufficient services such as speech, occupational, and physical therapy. Some were sent out for these services, but the majority of the children stayed in their cribs if they couldn't walk. She found Michael in his crib. One of the nurses had named him Joe.

He was under a blanket, and Lindy had almost missed him. She heard a sound, and when she turned she looked down into big brown eyes that captured her heart instantly. Lindy picked him up, unable to believe how small he was. He couldn't walk or talk. She tried to put him back down so she could read his chart, but he clung to her as if his life depended on it. One of the nurses had to help her get him back into the crib. He started crying.

"Don't worry about him, Doc. They all act like that. Just get on with your work and ignore the crying," the nurse on duty said.

"I just want to read his chart first," Lindy responded, still looking at the child.

He finally settled down after she pulled up a chair and consoled him by letting him hold her finger through the bars of the crib. When she read his medical history, Lindy was shocked to learn he was five years old. He was so tiny.

Weeks passed, and Lindy still couldn't shake the memory of the child. He stayed on her mind until finally she went back to D.C. General. She was tempted to do what she had promised herself she wouldn't do again after one of her professors at the hospital threatened to expel her from the internship program because she had practiced what he called 'voodoo medicine' on a patient.

Lindy remembered the incident as if it had happened yesterday. They were doing patient rounds with the chief resident, who related the medical history of a patient diagnosed with an inoperable brain tumor. She was a young woman pregnant with her first child. The mother-to-be was in a coma. They planned to take the baby by way of a C-section later that evening, and chances were the mother would not survive.

Lindy stared at the women and heard her say, "Help me."

No one seemed to hear what she had heard.

As the group was leaving the room, Lindy looked back at the woman, who briefly opened her eyes and again mouthed, "Help me." It was then that Lindy smelled lilies.

After the rounds were finished, Lindy returned to the young woman's room, making sure no one was in there with her. She lay there peacefully with her eyes closed. Lindy waited for her to open her eyes and say something again. She watched her for several minutes, but nothing happened. If she was going to do something, she had to do it now, since they would be coming to prep her soon. Lindy placed one hand under the woman's head and the other over her forehead, then began repeating the words Mary had taught her years before when she had healed her grandfather after a heart attack: *AUM MANI PADME HUM.* As she chanted, she did not hear someone enter the room. Standing behind her were her professor, Dr. Anthony Bryant, and a nurse.

"What in the hell do you think you are doing?" he shouted, moving quickly to the bed. "Take your hands off of her!"

Startled, Lindy quickly removed her hands.

"I was checking her for any bleeding," she lied. "I thought I saw something red on the pillow."

"You're lying. What are you doing in here, anyway?" he demanded, and then he heard the woman moaning.

When Dr. Bryant started examining the patient, she opened her eyes and stared up at them. Shocked, Dr. Bryant looked at her and then at Lindy.

"What did you do to her?" he asked Lindy, ignoring the mother.

"I didn't do anything," she again lied.

"Get Dr. Greer in here!" he ordered the nurse. Turning to Lindy, he said, "If anything happens to her, I am going to hold you responsible."

Difficult times followed for Lindy. Dr. Bryant rode her relentlessly, doing everything in his power to discredit her and to make it difficult for her to complete her medical training. She was a woman in a man's field. Dr. Bryant wrote a report recommending that Lindy be dismissed from the internship program for using unsafe medical procedures, but he could not explain what they were in his report. Because both the mother and baby were fine, his accusations didn't hold up. But Lindy had promised herself to never use the healing energy again. So she had decided to just give Michael tender loving care instead. Lindy would hold him and whisper in his ear, "I love you, Michael."

She had changed his name from Joe to Michael. Eventually, he began to eat and thus thrive. She wanted to adopt him, but she was single and it was very hard for someone single to adopt children. One day, Paul went with her to meet what he called his competition and fell instantly in love with Michael. Doing what they thought was best for the child, they got married. A year later, they were a family. People would stare at them not only because of Michael's disability, but also because she and Paul looked like two white or mixed-race people with a black child.

They were a happy family. Only one thing was missing—sex. Their marriage was never consummated. Paul agreed to marry her, but only if she took a vow of celibacy. He told her he was on a path of spiritual enlightenment that required him to remain celibate, and he wanted the same for her.

CHAPTER THREE

Margaret Johnson Lee Pierce clipped out Grace Perry's article and put it in the scrapbook with the other trophies she had collected about the Church of Melchizedek.

Soon she would have to buy a second scrapbook because the collection had grown over the years. Margaret used a magnifying glass to get a closer look at the article's photo of her daughter, Lindy Lee. How many years had it been since she had seen her in person? Margaret didn't want to stop to think about it. Lindy had made her bed, and now she had to lie in it. *There she was making a fool of herself. No sane mother or father would entrust their child to her for medical care. She was finished in this city as a pediatrician.* Margaret smiled. She must tell Papa about the article.

She found her father as she always found him, sitting in his wheelchair with his head down and saliva drooling down his chin. When she came in, the nurse stopped reading and started cleaning him up.

Good help, Margaret thought, *is so hard to find these days. It looks as if I will have to do everything for him. I'm going to get rid of this one soon. Besides, I don't like the way she looks at my husband, and that nursing outfit is too tight and short. She's got to go, and soon.*

Margaret dismissed the woman and then finished cleaning her father, who had suffered a paralyzing stroke a couple of years ago. It also left him unable to speak. When he had the stroke, Margaret had posted faithful church members outside his room in case Lindy tried to visit him. She didn't want Lindy near her beloved Papa to upset him as she had when he had his heart attack in '67, which she had caused in the first place.

Lindy had the nerve to send them invitations to several special-occasion events, but Margaret had simply sent them back, never mentioning them to Rev, as he was called by the congregation. Just before his stroke, he had talked about forgiving Lindy and bringing her back into the church family. He wanted to have a family dinner with the man Lindy had married and the child she had adopted. Then, the stroke happened. As much as she hated that it had happened to her father, it had served a purpose. There would be no reunion.

And when she received a photograph of the child, Margaret couldn't believe her eyes. *Why would Lindy adopt a tar baby? She always did like those darkies.* Margaret had torn up the photograph.

"Papa, I got some good news for you. Wait until you hear this." She smiled at the old man in the chair. *Does he understand me?* she wondered. Sometimes his eyes looked as though he understood; other times, they looked blank.

Margaret read the newspaper article to her father. When she mentioned Lindy's name, she noticed he became agitated.

"Oh Papa, I didn't mean to upset you. I just wanted you to know she is getting hers. Isn't it wonderful that the truth is finally coming out? Everyone will know she is involved with the devil and his worshipers. And that heifer who couldn't get a good black man and had to marry a Jew is getting hers, too. They did this to you, Papa. Oh, why are you crying? Here, let me wipe your eyes."

Margaret looked at her father, not knowing if he was crying because he was happy about the article or because he wanted Lindy back. But now he was hers and hers alone. It was just the two of them. Well, not exactly. Her husband, Alan Pierce, was there, too. But he was no threat. He did everything she told him to do.

Pierce was a fair to good minister. He just didn't have the passion needed for the ministry, unlike her father and her. The old-timers were still in the church because of Papa, but they were not attracting new members. It was that God-forbidden cult church having an effect on good Christian folks. Somebody had to put a stop to their doings. The Elder Healer was from the devil, not her God. They had to be stopped.

She walked around in front of her father and bent down so she could look directly into his eyes. "You were right, Papa; they're evil.

They are trying to hurt us good Christians with all that distorting of the Bible and God's words. We got to do something about them. And Lindy, I can't believe something as evil as that came out of my body."

Having no choice, the old man looked into the eyes of his daughter. He couldn't even turn away. He tried to form a word, but she didn't even notice his effort. She just kept on talking.

"I tried to tell you years ago, Papa, when you wanted to forgive her and let her come back to the church and family. She would have destroyed us, just as she is trying to do now. She came here one day after your stroke and wanted to see you."

A light briefly flickered in Rev's eyes.

"I knew she wanted to do some of that mumbo jumbo stuff on you. Talking about bringing you to that awful church of hers."

Rev again tried to speak.

"I wouldn't let her anywhere near you. Remember how she almost killed you when you had the first heart attack? I told that devil worshipper to never come here again. She wasn't my daughter. She didn't have any family here. Didn't I do right, Papa?" Margaret smiled sweetly at her father.

One tear rolled down the cheek of the old minister. If he could only say the word *forgive*.

CHAPTER FOUR

"Dois-tu partir, mon amour?" the long-legged model stretched out on the bed asked Nick as he packed his luggage.

"Oui, yes, I told you earlier I have to go. And I thought you were going to practice speaking English?" Nick Lewis looked up from what he was doing at the partially clad blue-eyed blonde.

She tried to say in English, "How-long-do-you-plan-to-be-gone?"

Nick knew she was asking these questions not because she cared about him, but because she needed to know if she should move on to the next prospect to get where she wanted to be—on a Parisian catwalk. In her business it was all about whom you knew, and he had to admit he was "The Man."

He decided to play with her mind. Or maybe the truth was he really didn't know how long he would be gone. "I'm not sure."

Nick continued speaking to her in English. He really didn't care if she understood him or not. It was over. Nick was tired of being used by women trying to get ahead in the industry. However, he was told many times by her predecessors that he used women. Over the years, he'd had his share of women. He didn't even remember the names of most of them.

Nick's work came first in his life, and now it was paying off. But why wasn't he happy? This one, Danielle, acted as though the award was nothing. How many times did he have to explain to her this was quite an honor? Nick Lewis, the son of a sharecropper from Alabama, was being honored by his alma mater, Howard University, for outstanding service and monetary contributions to the advancement of historical black universities.

"Danielle, we have to go. I don't want to miss the plane. *Il nous faut partir. Je ne veux pas rater l'avion."* He repeated his his command in

French to make sure she understood. She was giving him a ride to the airport.

Nick always flew first class, one of many luxuries he gave himself. Besides, he could afford it. When he arrived in Paris eleven years ago, he was on a shoestring budget, a starving artist. He knew he was a good artist, but quickly realized he was not good enough to get where he was today.

It was a fluke that he had become a sought-after photographer. He had picked up a cheap camera to take photos to send home. He entered a local contest and won. The judges told him that he was gifted and had "the eye." With the right equipment, they predicted he would do well as a photographer. Motivated by those words of encouragement, Nick borrowed money from a friend and bought an expensive camera. He sent his photos to numerous magazines in Paris and abroad and soon started getting assignments from several small magazines. Then along came Raquel.

They met at a party and she went home with him. He thought she was the most beautiful female on earth, except for one other he constantly tried to block out of his mind. He spent the next day shooting Raquel inside his studio and around Paris. Raquel's portfolio got her in the door of a top modeling firm. However, she didn't get the job; Nick did. Word of his professionalism and superb work got around, and soon many top magazines, modeling agencies, and designers were vying for his services.

Raquel lived with him for four years. But after expressing her desire to get married, a prospect that did not appeal to him, she returned to Spain. Last he heard she was happily married with two children.

Nick's most famous work was the result of a year spent shooting children who lived in the interior of Africa. The exhibit was a huge success in South Africa and was now on its way to the National Museum of African Art in D.C., then fifteen cities in the U.S, with Europe its final destination.

IT'S NOT OVER YET

By the time Nick boarded the plane, he found the seat next to his was already occupied by a young man about his age. He was relieved he wasn't sitting next to a woman. He didn't feel like being charming; he had too much on his mind.

It wasn't until he was seated and they shook hands that Nick got a good look at his seatmate. As a photographer, Nick felt he had an advantage of sizing people up. It was like a sixth sense. He knew a lot about them without them ever having to tell him. The gentleman sitting next to the window was pretty. Nick could think of no other way to describe him. He was what women called a pretty boy—with keen features, smooth olive skin, straight black hair, and a thin mustache one could barely notice.

They exchanged a few words in English and French. He had no accent, but Nick's best guess was that he was an American who lived abroad. Perhaps it was his clothing that made it difficult to know exactly where he was from. The man wore a dark-blue Nehru suit that accentuated his olive skin. The stranger's eyes were what really caught Nick's attention. They looked old and seemed to hold deep secrets.

Paul DeVorss looked at the man next to him, whose intense stare gave him the opportunity to study the person he would share space with for the next several hours. For a second, Paul thought he knew him. But from where? He knew the American was not the type he would associate with. He was ruggedly handsome. Women would find him extremely attractive and men would want to be in his company. He was athletic but thin, as if he had been ill.

The two men sat quietly, each lost in his own thoughts, as the Boeing 727 took off for Dulles International Airport in Virginia. Having been gone for six months, this was the longest Paul had been away from home. He recognized the strain his absence had put on his marriage to Lindy Lee, his exceptional wife. Paul thought she was the most beautiful woman to ever grace the Earth. She had a mysterious air about her that reminded him of the innocence of a young wild creature and an old spirit. After all these years, she still tantalized and fascinated him, even though she had promised her heart to another.

Right after graduating from Howard, he had left for India, but unable to get her out of his system, he returned a short time later at the instruction of his guru, who told him to go deal with his personal issues and then come back when he had them under control.

He remained in D. C. and won her over and they were married. He lived in two worlds: the world of his guru in an ashram in India, and the world of his marriage in D.C. He married Lindy not only because he loved her, but also because he wanted to give her what she wanted more than anything in life: to adopt the child she had fallen in love with. Paul too had fallen in love with the child, believing the boy and he had a karmic bond: they both had been abandoned at birth by their parents.

Paul was left on the doorsteps of a Texas orphanage one cold, rainy night. The sisters took him in and named him Paul, after the saint. He spent the first seven years of his life there. He was picked on by the older boys not only because of his small size, but also because of his love for reading. The books Paul often sneaked from the priest's office and his friendship with Jim DeVorss, the bus driver, were what brought joy to his life.

When Paul was seven, Jim told him to meet him at the bus, but not to tell anyone. That day, Jim stole Paul from the orphanage. He had taken a liking to the boy and knew he was in serious danger. Unbeknown to Paul, Jim had saved his life, because when boys at the orphanage reached a certain age, they were forced to undergo an initiation rite that included sexual assaults by the older boys.

Jim and his wife were good to him. They were simple folks, but they loved him. They taught him about nature and the beauty of God's work. By the time Paul was twelve, he had read the Bible twice and could even recite verses. He was told his purpose in life was to love and help all of God's creatures, especially the two-legged, who were the biggest sinners.

One day Paul returned home from school and found his parents packing up the family's belongings. They were missionaries, and their assignment had come through. This would be their last assignment abroad. They were moving to India to help the less fortunate.

With his light-brown skin and straight black hair, Paul fit in perfectly with the Indian children, looking more like them than he did his white parents. He quickly learned to speak Hindi and Bengali fluently. His parents struggled with the languages, and he often acted as their interpreter. He constantly asked his parents about the differences and similarities between Hinduism, Buddhism and Christianity. They would smile at him and say, "There is only one God, Paul. Nothing else matters." At the time, Paul didn't know what they meant.

Paul befriended a boy named Dharmesh, shortening his name to Dhar. They looked so much alike that strangers thought they were brothers. Paul spent many hours with Dhar and his family, assimilating easily into the Indian culture and lifestyle. Dhar's parents were deeply spiritual, following the path of Kriya Yoga, a scientific meditation through which one could have a direct personal experience with God.

Dhar talked often about finding a master. Paul finally asked him why he needed a master when he was free.

"No, Paul," Dhar laughed, "the master will be my spiritual teacher or guru."

"Guru?"

"A guru teaches you how to rid yourself of the darkness and find the light within."

This was Paul's first introduction into Cosmic Consciousness, and he wanted to know more. The language and words were foreign to him. However, it didn't discourage him from wanting to learn. Not understanding what Dhar meant by darkness and light, he asked his parents. They explained that when people were good, they were in the light, and when they were bad, they were in darkness. Paul understood, but felt their explanation was too simplistic, and he desired a more philosophical answer.

One day while waiting for Dhar, Paul stood staring at a large photo of the guru on the wall in his friend's home. The eyes of the guru were penetrating, and Paul felt as though he was being pulled into the photograph. He tried to avert his eyes, but could not turn away. Then he heard a voice distinctly say, "Your destiny is here in India." Afraid his parents wouldn't understand and might prohibit him from seeing Dhar, he never spoke a word of the experience to anyone, not even his friend.

The time for his parents' return to the United States coincided with Paul's last year of high school. He begged them to let him remain in India with Dhar and his family. He had an intense desire to live in an ashram and study under the same guru that Dhar had chosen. To his dismay, his parents denied the request since his father was not well and his mother might need him to help with his care. Besides, they wanted him to return to the States for his college education. They expressed that once he finished college, he could then return to India and live in an ashram.

Paul chose to attend Howard University, majoring in philosophy—first, to rebel against his parents for forcing him back to the States; second, because he wanted to learn more about black culture. Although he was not certain of his ethnicity, Paul thought it was quite possible that some part of him had black ancestry—at the least, perhaps a mixture of races and culture.

It didn't take him long to find out he had nothing in common with the black students at Howard, and that he preferred the company of the Indian students. After all, he had lived a large part of his life in India.

One day, Dhar sent him a small photo of his guru and urged Paul to leave the university and return to India. Paul would stare at the eyes of the guru in the photo and then meditate. Once again, he heard a voice giving him guidance. Afterwards, he wrote Dhar and told him it was important for him to finish his studies at Howard. He wondered why the guru had told him to stay at the university; he would have returned willingly if the guru had given his blessing.

To help pay for his education, Paul got a job under the work study program offered at the university and was assigned to the law office of Betty Goldstein, a black civil rights attorney. He took an instant liking to Mrs. Goldstein. Upon learning they had a common interest in spirituality, she wanted to hear all about Paul's life in India. She invited him to two events: First, an Awakeners' meeting, and second, a party she and her husband, who was a professor at the university, were giving at their home in the prestigious Georgetown area of the city. At first, Paul hesitated because parties with alcohol made him feel uneasy. However, he relented, and now looking back, Paul understood why his life unfolded as it had. Lindy was at both events.

The smooth flight the captain had promised the passengers turned out to be anything but smooth. Several hours out, they ran into a strong storm and severe turbulence that caused the plane to rock from side to side and dip terrifyingly low. Paul and Nick made small talk to ease their apprehension and to make time at least seem to go by faster. In an attempt to relieve the tension, Nick tried cracking jokes, but with the turbulence only getting worse, he soon found himself wishing he had taken a later flight.

Before the storm hit, Nick learned Paul was married and had a son. Nick instantly liked the stranger and wanted to know more about him. Being a good listener, Paul seemed genuinely interested in Nick's career and life. Nick found himself telling the stranger things about his life he would never tell anyone. He had heard how strangers traveling together revealed their most private thoughts, believing, they would never meet again. *Maybe,* he thought, *this was one of those times.* Whatever the case, he needed to talk to someone.

"I'm returning not only to receive an award, but to right some wrongs I committed many years ago," Nick confessed.

"You are very courageous to undertake such a task."

"Maybe it's because I'm getting older and want to clean my slate. But to be truthful, I was in Rwanda on a project and witnessed people get shot down as if they were animals. Women and children were lined up against a wall and slaughtered. I almost didn't make it out of there myself. From that point on, my work took on new meaning. The fashion photography I'd been doing didn't have the same passion for me. I knew I wanted to create something of significance. Gordon Parks is my inspiration. So I put together the *Children of Africa* exhibit," Nick explained.

"I know what you mean. I have something that I must do, also," Paul stated as the plane shook.

"I left things a mess when I left eleven years ago." Nick wanted to tell the stranger everything, feeling close to him for some odd reason. However, the plane's rocking and dipping stopped him from doing so as he fought the urge to upchuck the contents of his stomach. When the turbulence eased, Paul picked up the conversation.

"I admire that you want to set things right by asking for forgiveness."

"I never thought of it that way," Nick responded, pondering Paul's take on what he had said. "Forgive, huh? How do you go about that?"

"Just let your heart guide you. When you forgive, you free yourself of carrying around a heavy burden."

"Are you some kind of minister or cleric?" Nick asked uneasily. He hadn't been to church since he left home for college, and certainly didn't want to be preached to. Nick was raised Pentecostal. Hell-and-damnation sermons still rubbed him wrong. He didn't adhere to any particular religion, but he believed in God, having seen what God had done with his life.

"No, I am not. However, let me just say that much of the bad feelings between people happen because they don't know how to love truthfully and forgive themselves and others. Instead, they hide behind their egos and play games with each other."

Nick nodded his head in agreement, while desperately trying to stifle a yawn. Although he wanted to continue their conversation, he could hardly keep his eyes open. By now, the turbulence had subsided a little. While looking at his watch, he made a mental note to reset it because of the time difference between the two countries. Unable to fight off the fatigue, Nick closed his eyes and drifted off.

Paul was also tired, but he wasn't quite ready to sleep. What he had shared with Nick about letting your heart guide you were the exact words his guru had said to him just before he left India.

CHAPTER FIVE

Walking through the airport to the exit, where a black limousine waited to take him home to his son and wife, Paul recalled what Lindy had told him some time ago. Right before Paul returned home from one of his trips abroad, Michael would pick up his photograph and say, "Daddy come home." This occurred too many times for them to pass it off as coincidence. Besides, neither of them believed in coincidences. They knew Michael was special, a Rainbow child.

Swami Pranayama, Paul's guru, told him that Michael was way ahead of his time. The Rainbow souls were not due to arrive on planet Earth until 2012. The Indigo and Crystal souls would arrive first.

The aura of the Indigo child has predominant hues of purple and blue, the two colors mostly needed to help with the planet's transition to a higher level of consciousness. As they take on adult roles, the Indigo children are to serve as system busters, their purpose being to dispel the darkness in any government or organization that is not about truth. They are true spiritual warriors. The Crystal children are very similar, but are more gentle and sensitive in nature. Their auras have an opalescent essence of pastel hues. They will bridge the gap between the seen and unseen worlds through their telepathic abilities and will work closely with people in the art and literary fields. The highly evolved Rainbow children will possess all of the above attributes and more, with a significant amount of gold in their energy fields, or auras, to raise earth to a higher vibratory consciousness. Their purpose will be to unite the races of the world and heal the planet, but each will have his or her own special mission.

Swami Pranayama believed Michael came too soon to this planet, and this prematurity caused his birth defects. He needed the particular body to work through his karma so as to clear out old karma and prepare him for his mission.

As soon as he entered the house, Paul dropped everything and ran over to Michael, who was coming out of his room using a walker. He scooped him up into his arms, kissing him repeatedly. He loved this child. They were connected spiritually, as he was connected to Lindy.

Lindy watched the two most important males in her life from Michael's bedroom door. Whenever Paul was home, Lindy usually wore comfortable pajamas to bed. Tonight, however, she was dressed in a black lace gown she had purchased the week before from a high-end department store, and her waist-length hair was free of its usual pony-tail holder. Although she had entered into a pact with Paul to be celibate, she still wanted to be noticed as a woman, not just as a wife. But standing before him now, she was deeply embarrassed, feeling she had betrayed him by wearing something so sexy and revealing.

She walked over to Paul and embraced him warmly. He kissed her quickly on the lips and felt the heat in his body surge. The gown had not gone unnoticed. Part of him wanted to grab her and make love to her. Resting his hand lightly on the curve of her lower back, Paul leaned down and kissed her again. Afraid of losing his internal battle against temptation of the flesh, he quickly removed his hand.

"I'm so happy you're home. We both missed you so much," she said, gazing into his eyes.

"I missed you too." Seeking to redirect his eyes from Lindy's body and his mind from impure thoughts of sex, he focused on Michael.

"There's so much to tell you," she said, moving closer to him.

"I'll go unpack and wait for you upstairs while you get Michael into bed." Paul grabbed his suitcase and hurried up the steps.

While unpacking, Paul thought about why he hadn't come home sooner. A recurring dream had kept him in knots. He decided to discuss it with his guru.

"Sri, Sri, Sri Pranayama, I can't go home as planned." Paul said, sitting at the feet of his guru.

"Why?"

"I keep having this dream I'm afraid will come true."

"What you fear will only come to you because you are attracting it by your fear."

"I know, my guru. I have meditated on this dilemma, but the dream keeps occurring every night," Paul replied, swiping the sweat from his brow. Knowing the guru was quite aware the dream was of a sexual nature, he was embarrassed to be discussing it with someone held in such high esteem.

"When you first came here, Paul, you knew you were caught between two worlds. The world of materiality is pulling you toward it. Is this what you want?"

"All my life I have only wanted to follow the path of the yogi. Then Lindy came into my life, and I have tried to live in both worlds."

"Perhaps it is time for you to choose. Go home," the swami said. He then reached into thin air, and a flower, followed by an apple, materialized. He placed both in Paul's right hand.

Paul waited for her in the sitting room between their two bedrooms. For the sake of prying eyes, they maintained the appearance of sharing the same room. The truth is that they always slept separately, so as not to tempt fate.

When she entered the room an hour later, Paul pretended not to notice she had changed into something more modest: a long-sleeved, white cotton gown that covered her from neck to ankles. But he could still sense the tension between the two of them. Lindy sat on the sofa and set her big violet eyes on him as he relaxing in his favorite recliner. He looked away uneasily. She looked and smelled of sex.

When Paul finally returned Lindy's gaze, he could no longer contain the urge within. Feeling as though he was going to explode at any moment, he got up and took a seat next to Lindy on the small sofa, so close their legs were touching. Paul moved a few strands of her hair away from her face.

Take me, I'm yours. I want you, her eyes called out to him.

He could feel her hand on his leg, hot and enticing. Desiring to cup her breast, Paul began undoing the buttons on her gown. *What was happening to me?* he thought.

"Mommy, Mommy, Mommy!" a small voice cried out from downstairs.

Breaking away from Paul's embrace, Lindy ran down to Michael's room to comfort him. He had been having nightmares twice a week for the past several weeks. He would wake up in a sweat, screaming that a tall dark man was going to take him away. Lindy would reassure him that no one could take him away from them. Nevertheless, she felt a funny feeling in her heart.

Even as she lay cuddling her son, her thoughts drifted to Paul; she still craved him. She gently rocked Michael back to sleep, and hurried upstairs to the sitting room. By the time she returned, though, Paul had busied himself with reading Grace Perry's article. Frustrated, she returned to the sofa and started braiding her hair, patiently waiting for him to finish reading. They had never gotten that close sexually; however, the moment had passed.

"Who is this Grace Perry?" he asked.

"She's new to the area and wants to make a name for herself."

"She seems to be strongly focusing on you."

"I know. Betty called me earlier; she was upset about the article. I don't know why she even consented to be interviewed by this woman. Betty seems so different lately, almost reckless." Lindy looked at Paul, letting her eyes do the talking.

Paul swung around to face the desk; he knew that look well. Thank God Michael had cried out. It brought him to his senses.

⚬⚬⚬

Lindy later lay in bed listening to her husband moving around in the next room. Paul had explained numerous times that being celibate didn't diminish the love he felt for her, that it was part of their path and the way to high spiritual attainment. Still, it hurt, and lately she had felt differently. She had caught herself staring at men in a lustful way.

She was preoccupied with sexual fantasies and daydreamed about what it would be like to have sex with her husband. Would he be gentle or rough? She didn't even know if he had *ever* been with a woman.

Perhaps he had a lover or another family in India?

Lindy shook her head to clear her mind of such negative thoughts and reached for the phone. She had earlier promised to call Betty back, but time had slipped by with her busy schedule. Even though it was late, she knew Betty wouldn't mind.

"Hello," Betty answered in a husky voice that most men found sexy.

"It's me. Sorry it took me so long to get back to you. It's been that kind of day—one emergency after another." Not pausing for a response, Lindy continued. "Paul's home. He got here a couple of hours ago."

"Girl, what are you doing on the phone? I know we have to talk, but it can wait. Go take care of that man and give him my love."

Lindy felt a pang of deceit. She wished she could confide in Betty. For years, she had let her friend believe she and Paul were a hot item in the bed. Lindy never really said as much, but she never corrected Betty when the latter made "bedroom" remarks about her marriage.

"It's okay. We've talked, and he's in the shower."

"Well, go get in the shower with him. That man's been gone too long. I just wish."

Ignoring Betty's well-meaning remark, Lindy interjected. "Before leaving the office, I received a memo from Dr. Walker. He wants to see me tomorrow."

"Shit! Excuse my French. I'll come up and explain that you had nothing to do with any of this." Although she had kicked the habit years ago, Betty silently wished for a cigarette.

"It's okay; I can handle it. What are we going to do about that reporter, though? There is something about her. I can't put my finger on it, but she seems so familiar."

"I know; I get the same feeling. I have an SOS out to the Awakeners. We need to meet and take care of this. I am toying with the idea of suing the *Washington Star* and that damn reporter. I put the idea in the ear of someone who I know will take it to the right people."

Lindy smiled. Betty often reverted to her role as an attorney; even her language would change.

"Let's first see what the Awakeners want to do," Lindy cautioned. *What is really happening with Betty? She seems so different lately.*

—⁓—

Hanging up, Betty thought that if Stan were her husband returning home from a six-month trip, there is no way she would be talking on the phone. She just didn't understand Lindy and Paul. When they were all together, she could sense the sexual energy between the two. It reminded her of two people waiting to pounce on each other.

Betty stretched out on her beige satin sheets and stared at the phone, as if willing him to call her. "Where is he?" She hated when he didn't call her. She desperately needed to talk to him, especially today of all days.

As if on clue, the phone rang. She let it ring a couple of times before lifting the receiver. "Baby, I have been thinking about you all day," she answered in her most sexy voice.

"It's nice to know you care, dear. Let the others know we will be meeting in two weeks on a Saturday at our usual time." Ruth, the eldest of the Awakeners, responded in her crackly voice.

No words could describe Betty's embarrassment.

CHAPTER SIX

In the dim lighting of the restaurant, Nick looked at the woman sitting across from him and wondered how eleven years could have slipped by so fast. He had photographed plenty of top models in the business, but her sexiness and class were uniquely intoxicating. There was an air of success and money about her.

Her clothes were off-the-rack from expensive department stores. Impeccable jewelry accented the navy blue silk suit hugging her body. The three top buttons of the light blue shirt were undone, showing just enough cleavage to avoid appearing sleazy. Her hair was cut short, highlighting her bone structure and Native American heritage.

She was a class act and knew it. This was not lil' Diana from his hometown that he left behind years ago. Nick admitted to himself that he was surprised to see how well she had done, maybe even a little envious. She was married, had a successful career, but had no children. She had pulled herself up by her bootstraps and was now a genuine success story. Take away his career and Nick had nothing. Nick didn't want to bring up old stuff that needed to stay buried, but he had to open Pandora's box.

Diana's heart was fluttering. Every time Nicky looked at her with those big brown eyes, she thought her heart would leap out of her body. She wanted to smother him with kisses, to caress his body. Scratch that. She wanted to do more than caress him. He wanted to talk, but she wanted him to take her. What control did this man have over her? She hadn't seen him in eleven years, yet it felt as if they were sitting in the Kenyon Bar and Grill like old times. He was thin and his eyes had a look of sadness about them. Maybe he was just tired, she surmised. What had happened to him?

Nick looked across the table and searched Diana's face for any dispiritedness from the ordeal she had endured. Nothing. He had left her pregnant and penniless. Nick asked himself many times why she didn't hate him.

Instead, Diana had always kept in contact with him, sending him postcards or letters. And here she was sitting across from him, looking like a million bucks and giving him the sexiest and biggest Colgate smile he had ever seen.

"Exactly what happened eleven years ago?" he asked, unable to contain himself any longer.

"What do you mean? I told you everything in the letter. The baby," she said in a low, irritated voice, "was deformed—thanks to your little doctor bitch—and died at birth." *Why is he asking me about this? What does he know?* Diana stared at him, her eyes brimming with tears. "You're eleven years too late, Nicky."

"I know, and I'm sorry. I can only imagine that it was hell for you."

"Hell? No, Nicky, it was worse than hell, if that's possible."

"Forgive me. Can I compensate you in any way? There must have been doctor or hospital bills."

Diana looked at the man she still loved. She didn't want his money. She wanted him, not that he deserved her. And, she wanted him to suffer as she had. Yes, he could compensate her. She wanted his soul, body, mind, and spirit. He owed her.

She reached over and laced her fingers through his. "I'm not going to lie to you, Nicky. It was the worst time of my life." She picked up the white cotton napkin from her lap and dabbed at her eyes.

Nick slid around the booth to be closer to her, placing his arm around her shoulders. Although he hated being called Nicky, he allowed her to call him that. He had a lot to make up for. He had vowed that he would make amends for his past actions.

Diana felt his hot breath on her ear as he whispered, "Baby, baby, I'm sorry. Forgive me. I'm here now."

If only I could have had heard those words eleven years ago, she thought. Diana turned to face him and, barely opening her lips, said, "Let's get out of here."

They left the restaurant arm in arm.

—〜

Nick could barely open the hotel door before Diana threw her arms around his neck and kissed him hard on the lips. Nick felt the warmth of her lips and tongue and responded just as hungrily. He knew this was dangerous territory; he was here to rectify things and not create more issues. Nick tried to pry her arms from around his neck, but Diana wouldn't let go.

She pressed her body against his, and he felt the hardness of her nipples through the silk blouse. He didn't even know when she had unbuttoned her jacket. Her hands were all over him. Even as she tugged at his zipper, something in his head was telling him to stop her. But when her hands touched him, he lost all self-control. They were young, hot teenagers again, letting the heat and tension of their bodies take them wherever they needed to go. Groping each other, they left a trail of clothes on the beige carpet from the door to the king-size bed.

In the bed, Nick became the aggressor. He had learned the art of lovemaking from an older Spanish woman, Lilia, when he lived a short time in Spain doing a photo shoot for a Spanish magazine. She was the editor-in-chief, and they became good friends. One evening, after dinner on her veranda, she walked around the table and kneeled before him. Smiling, she pointed to his manhood and said, *"El postre"*—dessert. From then on, whenever she wanted sex, she would say in Spanish, *"Deseo postre."* The problem was she wanted dessert two and three times a day. He couldn't get anything done. Nick learned from that experience not to judge a person by his or her age. At the time, Lilia was fifty-five and he wasn't quite thirty.

Cleaning up in the bathroom, Diana could scarcely believe what had just happened. It had been so good she wanted to jump for joy. She couldn't even fantasize during the act. At one point, when she was on top, and riding him as if she would never get it again, she let out a scream that came out of nowhere. She wanted to beat her chest, but instead she grabbed the little hair Nick had on his head and begged him to go even deeper inside her. Looking at herself in the mirror, she could have sworn there was a light around her body.

Nick was snoring when Diana left the room. As she walked toward the elevator, she began to think about what lie she would tell her husband.

≈

Daniel Reilly was a political powerhouse and not easily fooled. He was fifteen years older than Diana, but in great shape. At one time, he had been head of the D.C. Personnel Department, and Diana worked as a classifier in his office. Was it fate or luck that she had bumped into him on the elevator one evening? He wanted to know why she was still in the office, assuming he was the only one who stayed late.

Director Reilly had been impressed that she stayed late most nights to do extra work while other government employees tried to break the door down at quitting time. They stood in the underground garage talking for several minutes. Diana was surprised how easy it was to talk to him. That chance encounter led to secret encounters that became a scandal within the department, especially when he promoted her to deputy director. Daniel left the District government and became one of the associate directors of the Federal Office of Personnel Management (OPM), doubling his salary. He guided Diana's career, and with his connections, she soon filled his old position as director.

Only one thing was missing in their marriage—children. They tried everything. Diana learned she had severe scar tissue around her fallopian tubes. Although the scar tissue could be removed, the chances of her getting pregnant were very slim. Diana had the surgery anyway, since Daniel kept pressing her to do it. Still, she never conceived.

Diana never told her husband about the attempted abortion she had while in college. Daniel was old-fashioned and very religious. She could never share that horrible experience with him. He was against abortions.

It was still a mystery to Diana what Lindy had done to her. Everything had happened so fast. By the time the paramedics arrived, the bleeding had stopped. They took her to Freedmen's Hospital anyway. The doctors examined her and checked the heartbeat of the baby. Unable to find anything wrong, they discharged her the next day.

She was on her own. Her family didn't even know she was pregnant, and Nick never sent her a red cent or tried to find out how she was doing. She couldn't go home that summer, and by the fall she was big. For a semester, she used her parents' money to cover her living expenses and never even registered.

One day she ran into the medical student who had performed what he thought was an abortion. He was shocked she was still pregnant, swearing up and down he had performed the abortion. He gave her his number and told her to call him if she needed him. He owed her one.

Diana was at the point of destitution when she started experiencing contractions twelve weeks before the baby was due. She had resigned herself to thinking that God really did want her to have the baby, even if she had to do it alone. But when she found herself in premature labor, she thought that maybe God didn't want her to have it after all. She called the med student.

Diana wished she could talk to that reporter, Grace Perry, and tell her about Lindy doing that voodoo on her. She lost her baby, and now she couldn't even have children. Ironically, she and Daniel were members of Lindy Lee's family church, Mt. Olive Baptist Church. Daniel wanted to go to that church because many of the city's power players were members. Appearance and status were very important to him. He was president of the board of trustees, and they even attended Bible study.

Daniel doted on Diana and thought she was perfect. If only he knew what really went on inside her head. She loved Daniel in her own way, and loved the lifestyle he provided her, but she was not *in love* with him. She loved Nicky. He was her heart and soul. After the abortion, she hated him, but hatred soon turned into sadness and that into pining for him. Through his parents, she found him in Paris. At first, he wouldn't answer her letters. Finally, he responded occasionally. Diana followed his career through magazines and newspapers.

IT'S NOT OVER YET

Out of the blue, she received a mysterious call from him. He told he was coming to the States and wanted to see her; he had to clear something up with her. Diana was so excited about seeing him, she almost forgot that there was a reason he wanted to see her. She had only one thing on her mind. God was giving her a second chance to be with the man she loved. She couldn't mess it up this time.

CHAPTER SEVEN

Grace Perry felt exhilarated when she awakened. She would feel even better once she completed her morning routine. Standing naked in her bedroom in front of the full-length, free-standing wood-trimmed mirror, she inspected her body, turning in all four directions to reassure herself everything was okay. She didn't need another cut or tuck anywhere. The spa treatments twice a week and workouts at the gym kept her in tip-top shape. She believed the many facials and body wraps had actually lightened her skin two shades. The medium golden-brown color of her hair softened her whole appearance. No longer was she the dark, skinny, ugly little girl she had once been. No, the woman who looked back at her in the mirror was striking—thanks to Billy Ray, a cowboy from Texas, who had arranged and paid for her makeover.

As she lifted weights, Grace thought about how connections and money made all the difference in the world. Moving to the treadmill, she reflected on the previous day's meeting with her editor. He told her that he had heard Rev. Betty Goldstein of the Church of Melchizedek might sue the *Washington Star* for slander. He wanted to review again her source of information. Grace reassured him for the hundredth time he had nothing to worry about. She was confident that it was just a matter of time before she would have what she needed to expose the cult and the fake healer. Then the good Christian folks would love her, and she would have her boss's job, if not a better one.

No cojones, she thought. *I have more balls than him.*

Grace wasn't worried about Reverend Betty Goldstein suing the *Washington Star*. She had some dirt on Professor Goldstein, and if she had to, she would play her trump card. Years ago, Nick Lewis was supplying the Professor with marijuana.

Grace decided the next thing she had to do was get to the church's building custodian again. She was sure he knew more than he was telling her, and with another fifth of scotch, his tongue would loosen up, although half the time he was incoherent.

Thirty minutes later, Grace stepped off the treadmill and wiped the sweat from her face and neck. She had to hurry; her hair appointment was scheduled for eight a.m. She planned to look exceptionally well for her appointment with none other than Mr. Nick Lewis, photographer extraordinaire. Grace took the Yves St. Laurent dress from her closet and cut the tag. She was really looking forward to today's meeting.

Across town, Margaret spoon-fed her father his oatmeal. Thank God he could still eat and swallow. At first, the doctors thought he would have to have a feeding tube inserted in his stomach, but having faith, she had called together her father's oldest and most trusted friends to pray for him. They prayed around the clock, begging God to spare Rev and revive his health. The next morning, their prayers were answered, and Rev was taken off the respirator and able to breathe on his own. A day or so later, he was able to ingest liquids. Whenever Rev had a crisis, they went to God and asked for his mercy. When Rev's condition didn't improve, Margaret was convinced it was not because of God; it was the devil's interference.

Now Rev was incapacitated, and it was up to her to save the Christians and slay the dragons of this great city. The voice told her how evil the people of the Church of Melchizedek were, and that next they would try to hurt her father. She had to protect him and, of course, herself. They were jealous of what she had accomplished over the years, and now they were out to destroy the church, Rev, and her.

Margaret wiped Rev's mouth and put a strand of hair that had fallen into his face back in place. After firing the nurse, some of the deaconesses and other women of the church had offered to help with him, but she knew what they were really after. They wanted to take Rev away from her. Margaret turned on the TV and wheeled her father in front of it.

"I'll be right back, Papa. I have to clean the kitchen. You behave yourself until I get back."

I mean, don't piss on yourself.

"Stop it!" she said out loud. "That's no way to think about Papa." Margaret hurried to the kitchen, as she didn't like to leave him alone too long.

Rev sat motionless in front of the television, drool running down the side of his mouth. There was nothing he could do about it; he tried to will his hand to move, but nothing happened. Now a tear formed in the corner of his eye and began to make its way down the side of his face. He thought about Amanda, his wife. He was glad she couldn't see him like this. A part of him wished he could see her and ask for forgiveness. He was so wrong. He wasn't strong enough to stand up to his father.

His father had called him weak. The words stung, and he had taken it out on Amanda. He had lost the wife he loved and his granddaughter, who had those same violet eyes. If only he could move, he would find Lindy and her husband. *What was his name?* Rev tried to remember.

Margaret peeped into her father's room, and saw that his bib was wet and a large spot had formed on the front of his pants.

CHAPTER EIGHT

Betty walked briskly to church, wanting to be there bright and early in case Stan called before his early-morning appointments. She desperately needed to talk to him about that stupid article in the *Washington Star*.

She hated when he would not call her for days. She yearned to call him, but he told her early on in the relationship that his receptionist was his wife's niece. She would get suspicious if he received too many calls from the same woman. Therefore, he would do all the calling, and Betty would wait, which she hated.

It reminded her of the relationship she had with her first husband and true love, Ali, who not only called all the shots in their marriage, but also in his marriages to his other wives. When he put her out because she couldn't have children, she tried to kill herself. It was the most depressing time in her life. She got hooked on prescription drugs, and that's when the visions started. These visions led to her involvement with the paranormal.

She now credited the visions and her second husband, Harvey, for saving her life. He nurtured and cared for her during her recovery, his love putting her on the road to hope. And how does she repay him for his undying love and support after all these years? By cheating on him. Their relationship had changed. She was too busy with her life to even see it coming. Eventually, she would have to face the unavoidable—another bad marriage—and the thought of it made her shudder.

Why didn't Stan call? Oh, God, I wonder if something happened to him at work, she worried.

After a couple of hours of sitting at her desk trying to write her sermon for the coming Sunday service, Betty had to do something to calm her nerves. So she resorted to stuffing her mouth with greasy, salty potato chips and nibbling on a piece of chocolate cake despite the earliness of the day. She would have much preferred a cigarette, but Lindy's words kept replaying in her head. *You need to kick the habit. Your lungs are already black from all those years of smoking.* She knew Lindy spoke the truth, since she was a human X-ray machine and could actually see the damage to her lungs.

Thinking of Lindy, Betty made a mental note to inform her and Paul about the Awakeners' meeting in two weeks. She picked up the pen she was using and twirled it between her fingers, a habit she had developed when she stopped smoking.

The Awakeners are so damn secretive, Betty thought. As much as she hated to admit it, Grace Perry was right; she *should* be on top of what happens in the church. She was the senior minister and a member of the Awakeners, but they still treated her as if she was a perpetual student. With her not knowing anything about the Elder Healer, how could she answer Grace Perry's questions intelligently? It's the Awakeners' fault. They made her look stupid.

The loud ring of the telephone startled her. "Please," she begged, looking down at the blinking light on her private line, "let this be him." Slowly, she lifted the phone's receiver.

"Reverend Goldstein. How may I help you?" Betty could feel her heart pounding rapidly.

"Why so formal?"

The rich sound of his baritone voice made her quiver. She felt as though she had gotten a fix. *What is happening to me?*

She got a hold of herself, although her voice had an edge to it. "Did you read yesterday's paper?"

"Yes, I did. I would have called you sooner, but my daughter came in yesterday from school and there was too much family around in the evening."

What about me? I needed you. It's always about your wife and daughter, Betty wanted to scream from inside her soul. "Well, what do you think?" she asked instead.

"What do you know about the Elder Healer?"

"Nothing."

"What do you mean 'nothing'? Who is she? Where did she come from?" Stan sounded as though he was talking to a child who needed reprimanding.

Should I tell him about the Awakeners? she pondered.

"There is this group."

"What group?" Stan asked, cutting her off with a voice laced with irritation.

"If you let me finish, I'll tell you. They're called the Awakeners. They are advisers to the church. It was their idea to have the first Friday healing sessions." Betty decided she wouldn't tell him everything about them. She didn't want him to think she was involved with a cult or anything of the sort. Stan, for all his brilliance, wouldn't understand. He was too left-brain oriented.

"Well, then, refer the reporter to the Awakeners. What's the secrecy surrounding who they are?" He didn't allow her a chance to respond. "Betty, you were a top civil-rights attorney and, at one time, a district attorney for the city. I can't believe you're telling me you would allow some group to run your church and you know *nothing* about them. They're making you look like a fool. Look, my next patient is here. I've got to go."

Betty quickly asked, "Stan, wait. When am I going to see you?"

"I told you that my daughter is home, and she brought her college roommate home with her. My wife has planned some family activities for us, so I may be tied up the next few days or weeks."

"Weeks? What about me?" Betty exploded into the phone.

"What you need to be concerned with is focusing on getting that situation straightened out and finding out whom and what you're dealing with. I expect more from you. Look, I've got to go. I'll call you."

Her heart ached at the sound of the phone clicking in her ear. *What went wrong?* she wondered. Stan was so attentive and different when she first met him. Always there for her, calling her every day and even sending her flowers. Then he started to drift away. There were no warning signs that she could remember. The calls simply didn't come as often, and when she did talk to him, he seemed distracted and close to being verbally abusive.

She was losing him. She knew it. Had she done or said something wrong? Could the one time that she suggested they get divorces and marry each other be the cause for him becoming distant? Was there another woman?

What do I need to do in order to keep my man? she wondered. For now, the only answer she could come up with was to have another slice of chocolate cake.

CHAPTER NINE

Dr. Lindy Lee sat quietly in the outer room of Dr. Herbert Walker's office suite, waiting for him to summon her. She knew he was deliberately making her wait just to rattle her nerves, another of his techniques used to instill fear into subordinates. It didn't matter if you were a doctor or the hospital custodian.

Paul, her guru, as she liked to call him, had tried to ease Lindy's anxieties by telling her there was nothing for her to be fearful of because Dr. Walker had no power over her. The power was inside her. These things she knew from her studies with the Awakeners and the many books she had read over the years. Still, it was always reassuring to hear the words of wisdom again, especially from those she knew loved her. She could rationalize that Dr. Walker did not have any control over her, but it was another thing to internalize the thought until she believed it.

So, as she waited to hear what he had to say about the newspaper article, she decided to do a relaxation technique Paul had taught her. He told her to release the negative thoughts surrounding any situation and focus on something pleasant to change how she was feeling. Right now, she was worried Dr. Walker would bring up that old mess from the time she was in medical school. Lindy kept telling herself not to focus on it, but to change her thoughts to something that would bring a smile to her face.

She was so happy Paul had come home. He instilled a feeling of tranquility in her soul and gave her discipline. His scent aroused her inner senses, as did the way he would sometimes touch her.

Stop, she told herself. Thinking about lovemaking with her husband would only frustrate her.

Lindy closed her eyes and visualized Paul moving around the house, making up for his long absence by cooking, cleaning, and caring for Michael. Paul was Michael's biggest advocate. Whenever Paul was home, he spent long hours at Michael's school, accompanying him to his therapies, talking and working with the therapists, as well as acting as a volunteer parent for Michael's classroom. Michael loved the attention he received from his father, and cried inconsolably when Paul left for India.

Paul promised he would take them with him one day, but days had now turned into years. Lindy wondered why Paul had not kept his promise. What was he not sharing with her? What pulled him back to India and kept him out of her bed? Could he have another family over there? *No, she told herself, not my Paul.* They were friends and honest with each other. Lindy shook her head, as if to shake the doubtful thoughts that had moved stealthily into her head, but they only persisted.

Lindy opened her eyes to see Dr. Walker standing in the doorway staring at her. Ten minutes later, she wished she was still in the waiting room, or better yet, that the meeting was over.

The short, bald-headed man sitting at his desk was a tyrant. He loved to flex his muscles, and was doing his best to intimidate her. Screaming at the top of his lungs, he told her Howard University Hospital could not afford any negative publicity, at least not under his watch. When he asked her point-blank if she was the Healer, Lindy at first sat there looking stunned. She had not expected him to be so direct.

Then she looked him straight in the eye and responded with one word: "No."

"I hope you're not lying to me, young lady, or the repercussions will be devastating for you," he threatened.

"I have no reason to lie."

"You are a member of this Church of Mel…Melchi…whatever?"

"Church of Melchizedek."

"Is this one of those New Age churches?"

"New Age is old wisdom, Dr. Walker. The name Melchizedek is taken from the Christian Bible. It's the name of the King of Salem, or you might know him by the name of Prince of Peace." Lindy felt herself gaining strength as she talked about Melchizedek.

"Um, well enough of that. I didn't ask you to come here to give me a Bible lesson. As I mentioned before, the hospital administration is very concerned about any bad publicity. You are well aware that as a black hospital we are scrutinized differently from the Georges." He picked up his cigar and lit it. "You know I am referring to Georgetown and George Washington hospitals, right?" he grunted.

Lindy nodded her head in the affirmative, wanting nothing more than to get away from the smoke and out of his presence.

"As one who took the Hippocratic oath, would you say the Elder Healer has medical credentials?"

Paul had warned her that Dr. Walker might ask her about the Elder Healer. Since Grace Perry had glamorized her existence, it stood to reason he would be just as curious as others who had read the story. Lindy chose her words carefully before answering, not wanting them to come back and haunt her later.

"The best way I can describe the Elder Healer is to liken her to Jesus Christ, the Great Physician. Like Jesus, the Elder Healer heals and performs miracles."

"You're saying she can walk on water?" he sneered.

"Didn't Jesus say we would do greater things than the ones he performed, if I may paraphrase?" Lindy fired back.

Dr. Walker stood up and clasped his hands behind him as he walked from behind his desk to stand directly in front of Lindy. He pulled his shoulders back to make himself appear taller than his five feet as he stood over her. He had heard from other doctors that she was not overly friendly, but a hell of a good doctor. Today, though, all he had learned was a lot of biblical nonsense. She was truly the grand-daughter of old Rev of Mt. Olive Baptist Church. Nevertheless, he felt he had to do his duty. He had to put her on notice. He couldn't let the other employees, and especially the doctors, think he had let this go unnoticed. The newspaper article was the talk of the hospital.

Lindy rose from her seat. "I can assure you, Dr. Walker, my involvement with my church and my job are two separate entities. I cannot control the media."

"You're right, and we must keep them separate. If they should happen to meet, I can only tell you that I will call a review board meeting." Before Lindy could respond, he added, "Oh, by the way, give my regards to that beautiful mother of yours and Rev. How is he doing?" he asked with a smirk.

Moving toward the door, Lindy turned back and looked at her superior. "Fine," she responded, letting the door close behind her.

CHAPTER TEN

On the way to her office, Lindy felt everyone she encountered was staring at her. She was flushed. Blood always rushed to her face when she was tense or upset. *He had deliberately asked me about my mother and grandfather, and he knows I'm estranged from them.* She grabbed her messages from the receptionist and hurried into her office, wanting to crawl into a shell and never come out.

She absentmindedly flipped through the several messages, her mind on her position at the hospital. She tried hard to fit in with the other doctors and hospital staff, but they shunned her. Was it because she didn't practice the same Christian faith? It was awkward when people asked what church she attended. She would get questions like, "What kind of church is that?" and "Do you believe in Jesus?" The rumors about her grandfather banning her from the church because she was supposedly possessed with the devil and practiced voodoo followed her wherever she went. *Will people ever accept me for who I am?* she wondered.

Betty had left a message about the Saturday meeting. Lindy felt relieved that the Awakeners had responded to Betty's call for help. Soon after she had read the last of her messages, the receptionist buzzed her office.

"Dr. Lee, there's a gentleman here to see you."

Paul? Lindy wondered. *He's probably stopping by to see how things went with Dr. Walker.*

"Send him in."

As the door to her office opened, Lindy looked up, expecting to greet her husband with a big smile. At first, she didn't recognize the tall, thin, bearded stranger standing in the doorway. Then Lindy caught her breath as she stared into the eyes of Nick Lewis.

"May I come in?" he asked. Not awaiting an answer, he closed the door behind him.

"Nick—Nick Lewis?" was all she could manage as she stood up. She knew he was coming to town, but did not expect their paths to cross. She wanted to see him, but felt it was better if she didn't. Now here he was standing in her office.

Nick took a seat in front of her desk and glanced around the office. The furnishings consisted of only a desk, two chairs, and two landscape pictures. Lindy, at a loss for words, remained standing. As their eyes met, she felt that he was undressing her.

"Have lunch with me?" He spoke the words as though they were young adults still attending Howard.

"After all these years, you waltz into my office, and without even asking how I am doing, and just like that ask me to have lunch with you?" Lindy moved in front of him, her hands on her hips, looking scornful.

Nick had to restrain himself from pulling her into his arms. He wanted so badly to kiss her. He had no idea he was going to react this way upon seeing her. *She's right; I'm acting like a schoolboy,* he thought.

Nick rose and walked toward the door; Lindy fought not to reach out and pull him back. She wanted to scream for him not to leave. Nick stepped outside her office door and knocked.

Cocking her head to the side, Lindy said, "Come in."

Nick entered a second time and greeted her with a big smile and a proper greeting.

After making light conversation, he asked her to lunch again. Her next appointment was not for another hour, and she needed to get out of the hospital, Lindy thought. *What the hell? Why not go to lunch with the man I've hated for over eleven years?*

Even during the day, the lounge in the Howard Inn was dark and secluded. Looking around, Lindy saw a couple of doctors and nurses she knew. They exchanged greetings, but it was clear their attention was on Nick. She didn't doubt that her little luncheon adventure would be fed into the rumor mill of the hospital.

Nick and Lindy sat at the table, pretending to look over the menu's selections. Nick couldn't believe how strikingly beautiful she still was, how little she had changed. It seemed as though time had stood still. Where Diana looked sophisticated and sleek, Lindy looked fresh and innocent. She was decidedly not Diana, who had fallen all over him. He was already regretting what had happened between Diana and him the evening before. She had thrown it at him, and he hadn't refused. It was just a piece. He hoped Diana realized that and wasn't reading more into it. Right now, all he wanted to do was savor every moment with the woman sitting across from him.

Lindy looked up from the menu to find Nick staring at her. "Why didn't you answer my letters?" he asked.

"What letters?" She looked surprised.

"I wrote you, trying to explain what happened."

"Where did you send the letters?" Lindy asked.

"To your house. I went there before I left for Paris, but your mother wouldn't let me see you."

"I wasn't there, Nick." Lindy went on to explain what happened that night and why she had come to his apartment early. The words stuck in her throat, and her face turned fire-engine red. It still hurt after all these years. She wanted to run again, but she forced herself to sit there.

Nick noticed the tears in her eyes. He instinctively knew the wrong thing to do was to try to console her as he had consoled Diana the night before. Lindy would probably think he was coming on to her; in a way, she would be right. *If I could only touch her,* he thought.

"Let's order," he suggested, aware they each needed a moment to regroup. After they ordered, he continued with the small talk. "I'm proud of you, baby. You did what you said you were going to do, which was become a doctor. What specialty?"

"I'm a pediatrician."

"Why did you choose that field?"

"I love children, and I have a son," she said, looking at him.

She had obviously moved on with her life. Nick tried to conceal any emotion this reality awoke in him.

"How old is your son?" he asked.

"Michael will be eleven at the end of the year." He noticed she glowed when she talked about him.

Eleven? Is he mine? he asked himself. Nick looked at her quizzically.

"Michael is adopted," she added, as if reading his mind. "We adopted him just before I finished my pediatrics residency."

"We?"

"I'm married, but I still use my maiden name at the hospital."

"That's why I could find you so easily."

What she said next came out of the blue, totally unexpected by Nick. "You were two-timing me." She glared at him between bites of her Caesar salad.

"I had dated Diana before I got involved with you. She got pregnant, but did not tell me right away. She decided to have an abortion, and I had to help her."

"Why didn't you tell me?"

"I would have eventually, after we were settled in Paris. I just didn't want you to get bent out of shape if you had found out beforehand. I guess I was wrong. I should have told you everything."

"She lost the baby that night?" Lindy asked, trying to get control of her anger. It was as if the clock had rolled back to the year 1967.

"No, strangely enough she lost it a couple of months later."

"It?" She looked at him disgustingly.

"I mean, the baby—the baby had birth defects."

"My son, Michael, was born prematurely and also has severe birth defects."

"What's wrong with him?" Nick looked concerned.

"He was born with hydrocephalus, water on the brain, and neurofibromatosis, a genetic disorder that causes tumors to form."

"And now, how is he?"

"He still has some health challenges, but he has come a long way. He uses a walker and his speech is limited." Lindy wanted to share with him that Michael communicated with Paul and her through telepathy and by pointing his finger. It was a joke in their household that Michael was a king, they were his subjects, and he ruled them with his little finger. Instead, she asked, "I read in the alumni magazine that you are a famous photographer. But what about your personal life? Are you married? Have any children?"

"No, I haven't had time," he answered, suppressing the impulse to tell her how he really felt. He paused before continuing. "Come to the reception and opening of my exhibit at the National Museum of African Art. Of course, the invitation is also extended to your husband."

"I'll let you know. I have to check with my husband." She couldn't look at him.

As they finished their lunch, Nick wished the moment would never end. Even though he could feel she was uncomfortable being with him, he could sense something else was wrong. Lindy looked calm on the outside, but his instinct told him that inside something was troubling her.

Declining dessert, Lindy quickly gathered up her belongings, looking drained and tired. The lunch had been too much for her on top of her meeting with Dr. Walker. She felt as though she was suffocating; she had to get away from him. Nick was amazed by how fast she moved. She was out the door before he could even say good-bye. Nick hurriedly paid the waiter, leaving more than a ten percent tip, and caught up to her just before she entered the walkway at the front of the hospital. She was walking so fast she didn't see the uneven pavement. As she was falling, Lindy felt a strong hand grab and steady her on her feet. Nick then gathered her into his arms. Lindy lifted her face to stare into the eyes of the man who was her first love and first hurt.

Nick wanted to kiss her mouth, chin, eyes, everywhere, but he knew that would only push her further away. He had to go slow. He was playing for keeps.

"I'll walk you back to your office," he said, releasing his grip on her.

"You don't have to. Thanks for the lunch, though."

"It's no problem. While I'm here, I want to check on some hospital records before my interview with Grace Perry."

"Did you say Grace Perry?" Lindy asked, also thinking, What could *he possibly need from the medical records department?*

"Yes, do you know her?"

"No, not personally, but she wrote a very disparaging report about my church." *Why am I telling him this? He doesn't care about my life. Probably just came back to gloat over his success.*

At the elevator, Lindy extended her hand to Nick, and with the sweetest smile she could manage, she bade him farewell. Ignoring her hand, he reached over and kissed her on the cheek, inhaling her natural scent. He had to get close to her at least one time.

"Come to the opening. I won't take no for an answer. I will sit on your doorstep. Besides, I want to meet the man who has your heart," he teased.

The elevator door opened and Lindy stepped inside without answering, while Nick stood looking at her until the door closed. He felt sad, but good at the same time. He had dreamt about this day for a long time. He knew it would take time to make amends, and maybe even get what he wanted, but he was willing to exercise patience.

As Nick walked over to the information desk, the women took note of the good-looking man, dressed in a white shirt and a blue double-breasted suit jacket that fit his body as if he had stepped straight out of a magazine. They hadn't missed him when he first entered the hospital and when he left with Dr. Lee. He carried himself as if he owned the world. Now he was standing in front of them asking for directions to the medical records office. What could he possibly want in MR?

CHAPTER ELEVEN

Timing was everything, or at least that's what her old tabloid boss used to tell her. And it seemed to prove true once again. Grace was in her little blue Beamer, driving down Sherman Avenue, when an accident brought traffic to a halt. Cars were being rerouted to Seventh Street passing Howard University Hospital. Grace couldn't believe her eyes when she saw Dr. Lindy Lee and Nick Lewis embracing. She quickly pulled over and grabbed her camera and took a few shots of the couple. *Wasn't Dr. Lee married?* Grace couldn't stop smiling; she knew an optimal time would present itself for her to use the pictures.

Nick entered the hotel's lounge and adjusted his eyes to the room's semi-darkness. He looked around and saw a woman rising from her seat and beckoning to him. It was Grace Perry. As he approached, Nick saw that she was attractive and wore an expensive designer suit. When he reached her corner table, Grace extended her hand and gave him a big smile.

After the handshaking and introductions, he pulled out a chair and sat down. He didn't care for this part of his work. He preferred to stay in the background. His publicity team had set this up as part of promoting the "Children of Africa" exhibit.

Before coming to the lounge, he had picked up his messages. Diana had left word that she would be by after work. He didn't want to deal with her tonight, but he needed answers. The hospital had no record of Diana being admitted on the date she had given him. The clerk, who had worked there for years, told him about an abandoned baby that had been brought to the hospital the same day. However, she couldn't give out any more details. She advised him to go to the public library and look it up in the newspaper. Right now, sitting across from Grace Perry was the last thing he wanted to be doing.

Grace's research confirmed that Nick had done well for himself. He was wealthy and well-respected in his field—and he was a ladies' man. She wondered what was going on with him and Lindy. Had they been seeing each other all these years? Is there a link between him and the Church of Melchizedek? If there was anything to uncover, Grace was confident her digging would find it. Just look how God had put her in the right place at the right time earlier that day.

She asked him the usual questions about his career and the exhibit, but right when he thought they were finished, she asked something that had nothing to do with his career or the exhibit.

"Are you in contact with your old friend Professor Goldstein? You two were close, right?"

"Who?" Nick froze. "Oh yeah, the Professor. He helped me to get into the University of France. Matter of fact, the Professor and his wife are coming to the opening," he answered offhandedly.

"Then you don't know?"

"Know what?"

She leaned over to whisper to him. There was no one near them, so Nick wondered why the cloak-and-dagger act. Nick's trained eyes told him that Grace had been under the knife, and he was willing to bet anything she had been under it more than once. She was not his kind of woman.

"In this city, you have to be selective about whom you associate with. You of all people should know that. Betty Goldstein, the Professor's wife, is the senior minister at one of those New Age churches. A lot of folks in the city are beginning to feel uneasy about what is going on over there. I gather some of the movers and shakers of the city will be at your affair." Seeing the tightness in Nick's face, she added, "Relax, Nicky. All I am saying is I would be careful mixing apples and oranges." Grace laughed.

She had called him Nicky, causing the hairs on the back of his neck to stand at attention. He didn't like or trust her.

"Thanks for the advice. I'll keep it in mind." He could only imagine how she would write the story. Nick decided it was time to end the pretense of an interview. Besides, Diana would be there any moment. Looking at his watch, he informed Grace that he had another appointment and hurriedly left, leaving her to have to yell at his departing back that the article would appear in the paper in a couple of weeks.

Emerging from the lounge, Nick spotted Diana at the hotel desk talking to the front-desk agent. As he walked toward her, Grace followed closely behind. She smiled as Nick approached Diana. For the second time that day, the heavens had smiled down on her. Nick was at it again, this time with the wife of the former director of D.C. personnel and head of the trustee board of Mt. Olive Baptist Church. With Nick and Diana heading for the elevator, Grace realized she didn't have much time.

"Nick," she called out, "I forgot I need a photo for the paper." Startled, the couple turned to face Grace's camera.

She quickly took the shot and raced across the lobby and was at the revolving doors before Nick or Diana could stop her.

CHAPTER TWELVE

Margaret dressed Rev in his best suit for the church meeting and pushed him into his old office, where her husband was working. She always liked him to look good when company came. He still was a presence to deal with. She only wished her husband carried as much weight. Alan Pierce, she thought, was a featherweight compared with her father.

Although they made a nice match, Margaret hadn't wanted to marry him. Nevertheless, it was the right thing to do to save the church from falling into the hands of the wrong people. Many of the deacons and assistant ministers wanted to walk in Rev's shoes. Years before, Margaret had seen the signs and had worked behind the scenes to position Alan in the right place at the right time. He was the most likely candidate to take over once her father retired. Good thing she married him when she did, because soon after, Rev had the stroke.

Despite all Alan's degrees and his pedigreed family, Margaret soon discovered he was weak. She had to show him how to do everything, including dressing himself properly. To her, the most disappointing thing was his lack of passion when delivering the sermon on Sundays. During the week, Margaret helped him to prepare the sermon and would go over it with him several times, telling him which words to stress and when to use hand or body gestures to make a point. As assistant pastor, he really never got a chance to preach much, but Margaret had thought with experience he would improve. Still, Sunday after Sunday he was dry and boring. Something had to be done. Membership was declining, a serious problem. This had never happened when Rev was preaching.

IT'S NOT OVER YET

Margaret waited until she heard the creaks in the floor as her husband pushed Rev's wheelchair down the hall. Certain they had left, she came out of the kitchen. She looked around the first floor of the house. It still looked great after all these years. The house was the parsonage, but she had made sure it was in her name and Rev's.

The pounding in her head had started again. She wanted to run up the stairs and lock herself inside her room. Well, she really wouldn't be by herself. They would be there. The voices had been there since she was a child. After the birth of her daughter, Lindy, Margaret tried to tell Papa about them, but he said she was suffering from postpartum depression and got her some pills.

Margaret stood in front of the large mirror in the vestibule. She adjusted her linen dress, and smoothed her hair, making sure not a strand was out of place. She turned to follow the path her husband and father had taken.

⸻

Reverend Alan Pierce wheeled Rev into the small meeting room on the first level of the church and positioned him at the table. The gospel choir was practicing down the hall with the door open. Alan could hear them singing "Sweet Hour of Prayer." The song gave him courage, something he would need in the coming hours.

Reverend Alan Pierce wiped Rev's mouth. He didn't know why Margaret insisted that Rev attend the meeting, especially when all Rev was capable of doing was sitting there and drooling. Alan believed Margaret wanted her father there to underline his authority. Every day she would roll Rev into the office and prop him in front of the desk where Alan was working. After a short time, Rev smelled of urine or feces. Alan would have to stop working and find Margaret or the housekeeper to clean him up. This would go on throughout the day. Alan felt like a babysitter, instead of the minister of one of the largest black churches in D.C. He couldn't stand to see the saliva run down Rev's chin, so he kept a set of towels handy to wipe away the drool. He couldn't believe this once-powerful man was reduced to having to wear

a diaper and bib. Sometimes he found himself talking to Rev, and when he looked into his eyes, he could swear Rev understood everything he was saying.

What disturbed Alan even more was that Margaret wouldn't let him touch her anymore. She stayed on her side of the bed, and some nights he would wake up and she would be gone. One night, he decided to go look for her. He checked downstairs and in the guest bedroom. He finally found her in the bed with her father. His first impulse was to drag her out of Rev's bed and whip some sense into her. Instead, he quietly closed the door and returned to their room, where he stayed awake for long time thinking about his wife and what he had gotten himself into.

He knew she was different and sometimes eccentric, but this was crazy. She had gone too far. He had to get her help. *Maybe*, he thought, *I could approach…no, I wouldn't dare talk to her daughter.*

Margaret hated her daughter as much as she hated her mother, about whom she never spoke. It was a forbidden subject in the household. All Alan knew was that her name was Amanda and that Lindy looked like her.

Staring into space, he thought about Margaret lying in bed with her father. In the early years of their marriage, they had normal sexual relations once or twice a week. She was just what he wanted in a woman. She had meat on her, something a man could grab hold of. But she had changed, and he couldn't remember when this transformation started. She became rough—biting him on the lips, pulling his hair, hollering and screaming obscenities. He couldn't figure out if they were directed at him or someone else. Once, he swore she tried to bite his sacred organ. Since that time, he hadn't let her mouth near it again. At times she would want to have sex for hours; other times, she acted as though she was completely uninvolved and would just lie there until he came. Afterwards, he would want to cuddle, but she would push him away from her, and begin crying or cursing.

After some time of going back and forth over several approaches to getting help for Margaret, Alan finally decided he must be the one that needed help.

⟞⟝

Reverend Pierce looked over the group that had gathered for the meeting. Rev. Thomas Jones, pastor of New Hope Baptist Church, and Rev. Benjamin Williams of First Baptist Church, were his buddies. They had attended Howard University School of Religion together and had remained friends through the years. Now each was the senior minister at one of the largest churches in the District. Deacon Coleman, Rev's right-hand man, and Margaret were sitting next to Rev. Daniel Reilly, the last to join them.

After the opening prayer, Reverend Pierce introduced everyone, more as a courtesy than anything else. He then got right to the point, explaining the gravity of the problem they faced: churches were losing members. The problem was more than just lack of attendance: people were migrating to other faiths.

What other church but that horrible place in Georgetown? Margaret asked silently, listening to Alan speaking about God and saving lost souls. *Why is he wasting good time on this foolishness? Tell them how Lindy and those other devil worshipers are out to destroy every Christian church in the city and take over the world.*

A voice whispered to her, *"You got to stop them."*

Margaret tried to catch her husband's eye. He ignored her.

"I have given this serious thought," Reverend Pierce said, while looking around the room and pointedly ignoring his wife's hostile look. "We must wage a campaign to bring people back to the church, or set aside a month in which every Baptist church in the city would have a special program to increase membership. What do you think?" he asked, opening the floor for others to speak.

"We used to have homecomings every August until that awful incident happened eleven years ago. I won't go into that, but I'm sure you all know what I'm talking about. Homecoming, that's what we need," Deacon Coleman chimed in.

"Homecomings are all right, Deacon Coleman," Reverend Williams of First Baptist Church responded, "but that's only going to get a few new members, and the old ones are going to just come to eat and then you'll never hear from them again. No, we need something more."

Margaret looked from one minister to the other as each offered his comments and suggestions. Her head was pounding again. She had to get this meeting on track so they could do what they had come to do. Margaret stood, and all eyes shifted to her.

At first, she didn't even recognize her own voice as she began to speak. It was different, as if someone else was speaking through her. The words just came out, calm but strong. She spoke with clarity and authority.

"Membership is declining and will continue to decline unless we address the underlying cause. People in this city are flocking to a false sanctuary of hope. Those healings in that forbidden place of devil worshipers have pulled the wool over our Christian brothers' and sisters' eyes. It's up to us to unmask the devil and bring God's sheep back home. This is not a new battle. It has been going on ever since Michael fought Satan in heaven. We must do the same. We can't afford to let outsiders hiding behind false prophets destroy the Christian foundation that has kept this city together. We need to take drastic measures."

"What do you have in mind?" Deacon Coleman asked.

"Expose them for who and what they are—-quacks and frauds." They knew to whom she referred without anyone mentioning their names.

"How do you suppose we do that?' Daniel Reilly asked Margaret.

"From the pulpit."

"From the pulpit?" the three ministers exclaimed in unison.

"You have the power every Sunday. Use it," Margaret said with force, and then sat down. "If Rev was still able, he would never let this happen." Reverend Pierce was about to say something, but Margaret hadn't finished. "I believe in my heart and soul my father would use the power of the pulpit to fight Satan. He would stomp down the devil."

Margaret stood again and placed her hand on Rev's shoulder. "Remember Rev the next time you stand at the pulpit. Think about what he would have done. Let the Holy Spirit into your spirit. Ohhhhhh, the Holy Spirit will not lead you astray! Cast aside your fears and stand up in the name of Jesus!" Margaret shouted, throwing back her head. She couldn't hold back any longer. She had to get the words out as the voice had instructed her. "Don't stand back and let Satan get a foot in the door. Fight back with the power of your ministry. Have meetings to find out what people want the church to do for them," Margaret stole a look at Alan. "Reach out to them by going to hospitals, homes, and anywhere you need to go to embrace the children of God. This is your power! Use it!"

"Do we know if these healings are real?" Reverend Jones interjected, not taking kindly to Margaret preaching to them.

"Good question. Let's ask around and try to find out," Reverend Pierce suggested.

Margaret shook her head. "We don't have to ask around. Everyone knows they hire people from out of town to act as if they are blind or can't walk. I keep telling you to use the power of the pulpit to expose them. Plant the seed of doubt."

"Where are you getting your information?" Deacon Coleman asked her. He had his own information about the healings, but decided this was not the time or place to tell all.

Margaret frowned and answered reluctantly, "I've been living here all my life, and people talk. Somebody needs to call that woman who calls herself a minister to task. Demand she put a stop to these Friday night satanic services. Who…"

"Wait one minute. Hold on now," Reilly interrupted. "We can't demand anything. Are you forgetting people have the right to worship as they see fit?"

Reilly had been quiet most of the night, having a lot on his mind, with the possibility of him getting a federal appointee position and Diana's recent bizarre behavior at the top of the list. He tensed up when he remembered Margaret and Reverend Pierce were on the list of people the investigators checking into his background planned to talk to. Listening to Margaret's rant that night, he cringed.

"Then what do you propose we do?" Margaret asked him angrily.

Reilly was used to working with professional woman who knew how to conduct themselves. This woman, he decided, was deranged, and knew something would have to be done about her eventually. Three prominent ministers were sitting there listening to her raving as if they were under a spell or scared to death of her. He was convinced she was the reason the church was losing members.

"I propose we offer Friday night prayer sessions at our respective churches."

"Hmmm, do you really think that will work? Haven't you heard that people who couldn't walk are now able to walk after leaving the healing service? And others are being cured of all kinds of cancers, diabetes, and blindness, so they say. How can we compete with that?" she challenged Reilly.

"By doing what you suggested, Margaret," her husband said, seeking to end the war of words. "We will expose them if they are using actors, use the pulpit to fight them, and have our own Friday night prayer and healing services. Jesus healed with prayer, and so will we." Hoping this would satisfy everyone, Reverend Pierce looked around the room.

"That's not enough!" Margaret shouted, before storming out of the room.

"God, what more does she want?" Deacon Coleman exclaimed.

Later that evening, Margaret lay in bed, her eyes wide open, listening to her husband's rhythmic snoring. His arm was across her breasts, holding her close to him. She wanted to push him away and run and hide in her father's room. There she would be safe. Rev wouldn't let anything happen to her. Margaret knew she wasn't the one speaking tonight; it was a new voice. This one was different. It didn't curse or call her bad names. It was an angel, she decided. It told her that she was the chosen one and had been anointed. Margaret fell asleep with that reassuring thought, but not before pushing her husband's arm away.

CHAPTER THIRTEEN

Lindy took one last look at a sleeping Michael and closed the door to his room. It was five in the morning, and they had to be at the house in Chevy Chase before sunrise. Marianne, the babysitter, had arrived ten minutes ago. She was one of the teacher's aides in Michael's classroom, and she loved Michael as if he was her own little brother. Lindy gave her last-minute instructions on what to feed Michael for breakfast and a list of activities to occupy their time.

On their way to their Toyota Corolla, they saw a large sign on the light post across from their car. It read: *Come one, come all to the first Friday night of the month prayer watch. Regardless of any challenge you may be having in your life, God will lift you up. God is the provider, the healer, and the protector. God loves you and will see you through.*

Signs and flyers listing dates, times, and participating churches had been distributed throughout the eight wards of the city. They were in libraries, beauty shops, barbershops, grocery stores, restaurants, banks, bars, and anywhere else the organizers could think to post them. The churches had even taken out full-page ads in newspapers, and public-service announcements were being aired on all the popular radio stations. For the last two Sundays, the ministers had preached on being fooled by false prophets and had invited everyone to attend one of the prayer services for spiritual healing. Lindy shook her head in disgust. She had no doubt that Margaret was behind this campaign to discredit the healing sessions of Melchizedek Church.

The car windows were down, and Lindy could smell the grass and hear the birds sing. She loved this time of morning. Lindy glanced at her husband, who was reading a couple of letters from his dear friend,

Dhar, in India. She knew he missed his life in India. He had just gotten home, and already she could see that faraway look in his eyes. Lindy prayed Paul wouldn't leave just yet. She needed him now more than ever to be close to Michael and her. There was just too much going on.

Why is it so hard for me to let go of the past? she wondered. Nick was back, and already she couldn't get him out of her head. Since the day he had just shown up at her office, she had been reliving their fun times together in his old dilapidated apartment. Then the awful night that changed her life forever would sneak into her thoughts, and a sharp pain in her heart would bring her back to reality, but her desire for him would not go away.

The day after she had lunch with him Nick sent her a dozen lilies, which only triggered memories of Mary, her spiritual teacher. Betty had told her years ago that she couldn't stop thinking about both Mary and Nick because she still had unfinished business with them.

The opening reception for Nick's exhibit was next month, but Lindy had already decided not to attend the affair. She again glanced at Paul, who was still very much absorbed in his letters. There would be no reason to tell him about Nick. After all, she probably wouldn't be seeing Nick again, anyway.

Shifting her thoughts to the first time she visited the Awakener's house, Lindy remembered that she had been afraid to enter, but a breeze had touched her face, and seemed to carry the message, *Doubt and fear keep you from the truth.*

From the outside, the Tudor-style house looked like any other house in the Chevy Chase area. However, the interior was sparsely furnished. Rows of folding chairs took the place of living-room furniture. Classes and meditation sessions were held in this room. In the early morning, sunlight would stream through the large bay window, and it was not unusual to see a rainbow on the white wall. Photographs of the pyramids of Egypt and Mexico, Stonehenge in England, Machu Picchu in Peru, and the Olmec heads of Guatemala adorned the walls.

Lindy had lived in the house in Chevy Chase off and on while attending medical school. Therefore, she knew the routine quite well.

Everyone was up before dawn, dressed, and assembled in the meditation room to face east for the sunrise meditation. At exactly sunrise, the house would vibrate with the ancient sound of *AUM*, and then for the next hour there would be silence. In one of her many lectures, Ruth told Lindy and the other students that spiritual knowledge flowed from the East and that the most powerful sound in the universe was *AUM*. Paul had told her that in the Hindu Upanishads, *AUM* stands for the primal sound of God.

While living in the house, Lindy was a vegetarian, and they ate raw food. Each member of the household had daily chores. Even with her medical school load, Lindy was still required to do her share of the household duties. She was also expected to attend the esoteric wisdom classes Ruth and Mark taught.

Paul also lived in the house for a short time. He told her it reminded him of his ashram in India, where they followed a very similar routine, but they meditated for hours. In the ashram, they were taught that the spiritual journey lies within, and that it is through meditation that one will reach a state of nirvana.

The group Lindy and Paul had started out with had dispersed. Lin Lee, the young Chinese woman who everyone called Lee because of the similarity of her name to Lindy, left to pursue mediumship with a group in Sedona, Arizona. Koto Omo returned home to Ghana and was studying the sacred healing practices of his tribe. After one or two meetings, Barbara Einstein never returned; Matthew was a librarian at the Library of Congress and was involved in the I AM movement. Lindy didn't know what happened to Adul and Maria. Just as the students came and went, so did the teachers. Only Mark and Ruth remained of the original six teachers.

Ruth had been in the country for over twenty years. No one knew much about her, except that she was originally from England, or so they believed, and had traveled quite extensively all over the world with her father, a historian and archaeologist. The photographs on the wall belonged to Ruth. Oddly, there were no people in them.

IT'S NOT OVER YET

There was no formal induction into the Awakeners. Students were simply accepted into the group after attending many classes and meetings. Ruth had told them the Awakeners would prepare them to enter the first level of the initiation into the mysteries. First, they had to learn how to master the emotional bodily and earthly attachments to reach higher levels of consciousness that led to the cosmic or celestial planes.

———

The three Awakeners were already seated in the front of the room. Lindy and Paul could hear the soft chant of the ancient sound as they quietly took off their shoes and joined the others. Paul took a dark-blue cushion from a seat and placed it on the shiny wood floor. He had become accustomed to sitting in the lotus position during his many years of training in the ashram.

Lindy felt a little antsy when she first sat down. She wanted to slouch in the chair and let her head fall forward, as the erect posture was so uncomfortable. The three Awakeners were sitting in armless chairs with their spines straight. Posture in meditation was just as important as breathing and directing your consciousness to the point between your eyebrows—the third eye. Energy would not flow upward if the spinal nerves were pinched due to poor posture.

Lindy hadn't meditated in months. Every day she vowed to put aside a little time to do so, but it never seemed to happen. But no matter what was going on in Paul's life, meditation always came first. He meditated faithfully every morning at four, at noon, and an hour before retiring for the night. She wished she could be as devoted and disciplined as he was.

Gradually, the chanting got softer and softer. Lindy began to focus on breathing—inhaling and exhaling. She tried hard to relax and keep distractions at bay, but thoughts of Nick kept intruding. Finally, she felt her body and mind relax. A small red sphere appeared before her eyes. Lindy watched as it grew larger and larger, and then everything went black.

Lindy heard someone calling her name. Her eyes popped open, and she was in a beautiful field of colorful flowers and bright sunshine. She turned toward the sound and saw a figure standing in the doorway of an octagonal-shaped glass building; gold beams intersected at each of the eight panels. In seconds, a force pulled her toward the building. She was falling, falling rapidly down a tunnel. Lindy saw she was in the house she grew up in. Fear gripped her. Her grandfather was in a wheelchair in his office, with saliva running down the side of his mouth. He looked so old and tired. She could hear his cries for help. She tried to let him know she was there, but he couldn't see or hear her. He was imprisoned in his own mind. Lindy's heart ached as she looked at the broken and crippled man who had once been larger than life. She had to help him. As she moved closer to him, a wall appeared, blocking her way. She couldn't get to him. Lindy pounded on the wall, and then she heard a faint bell, far away, getting louder and louder.

She opened her eyes to find Paul sitting next to her.

"You okay?" he asked, placing his arm around her.

"Yeah, I'm all right." She was shaking.

God, I am so blessed to have this man in my life. She took his hand and kissed the back of it. *There are two things I must do. Get Nick out of my mind and help Papa,* she thought. Lindy wanted to share her vision with the others, but the expressions on their faces told her this was not the time.

Ruth took the floor and informed them that the day's discussion would be on maya, or illusions.

"And not Grace Perry's newspaper article and what's going on with the churches?" Betty asked, looking distraught.

"What is there to talk about?" Ruth asked.

"They are attacking our credibility. Isn't anyone here concerned about what's going on?" Betty looked around the room, her gaze coming to rest on Lindy.

Before Lindy could respond, Mark said, "That's just it, Betty. It's not real. It is the darkness trying to get us to buy into the illusion of confusion and disharmony."

"No, you don't understand. This is real. These people are evil and want to destroy us. We have to fight." Betty took off her jacket and began to fan herself.

"Evil? Yes, I can see how you might think they are evil and are attacking us. Still, they are our sisters and brothers. From the moment you set foot on the spiritual path, you will encounter lessons and tests to help your growth spiritually. Our interactions with others bring us the lesson," Ruth offered.

"I know this, Ruth. Evil thoughts are all around us, but the difference here is they are aimed at us, the church. I need something or someone to help me fight back." Betty wouldn't let it go.

"Betty…"

Before Ruth could finish her sentence, Betty stood up and looked at the small group. With a trace of dismay in her voice, she said, "Grace Perry asked about the Awakeners. Soon she will be sniffing around to who you are." She nodded toward Ruth and Mark. "This reporter is a smart cookie, and soon she will put it together that the Awakeners and the Elder Healer are linked. Then she will let her hounds loose to track down identities. The kicker is she will probably find out who the Elder Healer is before I do." Betty's eyes landed on Ruth.

The silence in the room was too much to bear.

"I cannot at this time reveal the identity of the Elder Healer," Ruth answered wearily.

"Why not?" Betty asked, her voice hardening.

"I wish I could give you a more straightforward answer, but it's not that simple. I need you to trust me now. When the time is right, everything will be revealed. I can tell you that this is a lesson in oneness for everyone," Ruth replied.

"I can see that this is already happening. Once a month, churches across the city will be offering healing services to the community." Paul finally spoke out.

"And?" Betty asked sarcastically, pressing on.

"The multitudes of churches offering healing services will open doors for more such church projects to help people."

"I think you are way off base with this," Betty said. "They are offering these services not just to help people, but as a campaign against us."

Lindy could not hold back any longer. "What do you want us to do then, Betty?"

"I want the Elder Healer to come forth and let people know who she is and what she is about. Is this person so mysterious that she is not of this world?" Betty tried to lighten her request.

"Perhaps, my dear, you have finally forced my hand into at least saying you are partially correct."

"No, no, oh no…this is not good. You're telling me the Elder Healer is not of this world?"

"The Elder Healer is part of the mystical order called the Great White Brotherhood. The Brotherhood is a group composed of highly evolved spiritual beings such as Jesus, Buddha, St. Germain, Kuthumi, Serapis Bey, Mother Mary, Kuan Yin, and White Eagle—considered the caretakers of humanity and the master teachers of spiritual wisdom."

Mark picked up where Ruth left off. "They are often referred to as ascended masters or adepts because they are perfect and no longer bound by the law of cause and effect, or earthly karma." He added, "The Brotherhood mostly works on the etheric plane for the welfare of humankind, fostering love, peace, and wisdom. In some circumstances, they will choose to work directly among the people. By the way, the word white refers to the brilliant white light of their auras, not to any ethnic group."

Her voice weak from talking, Ruth stood up. "The Elder Healer is part of the Brotherhood's way of working on the earthly plane with humanity to bring about oneness and spiritual knowledge. It is part of God's plan that can only be revealed in God's time." Tiring, she threw a kiss at them and left the room.

"Years ago, you believed me when I told you Mary Magdalene came to me and gave us information about our past lives as the women disciples of Jesus. Why can't you accept this?" Lindy directed her question at Betty.

"This is different, Lindy. You don't have people hounding at your door. I'm the one in the hot seat. How do I explain the Great White Brotherhood to Grace Perry? She's not going to let up."

"Ruth is right," Paul spoke up. "We need to look at the spiritual lesson. The challenge that is presenting itself to us is a lesson and a test for each of us because we know the laws. Don't let Grace Perry and the others pull you down into this maya."

"Pull me down? Ha! I'm already knee deep in the mess." Betty picked up her purse and, without saying another word, left Lindy, Paul and Mark looking lost.

CHAPTER FOURTEEN

From the first seat in the senior choir loft, Margaret had a clear view of everyone in the congregation. To her dismay, the church was still not as full as she would have liked. She remembered how the church would be packed twenty minutes before Rev would get started, and the collection plates would be overflowing. The big checks written by those high and mighty district and federal government workers kept them going, not that she was complaining. But Margaret figured they could be gone tomorrow. Then what?

Wearing long black robes, the senior choir members stood as the organist began to play. After Alan became senior minister, Margaret joined the choir to keep her hands in church business. With a new president to the trustee board, she was no longer handled the collection plates or paid the church bills. The board had stripped her of her unofficial role as treasurer of the church. The trustees were now the overseers of the church's money. Margaret wanted to laugh when she thought about the plaque they had given her for her many years of devoted service to the church. Hell, her father founded the church. A plaque was a slap in the face.

The board had the church financial records audited. Margaret felt a rush of anger come over her as she relived the humiliation of them poring over the records. They didn't find anything. The voice had warned her to keep a second set of books locked up in her desk drawer. Tomorrow, she promised herself, she would get rid of them.

Margaret perked up when she saw Grace Perry take a seat in the back row, and made a mental note to greet her after the service. She looked around again and saw that the church was slowly filling up. A good sign. Diana Reilly was sitting in the row behind the deacons and trustees. Margaret tried to be courteous whenever they met, but Diana had an uppity air about her, even though she was from a piss-poor dirt farm somewhere in Alabama. She was the same age as Lindy, and had also attended Howard. Diana had it all. She was married to Daniel Reilly, a powerhouse in D.C., and had a high-level job. Rumor was she had slept with him to get where she was.

Give them a halfway good job and position, and the darkest and ugliest ones try to be more than they are. Margaret decided it was the expensive clothes and hairstyle that made Diana look almost presentable.

Margaret looked at Daniel Reilly sitting in front of his wife, noting that he was at least three shades lighter than Diana. *Wonder why they never had children?* Daniel probably didn't want to take a chance they would come out the wrong color. Her husband's voice brought her back to the present; he was reading from the Bible. She looked out at the audience and saw a sea of bored faces. Margaret wished she could figure out how to put the fire in him. She suffered through the rest of his sermon, hearing him call her to the pulpit to talk about the healing sessions to be held at the Mt. Olive church and other churches throughout the city.

Margaret had to step over several women as she left the choir loft. She wished she could take off the heavy robe. She was wearing a lovely and very expensive beige suit, which she had caught on sale for $350. She had taken the money out of Rev's account, since she couldn't take it out of her account with Alan. Margaret didn't feel like arguing with Alan over a few pennies for a suit. He was so cheesy, counting every dime, constantly telling her to curb her spending habits. She missed Cissy. Cissy could get her the best designer clothes, for which she paid hardly anything. Margaret never asked Cissy where she got the clothes. The rumor was Cissy was a booster. *Nonsense. I wouldn't deal with a thief.* If anything, Cissy was a liar. She had lied about Lindy being pregnant by Nick. Margaret knew she could never trust Cissy again, even if she showed up on her doorstep today—not unless, of course, she had a few nice pieces.

By the time Margaret reached the pulpit, Reverend Pierce was sitting down in the new chair he had the church purchase for him. Over Margaret's objection, Rev's old chair was in the basement.

"Um, um, good morning," Margaret said, looking out at the congregation. "I am not going to mince my words this morning. I'm standing in front of you today to talk about the first Friday night healing prayer meetings. This church, and every church in the metropolitan area, is in grave danger of being attacked by a dark satanic force." Reverend Pierce saw trustee Reilly looking at Margaret as if he wanted to strangle her. That didn't stop her, though; Margaret just kept going.

"The devil is alive and coming after us. As my father would say, don't be fooled by the disguises he is wearing. Get behind me, Satan," Margaret screamed. "Do you hear me, Satan?" She raised her voice even higher. "I said get behind me!"

"Amen. Preach, Sister Margaret," Deacon Coleman hollered. He was getting a kick watching the shock on Reverend Pierce's face, who by now was leaning halfway out of his chair.

Margaret had been waiting for this moment for a long time. The pulpit was all hers, and so was the congregation. One of the older members stood and waved her arms to and fro.

"The devil wants a fight and we are going to give him one. We are not going to stand by and let him belittle and ridicule Christian soldiers, are we?" she shouted.

"No!" the congregation screamed back.

When Reverend Pierce stood and made a move towards the pulpit, Margaret moved across the pulpit, beseeching the crowd, "Won't you join the army of our Lord and savior Jesus Christ? Don't stand by and let false prophets steal away your family and friends. We have to save those who have been tricked into a deceitful way of believing that they are being healed."

As she spoke, her face and body changed. She actually seemed taller. Margaret leaned back, just as she had seen her father and grandfather do. She really wanted to get down on one knee, but the skirt stopped her. She bellowed, "God, help us! Help us, Father!" Margaret stomped her feet and shook her head so hard her hair came loose. She started to jump around, shouting, "Jesus, God, help your children!" By this time, the congregants were on their feet, shouting with her.

Margaret looked up to the ceiling, as if expecting God to descend and take her up to the heavens. Her arms went up, and she started moving them back and forth. She looked out at the people waving their arms in unison with her. Tears streamed down her face. Margaret Johnson Lee Pierce wanted to never move from that spot. It belonged to her, and for the first time in her life, she felt truly happy.

Reverend Pierce couldn't believe his eyes. Margaret had done what he couldn't do in eleven years. Thankfully, she paused, and he seized the moment to signal the organist to play. Reverend Pierce moved in and grabbed her arm, squeezing her elbow. He led his resisting wife off the pulpit. He wouldn't look at Reilly as he led Margaret back to her seat.

At the end of the service, Margaret could not get out of the choir loft; as many of the old members were crowing her, and trying to shake her hand or to hug her. They all promised to show up on the first Friday. "You got to stand up for God," she told them.

The last person to approach her was Grace Perry. "Quite a sermon you gave, Mrs. Pierce. You sounded like your father," Grace said.

"I thought you were new to this area. My father hasn't preached in years."

"I passed through D.C. once or twice." Opening her notebook, she quickly stated her business. "If you have a moment, I would like to ask you some questions."

"You sure do remind me of someone."

"They say everyone has a twin," she replied.

"No, not in looks; it's your mannerism and speech. It's not important, though. So what do you want to ask me?" Margaret wanted to get it over with so she could bask in her triumph. *Where is Papa? Did he see me?* She couldn't wait to go over it with him.

"About the first Friday healing and prayer meeting, could you tell me a little more about it?"

"Yes. As good Christians, it is important we do our missionary work of bringing the lost sheep back to the Lord Jesus our savior, especially delivering them from unchristian-like folks."

"How do you plan to do this?"

"We are asking that everyone attend one of the many prayer services and bring a family member, friend, or whomever along. We will pray for them and teach them to rely on Jesus our Lord for guidance and healing. We will reinforce the Christian doctrine that it is the spirit of God through Jesus that performs miracles and healings, not just any ordinary man. It is very important people understand that."

"So, you think the healing miracles taking place at your daughter's church are not real?" Grace Perry asked, deliberately referring to Lindy.

"Miracle healings? Ha! Did you hear what I just said?" She gave Grace Perry her best face.

"You know, people being able to see after having been blind for years?"

"I don't know anything about these people being blind or crippled. Have you seen their medical histories?" Margaret asked harshly.

"You are saying they are faking the illnesses?"

"I'm saying don't judge a book by the cover until you have read everything in it."

"May I quote you?" Grace Perry asked, smiling smugly.

"Why not? I'm only saying what others are thinking. Maybe you're looking in the wrong places. The truth might be right under your nose." Margaret shook as chills ran up and down her spine. It was the voice making her talk as if she had authority.

Grace Perry snapped a photograph of Margaret, and then hurried out of the church to make her other important appointment. Grace reached under the seat of her car and felt for the bag. The bottle inside was hot because it was one of the dog days in D.C., the temperature reaching into the nineties for the third time that week. The liquor had been locked up in the car since she purchased it the night before. As Grace Perry headed across town, she thought the old drunk wouldn't care if it was hot or cold…as long as it tasted like scotch.

CHAPTER FIFTEEN

Diana sat across the kitchen table from her husband, Daniel Reilly, sipping her first cup of black coffee of the day. He was staring at her with the most horror-struck look on his face; he had just read the morning paper. Daniel spread the paper on the table so both articles could be seen. The article about Nick was harmless enough, but the two photographs with their captions implied more was going on. Diana peeked at the photograph of Nick embracing Dr. Lindy Lee. The caption read, *Renowned photographer Nick Lewis is welcomed home by Dr. Lindy Lee and Diana Reilly*. She should have followed her first instinct to tell him about her dinner with Nick. *Damn that Grace Perry!*

Diana folded the paper and threw it into the trash, but Daniel retrieved it.

"Daniel, please. You of all people know how reporters lie. They twist the truth." Diana reached for Daniel's hand, but he quickly pulled back.

"But photographs don't lie! What is this Nick Lewis to you?"

"He is my homeboy. We grew up together in Alabama!"

"What were you doing with him at a hotel?" he demanded.

"You act as though you don't trust me. We had dinner together to catch up on old times, and he wanted to invite us to the opening reception for his 'Children of Africa' exhibit at the museum."

"Why haven't you told me about this? I had to find out from an article in the *Washington Star*." Daniel pushed his chair back and stood at the sink, glaring at his wife.

Diana got up and walked very seductively over to her husband, placing her arms around his neck. "Baby, you sound as if you're jealous," she teased.

He removed her arms. "I have told you numerous times appearances are very important. I have been waiting to tell you that I'm being considered for an appointed position. It hasn't been announced, but I can't afford any bad press."

"What? You never told me about any appointed position. You mean by the President?" Her voice had a trill to it.

"Yes, who else would I be talking about? This would definitely project us into a whole new social stratum. Now do you understand why I can't afford the least little rumble?"

"Daniel, you don't have to worry about anything. This Grace Perry woman was looking for something to say about Nick because he's like a star. You know how the media likes to dig up all kinds of dirt and start rumors about folks, especially those in the limelight." Diana grabbed him again.

"Maybe I did make too much of this, but my nerves are on edge waiting to see if I get the position. I wanted to surprise you with the news by taking you out on the town." Daniel kissed her gently on the lips.

"We can still do that. Come with me; I know what will calm you down." She turned around and pushed her behind into him.

"Although your offer is tempting, I have a meeting at nine this morning and can't be late. They're watching everything. By the way, when is your friend's exhibit?"

"I don't remember off-hand. I have to look at the invitation," Diana stated.

"Find out. If he's that famous, then a lot of the right people will be there. I think for appearance's sake we should go."

"The invitation is in my office. I will call you with the information so you can put it on your schedule." Diana blew him a kiss and hurriedly moved toward the living room before her husband could respond.

Daniel folded the paper neatly and placed it under his arm. He wanted to read the other article Grace Perry had written, the one with the picture of Margaret. The look on her face said it all. Mad. He had to do something about her if that weakling husband of hers couldn't keep her in check.

≈

Paul did not read newspapers. He felt the stories influenced one's mood for the day, as they were filled with violence and despair. Still, Lindy felt it was better if she told him about the photograph in case he somehow found out. She stared at the photograph of Nick and Diana. They looked good together. She bit down on her lip, tasting blood. She pressed a tissue against her lip.

What difference does it make to me? I don't plan to see him again.

Lindy's call took Paul by surprise; usually, she was too busy to call so early in the morning. Paul had decided to keep Michael home after he had another nightmare in which someone was trying to take him away from them.

Her voice sounded troubled when he answered the phone.

"There's another article by that reporter, Grace Perry, attacking the church."

"They're not going to stop, but we have to maintain peace and love in our hearts for them," Paul responded.

"I know, but it must be difficult for Betty."

"What do you want to do?"

"I don't know. I just don't want her to feel as if she is alone."

"Then let her know we are with her," Paul replied.

"With her how?"

"We can ask for inner guidance from the spirit."

"What are you saying?"

"It's time you use your gift."

Lindy cut him off before he could finish. "You know I don't do that. I wouldn't know where to start."

"The dreams and visions you have been having lately are pulling you back."

"Stop, Paul! I can't do it. Mary deserted me. I don't want to give Betty false hopes. She wants someone to stand up with her, not contact a spirit."

"How do you know she wouldn't want it?"

"Trust me, she's different now. Didn't you hear what she said at the meeting?"

"Yeah, but another article has come out, and from what you told me, your mother is saying the healings are fake. Okay, then, let's find out what Betty wants to do before jumping to conclusions."

"Yes, that's good," Lindy answered.

"Don't worry. Everything will be okay."

"There's something else."

Paul braced himself.

"Remember Nick Lewis from Howard?" Lindy could hardly get the words out.

"The Nick Lewis that you were going to run away to Paris with?" The words came out so quickly they sounded harsh, although Paul didn't mean for them to sound that way.

"Yes. He's here in D.C."

Silence. "Paul? Are you there?"

"Yes."

Lindy told him about the day Nick came to her office and surprised her, that they'd had lunch, and that he had extended an invitation to them for his opening exhibit. Then she told him about the newspaper article and the photograph taken by the reporter, and how Grace Perry had insinuated there was more to it because of their past.

Again, silence.

"Paul, it was a harmless lunch. I don't plan to see him again, and I'm definitely not going to the exhibit."

"We should go," he responded, his voice devoid of emotion.

"Why?"

"Why not? It will put a stop to any gossip. I'll be there with you."

"Okay," Lindy said, ending the call.

This was so unlike Paul to want to go to a social event. She usually had to beg him to accompany her to any of Betty's parties or the hospital functions. Now he wanted to go to Nick's exhibit.

She tried to read the case history of a young patient she had to examine later that day, but her thoughts kept returning to events of the last few weeks. Nick was back in her life. *No, he's not. He's with Diana.* Lindy picked up the newspaper and stared at the two of them. She wanted to scream. She had to get out of the office. It hurt so badly. As she hurried to leave, she was startled by Nick's presence on the other side of her door.

"What are you doing here?" Lindy asked in a stern voice.

"To give you the invitations to the exhibit."

"You could have mailed them."

"I don't know your address. Care to give it to me?" he joked.

"Did you read the *Washington Star* this morning?" She ignored his jesting.

"Is that what's bothering you? Can we go into your office before more pictures are taken?" Nick laughed.

"Nicholas Lewis, I don't know what you think is so funny. This Grace Perry has some type of vendetta against me. Why? I don't know. I don't even know the woman." Lindy backed into her office.

"She did ask a few questions about you at my interview," Nick shared. "Perhaps it has something to do with your church."

They were now standing in the middle of the floor. Close. She kept telling herself to move away, put some distance between them. The cologne he was wearing was intoxicating. He moved closer and gently cupped her chin. Lindy tried to push his hand away, but not in time. Nick bent down and kissed her—gently at first, and then his tongue was parting her lips. Lindy found herself giving in to him as his hand lightly touched her breasts. A light knock on the door brought an abrupt end to the kiss.

"Come in," Lindy said loudly as Nick walked over to a chair and sat.

"It's just me, Dr. Lee. I have some messages for you. Oh, I didn't know you had company," Pearl, the receptionist, said with a slight snicker.

"Thanks." Lindy took the messages from her. "I'll be leaving for my eleven a.m. consultation in a few moments." *By lunchtime, I'm sure it will be all over the hospital that the man in the photograph with the married Dr. Lee was in her office again.*

"Sure, Doc," Pearl said, smiling at Nick as she shut the door.

"Don't ever do that again. In case you've forgotten, I'm a married woman with a child. Happily married, I might add." She stared angrily at him.

"For old time's sake, Lindy, married or not, you have to admit you wanted it." He sounded like the Nick she remembered.

"You should leave. Besides, your friend Dinah—Diana, or whatever, is probably waiting for you."

"The article and photographs were used to twist the truth. Diana and I had some unfinished business. As you know, I left her in a bad way, and I needed to make amends."

"So you told me."

"I can't find any records of the birth or death of the baby at this hospital."

"Why are you looking?"

"I'll tell you at lunch. It's a long story."

"No, Nick, I don't think that's a good idea," Lindy said weakly. They had already gone too far today. Her nipples were still hard, and she felt aroused.

"About what time will you finish your appointment?" he asked, ignoring her.

"Around twelve-thirty." *Why am I telling him this?*

Moving toward the door, Nick said confidently, "I'll see you at one o'clock at the same restaurant, baby."

Lindy felt her skin flush.

CHAPTER SIXTEEN

Betty picked up the paper, wanting to read those few lines again, even though she had read them several times already.

"Who are these people being healed? Mrs. Margaret Pierce wants to know. She claims there is no medical documentation to substantiate their claims of illnesses or healings."

Betty slammed down the newspaper.

And we're supposed to turn the other cheek. No way. I'm going to stop her. Stan is right. I am in charge of this church, and I need to get a hold of things. How does Grace Perry know the intimate details of what is going on here? Betty wondered.

Betty skipped over several paragraphs until she came to another part of the article quoting Margaret. Adjusting her new reading glasses, she continued reading:

"It was a lively service at the Mt. Olive Baptist Church. Margaret Johnson Lee Pierce, daughter of Rev. Perlie Johnson, former senior pastor of Mt. Olive, and wife of the present minister, Rev. Alan Pierce, brought the congregation to their feet with exhortations to seize the opportunity to bring lost and straying members back into the fold.

"In an interview after the service, Mrs. Pierce expanded on her impromptu sermon:

"The Christian churches of the city plan to hold their own prayer and healing services on the first Friday of the month. As good Christians, it is important we do our missionary work of bringing the lost sheep back to the Lord Jesus our savior, especially delivering them from un-Christian like folks. We must reinforce the Christian doctrine that it is the spirit of God through Jesus that performs miracles and healings, not just any ordinary man. It is very important people understand that."

What more did Ruth and the others need to wake up? Margaret was calling the Elder Healer a fake and the healing sessions bogus, a slap in the face for everything they stood for. If the others didn't do something soon, she sure as hell planned to use all the legal power she still had in D.C. to let Grace Perry and Margaret Pierce know she wasn't going to take this crap. Betty examined the article once more and picked up her legal pad.

Thank God she had followed her instincts and had kept records, such as the names and addresses of all the people the Elder Healer had healed.

Pacing anxiously in her small office, Betty's mind was racing. The ringing of her private line put a stop to her pacing and twirling. Betty let it ring a few times before answering it. When she heard Stan's voice, she silently said, *Thank you, Jesus.*

"What are you doing?"

"Working on my sermon for Sunday," she lied.

"Meet me in thirty minutes at the usual place," he said.

She hesitated.

"Something wrong?"

"No, I'll be there."

"Don't keep me waiting."

So much for the work she planned to do. She couldn't afford not to meet him. She had gone long enough without seeing him. Besides, she needed a little TLC.

Betty removed her purse from the desk drawer, and was headed out when the phone rang again. "Oh, God, don't tell me he's calling back to cancel." Betty stared at the phone. Finally, she grabbed the receiver. Betty let out a long sigh of relief when she heard Lindy's voice.

"Lindy, I can't talk now. I'm on my way out." Holding the phone between her head and shoulder, she checked her image in the mirror.

"I'll make this short. We want you to come to dinner tonight."

"Tonight?" She looked at the work before her. "Okay, I'll be there," Betty promised.

IT'S NOT OVER YET

Checking her watch again, Betty stuffed her makeup case into her purse. Stan didn't like her to be late, so she had better hurry. She could put her makeup on at traffic lights. Betty closed the door to her office and did something she had never done—locked it. She was sure there was a rat in the church, and she was going to smoke the creature out.

Stan had already arrived at the motel off Route One in College Park, Maryland. He had insisted they meet outside D.C. Stan told her constantly he had too much to lose if his wife found out. *What happened to the Stan who used to parade me around the best restaurants and hotels in D.C. when we first met? Is he pulling away from me?*

Betty admitted to herself she wanted more out of the relationship. She had gotten involved with Stan out of boredom and lack of good sex. The relationship with him was supposed to have been an outlet for her frustrations, but it had taken a different turn. She wanted Stan to be there for her. *Is it time to set an ultimatum? Leave your wife or I'll leave you!*

How about her own marriage? Harvey was gone. Every chance he got, he went to Israel to be with his family. A postcard or letter now and then was not enough.

Betty looked at the car's clock as she pulled into the parking lot of the motel. She was ten minutes late, which was not good.

Stan opened the door and pulled her into the room, wearing only his jockey shorts. He kissed her long and hard on the mouth and rubbed against her. Then he began to unzip the back of her dress. She felt his large hand tugging at her bra.

"Wait—wait." She gently pushed him away. "I haven't seen you in a while and this is how you greet me?" Betty tried to sound as though she was teasing him.

"You were late, and I don't have a lot of time. A patient canceled and I thought we could get together like old times—in between patients," he said with contempt.

"I need to talk, Stan. There's so much going on. I feel as though I'm going out of my mind."

"Then make an appointment to see me." He pulled her down onto the bed. "Let's not go there today. Want a drink? I brought some wine." Stan got up and poured some wine into two styrofoam cups.

What happened to the nice hotel with crystal wine glasses?

Betty sipped the wine slowly, deciding she was going to drag this out as long as she could. But Stan had another plan. He took the cup from her hand and placed it on the nightstand, and then he pushed the top of her dress off her shoulder and kissed her neck.

Betty lay there without responding. She had been waiting for this, but now that she had it, she wasn't enjoying it.

"Okay, what in the hell is going on?" He stopped and sat up. "Is this about the church or what?" he asked, his voice rising.

"That and a lot of other things." She also sat up.

He pulled her close to him. "You know all day long I listen to my patients' stupid problems. When I'm with you, I feel like a million dollars. You make me forget the hospital and my problems. Our time together is special. Every morning when I am sitting on the toilet taking a crap, I think about you. Now, let the doctor relax you." Stan pulled her dress down to her waist and slipped her bra off.

He loved her breasts. For a woman in her forties, they were still very perky. He gently started to kiss and suck each nipple until they got hard. The wine started to put Betty in a relaxed state. As his tongue darted in and out of her ear, he pulled the rest of her clothes off.

They were like two animals in the jungle. Betty tried to wrap her legs around his waist, but he pushed her away, turning so that his member hung over her mouth.

Betty reached up and began to use her tongue to circle around the tip of his manhood; he tried to get her to take it all. She knew what drove him crazy, just as he knew what she liked. They were so sexually compatible.

"Give it to me, daddy!" she screamed as he turned and inserted his engorged member into her. He then flipped her over. Betty loved being on top. She could feel the penetration better. The bed creaked as she rode him. Just as she was about to come, he flipped her over again. Drops of sweat from his brow dripped into her mouth and eyes as he pushed harder and deeper into her. The steady rhythm of their bodies was like an orchestrated dance. She felt herself entering a zone that could be comparable to a meditative bliss. At last, she felt his body tremble as she came, too. Stan collapsed on top of her, his weight crushing her beneath him. She couldn't breathe. Finally, he rolled over onto the other side of the bed, and Betty pulled the sheets up over her.

"What time is it?" He reached for his watch on the nightstand. "It's late. I got to go."

"Wham, bam, thank you, ma'am," she muttered to herself.

Stan headed for the bathroom. "Come on, lazy. Don't you have to get back to work?" he joked, closing the bathroom door.

Betty checked her watch for the time. It was one; they had been there less than an hour.

Why don't I feel good? she asked herself while gathering up her clothes.

At the Howard Inn, Nick Lewis looked at his watch. One p.m. and still no Lindy. He ordered a drink and took out the papers from his briefcase to read over the 1967 news article. He had gone to the public library to search the obituary sections of the *Washington Star* and *Washington Times* from the year 1967. The librarian in the Washingtonian Division of the public library was very helpful and showed him how to operate the microfiche machine.

The clipping he had was not an obituary, but an article about an abandoned baby found in the dumpster behind the girls' dorm of Howard University. The baby was described as a boy, dark brown with light brown eyes, 19 1/2 inches long, weighing 3 lbs., and only a couple of hours old. The day was December 17, 1967.

No, it can't be! He began to scribble dates on the back of the napkin. *When did Diana tell me she was pregnant? It was during the summer of '67. She was getting ready to enter her second trimester when she had the botched abortion.*

Nick was so engrossed in re-creating the events of the past he didn't see the waitress standing at the table.

"Are you ready to order, sir?" she asked.

Still no Lindy. Nick wished hadn't been so forward with her earlier. She looked so innocent, but seductive at the same time. He had reacted with the head below the belt, instead of above. He could feel the heat from her body; she wanted him, too. *It's just a matter of time.*

"Let me have the steak, medium rare, mashed potatoes and gravy, cornbread, and some okra."

CHAPTER SEVENTEEN

Lindy deliberately kept the parents of the child she was referring for surgery in her office longer than needed, but not long enough. The meeting ended at one, still leaving enough time to meet Nick. Afraid he might return to her office looking for her, Lindy made her rounds earlier than usual, and then decided to go home to avoid the temptation of going to meet him. Paul and Michael were surprised when she came home early. They were, nonetheless, excited to see her.

After spending an hour talking to her husband and playing with her son, Lindy went upstairs to take a bath before having dinner, which Paul had already started preparing.

While soaking in her favorite rose-scented bath fragrance, Lindy closed her eyes and let the warmth of the water soothe her body and mind. Her thoughts soon flashed back to the morning, and she could still smell Nick's cologne and feel his thick lips on her mouth. She experienced a tingling between her legs as the water warmed her body. As she imagined Nick covering her with kisses and penetrating deep inside her, Lindy reached under the water until she felt the softness of her vagina. She then pleasured herself.

She let out a muffled moan, suppressing the urge to scream out Nick's name. Tears collected in her eyes. Then she leaned over the tub and quietly sobbed.

It's Paul's fault. He's pushing me toward another man by not wanting me. If only I hadn't agreed to that stupid vow of celibacy.

Lindy stepped out of the tub and towel-dried her body and hair. She put eye drops into her eyes, promising herself at that moment she would not see Nick again. Tomorrow she would tell the receptionist to tell him she was busy if he showed up at her office. She could not trust herself, especially after what had happened that morning.

Putting on a pair of slacks and one of Paul's old shirts, Lindy twisted her wet hair and secured it on the top of her head with a pin. As she descended the steps, she wondered what Nick had wanted to tell her.

Betty joined them for the Indian dish Paul had prepared. They made small talk during the meal and later played with Michael until bedtime. After the three settled in the family room with their cups of chai tea, Betty pulled out a letter and handed it to Lindy and Paul to read. It listed everyone the Elder Healer had healed from the first Friday night healing session.

"I didn't know you kept these kinds of records," Lindy exclaimed. "They are so detailed."

"Yes, I had Sandra, the church clerk, record the name, address, phone number, and health issues of each person healed. I guess you can say it's the lawyer in me," she kidded.

"She even made notes regarding what they had been healed of," Paul added.

"Look at number five, Stephanie Preston." Betty pointed out. "Ms. Preston called the church and reported that the breast tumor she had disappeared. She went for another examination and the doctors couldn't find it. Number seven, Roland McKinley, had a rare blood disease. After being healed by the Elder Healer, he was also examined by his doctor and had no trace of the disorder. He sent a hefty contribution to the church. The list goes on and on like that. I also have copies of letters and thank-you notes sent to the church from people the Elder Healer has helped. It is overwhelming."

"What are we going to do with the information?" Paul asked.

Betty handed them a second letter. The short-lived fiasco with Stan had left her with plenty of time to complete it. "This is a rough draft of a letter I want to send to the editor of the *Washington Star*. I want you to read it and tell me what you think."

Paul and Lindy settled back on the sofa and read the letter. It described the wonderful healings the Elder Healer had performed and stressed that the mission was to simply perform these healings without compensation. The letter went on to express the Elder Healer's wish to remain anonymous to protect her privacy and that of those requesting the healing. It also stated that she believed the healing work was more important than who she was.

The letter also declared that the minister and board members of the Church of Melchizedek were delighted to see other churches in the metropolitan area planning to hold first Friday healing and prayer services, and that they firmly believed such outreach services could be the bridge that would link the citizens, and perhaps serve as a prototype for other cities, nations, and countries. In closing, Betty cited the names and health challenges of several individuals who had given their written consent.

"What do you think?" Betty asked when they had finished reading.

"I think the letter is perfect. But there is one problem," Lindy hesitated. "Knowing my mother, she will not stop if you don't identify the Elder Healer. And I don't think Grace Perry will stop, either."

"But it will buy us some time. We all know the other churches are threatened by what we believe and our way of doing things. Listing the names of some of the people who received healings should stop them from referring to the healing sessions as bogus."

"I don't think so. It goes deeper than that. My mother wants to destroy us. We can offer all the proof we have, and she will not be satisfied until she runs us out of town," Lindy replied, frowning.

"The letter would temporarily deter them, though. I'm going to ask Ruth again to reveal the identity of the Elder Healer or..." Betty paused before continuing. "Lindy, you could try and communicate with the Healer."

"Paul also asked me to do this. I don't know. Are you forgetting it was Mary who contacted me? Or I would have a dream, vision, or whatever you want to call it."

"All we are asking is that you try," Paul pleaded with her.

"Let's call Ruth, tell her about the letter, and ask her again to tell us who the person is. I don't want her and Mark thinking we are conniving behind their backs. I don't feel comfortable trying to contact the Elder Healer without Ruth knowing about it." Lindy reached for the phone.

"You're right, Lindy. Call them," Betty said halfheartedly.

"Wait!" Paul put his hand up. "We are not doing anything behind their backs. We have always functioned independently. Ruth taught us that we have choices and need to think for ourselves."

"I can't do this," Lindy begged off, cringing.

"Yes, you can. Let go of the doubt, Lindy. Try. That is all we are asking you to do." Paul hoped telling Lindy that they believed in her would persuade her to change her mind.

"All right, but if nothing happens…"

"Then at least you tried," Paul reassured her.

"Well, let's get started," Lindy said, giving in.

Paul dimmed the lights. With hesitation, Lindy stretched out on the sofa and, concentrating on her breathing, tried to calm her nerves. Betty and Paul had more faith in her abilities than she did, expecting her to contact the Elder Healer and discover her identity. It wasn't that easy. She had no control over seeing colors, knowing information about others, and healing.

Suppose this doesn't work, Lindy thought. *Stop. Let go of all doubt. Focus.*

Lindy began to feel her body relax. As she focused, she felt herself drifting off to sleep. She refocused by moving her body slightly. In a feeble attempt not to go to sleep, she kept chanting silently. The octagon building loomed before her. The person was standing in the doorway again.

Who are you? Lindy formed the question in her mind.

She thought she heard the words 'Elder Healer', but before she could respond, the scene changed and she was back in her grandfather's office. He was reaching out to her, begging her to help him out of hell.

Just as she was about to extend her hands, Lindy found herself in an area dense with green foliage. She could feel herself being pulled until she stood in front of a cave. A faint light glowed from inside. Terrified, she stood there until she heard her name being called. It was Nick's voice. He needed her. She was no longer on the ground, but high up in the cave looking down on him. He was naked and shivering. Nick had beads of sweat on his face and he was very thin. Lindy felt another presence in the cave. She couldn't see the person, but heard a soft chanting of the words 'love heals'.

The Presence was directing her to send love to Nick. The dark color around Nick's body began to change to a greenish pink.

"Love heals, love heals, love heals," Lindy began to chant with the Presence.

Paul was gently shaking her. Lindy felt groggy and disoriented. At first, she thought she had fallen asleep and nothing had happened. However, as she regained consciousness, a flood of thoughts flowed through her mind. She looked around the room. Paul and Betty were both looking intently at her.

"You were chanting 'love heals,' " Paul stated, looking confused.

"How long was I out?" Lindy put the crystals she was holding on the table and swung her legs around so that her feet touched the floor.

Betty shrugged, "Not long."

"Here, drink this water and then tell us what happened." Paul placed the glass in Lindy's hands.

The water was cool and soothing. Lindy handed the glass back to Paul. "Give me a moment." She rushed to the bathroom and wiped her face with a cool towel. She had to think. She couldn't tell them about Nick.

She stood in the doorway a few moments, looking anxiously at her two best friends. "I don't know what happened," she finally said.

"What do you mean you don't know what happened?" Paul looked surprised.

"That's just it. Nothing happened."

"Nothing?" he pressed. "What about the statement 'love heals'? You kept repeating it."

"I don't know what to say. I felt the presence of someone in a cave chanting. You're right. He or she was saying, 'love heals.' " Lindy made a point of leaving out the part about Nick being in the cave.

"Hmmm, love heals. It doesn't make any sense," Betty said.

"But it does. *Love heals*. That's the message. It's oneness based on love. If we stay in a vibration of love and our intention is always about love, the healing or the oneness will happen. The Law of Attraction says what you desire will come to you if you stay in vibratory alignment with it!" Paul exclaimed excitedly. He kissed Lindy, and she couldn't help but think it was more for show because of Betty being there.

"I don't know. You may be taking this too far," Lindy replied, reaching for the glass and avoiding eye contact. She didn't like to withhold the truth, especially from the most important people in her life.

~~

As Lindy walked Betty the short distance to her car, she asked about her husband, attempting to ground herself in everyday life issues again.

"The Professor is the Professor. I think he wants to move permanently to Israel. He keeps hinting he's not getting any younger and wants to be near his family." Betty pulled out her keys.

"So he's not coming back anytime soon?"

"Believe it or not, he's coming home for Nick Lewis's exhibit." Betty looked Lindy in the eye. "I saw the photographs in the paper."

"The whole world did, and it's not what you think. We met for lunch, that's all."

"I'm not saying a word. Just remember you have a good thing here at home, girl."

"I know. It's just that in a way I feel we are back in 1967—turmoil." Lindy wanted to tell Betty what really happened in her vision, but decided to leave well enough alone.

"Maybe it's time to face whatever you are running from." Betty blew Lindy a kiss as she got into her car.

———

Betty decided not to wait until the next day to talk to Ruth. It was late, but she didn't care. She arrived at the house in Chevy Chase a little after eleven p.m. Ruth and Mark had just finished their evening meditation. Betty didn't waste any time explaining why she was there. Both Awakeners read the letter, noting how well written it was, and agreeing it was up to her to do what she wanted to do with it. Betty once again asked Ruth to reveal the identity of the Elder Healer, and once again she refused to do so.

Tired and devastated, Betty went home. She changed into something more comfortable and relaxed on her chaise lounge, sipping a glass of chilled wine and nibbling on crackers and cheese. Her attention was not on the television program, but on her conversation with Ruth. She had asked why they were refusing to do anything to clear the name of the church and the Awakeners, or to defend the principles they stood for.

"What they say is not important. Jesus's life demonstrated that one must remain in love no matter what the outer appearance may be. This campaign against us, the healings, and our beliefs doesn't exist in our world; therefore, there is nothing for us to do. We only see love, and love heals," Ruth explained.

Betty fell asleep on the chaise with the words 'love heals' on her lips.

CHAPTER EIGHTEEN

Huffing and puffing, Grace Perry stepped off the treadmill. She was exhausted after running for an hour, lifting weights, and contorting her body into a variety of positions. Wiping the sweat from her forehead and inspecting her small frame, Grace swore she would never again be fat. After a quick shower, she put on a halter top and shorts and went out on the balcony of her prestigious Wisconsin Avenue apartment to enjoy a cup of black coffee and scan the morning papers.

Girl, you've come a long way, she told herself, *from that hell hole you lived in years ago*. But she didn't want to think back to those times. Looking down at the neighborhood, Grace smiled. *This is the good life. Now, what's on the agenda for the day? First I have to find a way to get into that room in the church basement. That drunken fool claims he doesn't have a key, but another bottle of scotch, and I'm sure he'll find one. Billy Ray always said you could buy anyone and anything for the right price.*

The ringing phone cut Grace's plotting short. She pushed the sliding glass door open and picked up the phone.

"Hello."

"Baby...oh, my baby." Only one person called her baby in that tone of voice.

"Billy Ray? Is that you?"

"That's right, baby...your long-lost, loving man."

"H-h-how are you?" she stammered.

"How in the hell do you think I am, bitch? You left me high and dry."

"Wait a minute, Billy Ray. Before you go and get all ugly, I can explain everything."

"You do that, but not now. When I see you."

"See me? What do you mean 'see me'?"

"There's no hole you can crawl into that I won't find you. I do read!" He slammed the phone down.

"Damn, what am I going to do?" a panicked Grace asked herself, gripping the phone. "Billy Ray can't come here. It would spoil everything." Grace walked back and forth in the same spot until she almost wore a hole in the carpet. Deciding to go on the offensive, she phoned an old buddy of hers. It was still early there, in California, but she couldn't wait. Billy Ray's call had really shaken her. The biggest story in her career was about to break, and she didn't need him showing up and spoiling everything for her. She wasn't going to let *anyone* mess up what she had spent a lifetime wishing and plotting for—which was acceptance from the right people in D.C.

She briefly agonized about calling Jacko, but he was the best man for the job. She trusted him because he had a reputation for doing good work for the right price. Grace was not going to spare any money for something as important as this.

When a groggy-sounding Jacko answered his phone, she told him to find out everything he could about Billy Ray's case. Was he appealing? Would he be paroled anytime soon? She wanted to know the word on the street.

She hung up and turned to another pressing problem: What should she wear to make her look influential but pretty?

By afternoon, the clouds had disappeared and the sun was scorching the streets. Diana was in her air conditioned office finishing a report for the mayor. She had taken care to look exceptionally appealing today for her lunch date with Nicky. He had called the day before and invited her to have lunch with him at the Flagship. Daniel would be tied up in meetings all day, so she didn't have to worry about him. He had been spooked ever since that damn newspaper article. The expected appointment had made him jumpy. What a coup that would be for them. Diana checked her makeup and brushed her hair several times before leaving her office.

Nick was already there when she arrived. He was standing at the front desk talking to the hostess, a pretty young thing, who was grinning up at him as if he were a bronze god.

Men. They're always trying to stick it into anything wearing a skirt.

Walking toward him, she looked around to make sure there was no sign of Grace Perry lurking about. Diana wasn't taking any chances. She would have preferred meeting him in his hotel room; it was safer. And who knows what it might have led to? She walked up behind Nick and slipped her arm through his to claim what she believed was rightfully hers.

"Bonjour mon ami," she said in French, ignoring the hostess.

Dinning on fresh lobster tails, scallops, baked potato, salad, string beans, and hot rolls and rum buns, they made small talk. Hidden from view by the long white tablecloth, Diana kicked off her shoe and worked her foot up Nick's pant leg as far as she could.

"Did you ever see the medical student who performed the abortion?" he blurted out.

Diana brought her foot down hard on the floor. "What? Where did that come from?" She was furious. "I thought we had finished with that the last time we talked."

Leaning forward, Nick spoke quietly, "I can't find any record of the baby's birth or death."

"Now it's a baby? If I remember correctly, according to you it wasn't a baby." Diana looked him in the eyes. "Why do you keep bringing this up? It's dead, Nicky. Dead."

"If that's the case, why aren't there any records?" Nick pressed.

She sighed. "In those days, hospitals didn't keep records of still-births."

"You know that's not true!" He moved his chair closer to her.

"I have to go to the bathroom. This is upsetting me," Diana said, grabbing her purse.

"I'll meet you in the lobby." Nick pulled out his credit card to pay the bill.

"No, at your hotel. Too many ears around here." Diana walked off. She needed time to think, to get her story together. *Why is Nick bringing this up now? He never wanted a baby. In fact, it was his idea for me to have an abortion. I took care of the problem, and now he's all over me about it.*

═══

Nick waited for her in his room. She was hiding something, and he had to get it out of her. Fearing he had scared her off, he didn't relax until he heard the knock on the door. When he opened the door, Diana was standing there, tears in her eyes, her makeup smeared. She looked as though she had been in a car wreck.

Nick pulled her into his arms and pushed the door shut with his leg. "Ah, baby, come on now," he crooned.

"I was alone and had to do it by myself."

Nick held her back a bit and looked at her. "What happened to your mother? You told me that your family was going to help you."

"Why do you keep bringing up the most hurtful time in my life?" she asked him, still weeping.

"All I want, Diana, is for you to tell me what happened," he said, guiding her to the sofa.

"Okay, Nicky, I didn't have the baby in the hospital because I couldn't afford it, and I never told my parents about it. The medical student helped me. The baby died at childbirth. It was severely deformed. He got rid of it."

Nick walked over to the window and stood with his back facing her. "How did he get rid of it, Diana?"

"I don't know. I was so sick after that. I barely made it. What about me?" She went over to him and put her arms around his waist, resting her head on his upper back.

Nick didn't move. "Was it a boy or girl?"

"It was a boy, damn it!" she shouted, letting him go. "A messed-up, deformed boy, thanks to your half-white fake doctor. You want to blame someone? Blame her, and don't forget to include yourself. If you hadn't made me have that botched abortion from that quack doctor our son would be alive today."

"Maybe he is alive."

"What are you talking about? Don't play with me, Nick Lewis!" Diana screamed, her hands clenched at her sides.

The medical student told me the baby would not live more than a few hours, if that long. His lungs were probably damaged. I couldn't handle being saddled with a child with severe multiple disabilities for the rest of my life. It's not possible for the baby to be alive. Daniel would leave me if he found out any of this.

Diana sat on the bed sobbing. She looked up at Nick, who was now standing in front of her. "It's impossible, Nick. The baby is dead. You have to let this guilt trip go. I told you I forgive you. It's the past. Remorse is eating you alive." Diana stood and leaned her body into his. "Please let it go. There is nothing we can do about the past. I'm not carrying it, and I am the one who can't ever have children."

"I'm sorry. You're right. I have to let it go." He released her and went to the bathroom. She could hear the water running.

Diana was reapplying her makeup when a knock on the door startled her. Nick didn't respond, so she walked to the door and opened it. She couldn't believe her eyes.

Dr. Lindy Lee stood there with her mouth half open.

What is she doing here? Diana wanted to rip Lindy's violet eyes out of their sockets.

"Yes?" Diana smirked.

"Is Nick here?" Lindy had debated with herself all morning whether to come, finally deciding Betty was right; she needed to face the demon that was destroying her. Maybe, just maybe, she could forgive him and move on. But here she was, feeling foolish while Diana stood there looking smug.

"He's in the bathroom."

"Oh, well just tell him Dr. Lee stopped by. Thank you." *Look at her. She looks as if she just got out of bed with him. Why didn't I just call?* As Lindy turned to leave, she heard Nick call her name. He came to the door and pulled her into the room. "Diana was just leaving." He looked at Diana.

"I can come back another time," Lindy lied.

Diana gathered her belongings and reached up to kiss Nick on the mouth. Stepping aside, he turned his cheek to her lips.

"I'll call you," she murmured, brushing past Lindy.

"I can explain about Diana," Nick began.

Lindy held up her hand to silence him. "You don't owe me an explanation. I better go." She turned to leave, but he grabbed her arm to stop her.

"No, wait. You came here for a reason. What is it?"

"I wanted to apologize for not showing up for lunch the other day. I got caught up with my appointments, and then I had to go home early to help my husband cook because we were having a guest for dinner." Lindy bit her lip. She was getting good at lying.

She was supposed to tell him she couldn't see him anymore, but instead she was making small talk and wishing he would sweep her off her feet and make love to her. Lindy knew she had to get out of there before she did something she would regret later. When she tried to leave a second time, Nick grabbed her by the arm again and pulled her down onto the sofa.

He knew that look in her eyes. He had seen it in enough women who begged for it through their eyes, but wouldn't come out and ask for it. Then when you approach them, they back off. *No*, he told himself, *I'm not going to be rejected by her again.*

"Lindy, how old did you tell me your son is?"

"He'll be eleven this year."

"Eleven?" Nick repeated, with a weird expression on his face. He moved closer to her. "Tell me something, where did you adopt?"

"You mean what state or agency?" Lindy looked puzzled. *Why was he asking about Michael?*

"Yes…state, agency, whatever."

"We adopted him here in D.C. He was abandoned by his parents. I found him—I mean, I first saw him when I was doing my internship at Howard and was volunteering at D.C. General."

"This happened when?"

"He was about five. He was so little and sad. If only you could have seen his eyes, the eyes of what we call an old soul."

"How does your husband feel about him?"

"He loves him. Paul travels a lot, but when he's home, they are inseparable." *Why is he asking me all these questions about Michael?* Lindy looked at Nick and saw the loneliness in his eyes.

"What else did they tell you about his birth or the parents?" he asked, sounding anxious to learn more.

"It's not a nice story, Nick. Horrible people!"

"Tell me."

"They left him in a dumpster to die, probably because he was deformed at birth."

Could it be? He didn't want to dig up all of this mess, but he had to set things right. He had made a promise to God, and to the one who had saved his life.

"What did you want to tell me?" Lindy asked, changing the subject. "Remember, you mentioned you had something important to tell me?"

"I did, but I don't remember now," Nick responded, feeling it was not the right time to say anything about his suspicions to Lindy, at least not until he had more proof. "Well, I hate to cut your visit short, but I have to meet the curator of the museum about the exhibit." Nick took his jacket off the back of the chair.

At the elevator, he made an unexpected request. "I would like to meet your son. Do you think that would be possible?"

"Yes, of course. Why not?"

"You sound surprised that I would want to meet him."

"It's the last thing I thought you would want to do, but life is full of surprises."

"Tell me about it," he laughed.

CHAPTER NINETEEN

Thirty minutes later, Lindy was sitting in traffic inching along Wisconsin Avenue. One drop of rain in D.C. and traffic came to a standstill. She looked out her side window at the darkening sky. Was this an omen of what she might have to face when she reached her destination, Georgetown Hospital?

How she wished she was anywhere but in her car on a hot, stormy summer afternoon about to face another one of her biggest fears: coming face to face with her grandfather. She had already failed one test of fear today—facing Nick. It had gone all wrong. Lindy thought about how she lied to herself about never wanting to see him again. She had used facing her fears as an excuse to see him. All the way to the hotel, she trembled inside with anticipation of what might happen between the two of them when they were alone in the hotel room.

Seeing Diana had brought her back to reality fast. The entire time she was making small talk with Nick, her one thought was how stupid she had been to think he still wanted her. He was obviously involved with his old flame. She wanted to kick herself for the risk she almost took, which could have hurt others. Maybe she should thank Diana for saving her from herself.

Paul told her souls often reincarnate at the same time, to complete unfinished business or karma they carried over from previous lifetimes. One soul sometimes volunteers to play the role of the adversary, to help the other soul to evolve spiritually. We forget that we make pacts with one another before reincarnation. She had read about twin flames and soul mates. The twin flame is when the flame splits in two parts, which are of the same soul essence. To her surprise, she discovered a person can have several soul mates, and that they don't have to be the opposite sex. A good friend or sibling could be your soul mate.

Is Nick or Paul my twin flame?

The traffic finally started moving. She had to be on time or everything could go haywire. Earlier in the week, she had called an old classmate of hers who owed her a favor because she had helped him through medical school. Because he trusted her, he had sent her copies of her grandfather's medical records.

After pulling into a vacant parking space on a side street not far from the hospital, Lindy reached over and took the medical records from her briefcase. Holding the folder close to her chest, she imagined how difficult it must have been for her grandfather to depend on others to care for him. He had been such a strong and proud man. Rev had made his mark in the city, and the people loved him.

Lately, she had been thinking about her old church, Mt. Olive. She loved that church. But in an interfaith church, such as the Church of Melchidezek, one could still worship however one wished. Outsiders thought they were heathens and didn't believe in Jesus Christ. If they only knew how much they loved and worshiped the Master. They also revered all the saints of all religions. They practiced acceptance and inclusion of all faiths, and they didn't believe there was only one way to go home to God. There were many spokes on the wheel of life.

Lindy placed the folder back into her briefcase, and quickly inspected her face in the visor. Satisfied with her appearance, she exited the car. Dodging rain drops, she hurried to the hospital, praying that her face-to-face with Rev would go better than her meeting with Nick.

Visions of her grandfather reaching out for help haunted her, and she was so preoccupied with her thoughts she didn't see the little old woman in her path. They collided with such force, it was amazing neither one was hurt. The elderly woman had a very strong grip as she clung to Lindy's white medical coat.

"I'm so sorry. It was my fault for not looking where I was going," Lindy said, steadying the woman. "I'm a doctor. Are you all right? Come sit over here for a moment."

"It's all right, child. I don't need to sit. I'm just going a few feet down the way to the X-ray room."

"Are you sure?" Lindy looked into the woman's deep violet eyes, which looked so much like her own.

"I didn't fall, now did I? I just lost my balance a little."

"I could help you to the door. I am going there too."

"Now that would be nice of you." The woman put her hands in Lindy's, as if she were a child. Lindy prayed the woman wouldn't want her to go into the waiting area with her. She didn't want to take a chance of running into Margaret. Suddenly, Lindy's hand felt hot, as if it was on fire. When they reached the door, the elderly woman grabbed Lindy's other hand and said, "Believe in you."

The door opened to let a patient out, and the woman slipped through before Lindy could respond. Lindy looked down at her hands; both of them were burning. All she wanted to do was find a bucket of cold water and submerge her hands in it. They were tingling and now a little swollen, but that didn't bother her as much as the blue and green glow they radiated. She wanted to find the woman and ask her who she was and what she had done to her hands, but she had to get to her appointed place, so she made her way to the side door.

The man behind the door quickly opened it and motioned for her to enter. It was the back door to his office. Lindy had used it once before to visit her friend Tom Bingham.

Looking at Lindy with a gleam in his eyes, Dr. Bingham gave her a big hug. He still had a crush on her, imagining how it might have been with them. They had spent many nights together, burning the midnight oil studying. They were now doctors and married with children. They kept in touch by phone only.

"You have a short window to do whatever it is you plan to do. Your mother will be waiting just outside that door. I had to pull a lot of strings to get his doctor to consent to him getting X-rays."

"Big," Lindy said, using her nickname for him, "I wouldn't have asked you to do this if it wasn't important."

"Just do whatever magic you're going to do. I just don't want to know anything about it." He smiled at her.

"Thanks. I owe you."

While waiting for Big to bring Rev into the room, she examined her hands. They weren't pulsating as much, and they weren't glowing. Lindy wondered who the elderly lady was.

Fear gripped her as she heard Big pushing Rev's wheelchair to the door. *How will Papa react to me? What have I gotten myself into?*

When the door opened, Lindy stepped back out of view. She could hear her mother demanding to come into the X-ray room with him, but Big firmly told her it was against regulations, refusing to be intimidated by her tyrannical behavior. After rolling Rev into the room, Big locked the door. He then pointed at his watch as a reminder of the time and left by the side door.

Lindy took a deep breath and slowly approached Rev from behind. She then walked around to the front of his wheelchair. Nothing happened. Rev simply sat there motionless, his head down and saliva oozing from his mouth. Lindy reached for a tissue to wipe away the drool. She then bent down on her knees until she was face to face with the only father she ever knew and kissed him on the cheek.

At first, Rev thought he was dreaming. Amanda was here. *How?* He wanted to shout her name, but the words wouldn't come out. He couldn't move. He longed to reach out and touch his wife. Lindy wiped away the tear that ran down his cheek. She could sense his distress. He was groaning and making gurgling sounds, trying to communicate with her. She checked his pulse; his heart was beating rapidly. She had to do something. She didn't want him to have another stroke. It could be fatal.

"It's okay, Papa." As her own eyes filled with tears, she attempted to calm him.

Why is she calling me Papa?

Lindy caught a glimpse of the blue and green light around her hands and felt them getting hot again. A vision of the Elder Healer came to her. She knew what she had to do, but fear stopped her as she moved around to the back of his chair. *Who am I to think I can heal him?* She was not Ruth or Mark, who had acquired their healing skills through years of study and performing many healing sessions.

Rev was still very agitated. "Please calm down, Papa. You have to relax."

The words of the old woman came back to her: "Believe in you."

"Yes, believe in myself. I do. I do believe in myself," Lindy assured herself. At that moment, she felt her hands getting heavy and hot. Guided by a power she didn't yet understand, Lindy gently placed both of her hands on her grandfather's head, closed her eyes, and began to breathe deeply. After a few minutes, she repeated the ancient Sanskrit words over and over again that Mary had told her to use when Rev had suffered a heart attack—AUM MANI PADME HUM. It was the same words the Elder Healer used in her healing sessions.

I can do this, she thought, as she continued intoning the words. *If only Mary was here,* she thought, wavering. Her hands were on fire, and Lindy knew she had to release the energy. The blue-and-green light formed a visible vessel as it circled his head and extended two to three inches outward. The energy moved down his body, stopped for a few seconds at his heart, and finally moved down his legs into the floor. Her hands still pulsated and felt hot, but the light had vanished as quickly as it had come.

Love heals. She heard the words far off in the distance. Lindy lifted his wrist and checked his pulse. It was normal. Rev was very peaceful. Misty-eyed, he looked at her.

"Papa, blink once for no and twice for yes." She repeated the instructions a few times before asking, "Papa, do you know who I am?"

Of course, I know who you are. You're Amanda. Why would you ask me such a dumb question?

Lindy was kneeling before him again. Nothing. But when she started to get up, Rev reached over and grabbed her wrist. Lindy looked into his eyes. He blinked twice. Elated, she hugged him. "You understood?"

He blinked twice again.

"You also moved," she exclaimed.

A soft knock at the back door, and Big entered.

"It's time," he said.

Exultantly Lindy explained to Big that her grandfather could respond through blinking, and that he had to be the one to tell her mother he had accidentally discovered Rev could do this.

Margaret paced the floor of the crowded waiting room. The only seat available was next to a little old lady who looked as if she was on her deathbed. Tired of standing, she sat down next to the lady without acknowledging her. Minutes later, Margaret looked up as the doctor wheeled Rev back into the waiting room.

"Hold on, child, just hold on. Everything is going to be all right. God loves you, and so do I," the woman said.

When Margaret turned to look at the woman, she was gone. How was that possible?

Now why would a stranger tell me she loves me? Margaret couldn't remember the last time someone had spoken those words to her.

Lindy waited until Big returned to his office.

"Your mother complained I kept him too long, and she didn't seem happy at all when I said he could respond to yes or no questions by blinking. She said it was impossible."

"Did you demonstrate it?" Lindy asked.

"Yes, I did."

"And what happened?"

"I don't think she cared one way or another. She was too busy looking for an elderly lady with violet eyes."

Lindy flopped down in the nearest chair to keep from hitting the floor.

CHAPTER TWENTY

Margaret wheeled Rev into his room. His chin was on his chest, and he was snoring lightly. Margaret lifted his head up and looked at her father. He never opened his eyes. She gently let his head rest on his chest again. She was visibly upset.

The army of the devil is everywhere, she thought.

The doctor at the hospital was trying to trick her into thinking her father could communicate by blinking his eyes. She stood in front of Rev, who remained still.

"Spies, spies—the devil has them everywhere," she said aloud to her father. "They are trying to confuse me so I can't do what God wants me to do—crush that house of the devil and bring home the children of the Lord. Papa, what am I going to do?" She looked at him. "I wish you could talk to me. You would tell me what to do."

No, he wouldn't, the voice said. *You're stupid. He wouldn't let you preach, would he?*

Margaret sat on Rev's bed and covered her ears with her hands. "That's not true. Papa loves me."

If he loves you so much, why aren't you the minister of the church? You're nothing, the voice insisted.

Margaret rose, walked over to the cherrywood dresser to get a tissue to wipe her tears. She didn't understand why the voice was sometimes nice to her and sometimes hateful.

The words of the old woman came back to her. *Hold on, child, just hold on. Everything is going to be all right.*

"Yes, she's right. I just got to hold on. I'll show them. Everybody will be talking about Margaret Johnson Lee Pierce."

Walking to the door, Margaret looked back at Rev, who was still asleep. *What in the world did they do to him in that room?*

He's not drooling, the voice said.

"Shut up!" Margaret yelled. She didn't want to hear any more from that voice.

—

Rev heard the door shut, but waited a few more minutes before opening his eyes. For the first time in years, he felt like himself. He slowly lifted his right arm, then his left. He wanted to try his legs, but was too scared. What if they didn't move? He sat there staring into space, thinking about his wife.

There was so much he had wanted to say to her, but he couldn't utter a word. She was still a beautiful woman. She hadn't died! Amanda was alive. She had healed him for the second time in his life. When he was a young boy and dying, she prayed over him and used herbs to remove the fever from his body. She was his angel. He and his father, as well as the people of the old family church in Virginia, never understood Amanda's gift of healing. They were ignorant of the wisdom God had given her. They thought Amanda was possessed by the devil. They were scared of the power she possessed, power they feared she would use against them. His fear of his father and his stubbornness had caused him to miss out on a life with her.

Where has she been all these years? Didn't she know Margaret needed her? Poor Margaret. That's what's wrong with her. She missed out on having a mother to guide and teach her.

Rev looked down, noticing his foot was no longer resting on the wheelchair footrest, but on the floor. It must have moved involuntarily. "God is good! My God is good all the time," he cried. God had given him a second chance to redeem himself.

It was through the birth of his granddaughter, and what did he do? He treated her as if she was the devil himself. Lindy was a woman now. His stubbornness had caused him to also miss out on so much of her life. She was married to that fellow Paul. Despite their religious differences, Rev remembered how much he liked the young man. He had met him in the summer of '67. They had a child. No, they had adopted a child with medical problems. It was just like his Lindy to want to take care of everybody. She couldn't settle for being a doctor; she had to bring the problems home with her. Amanda and Lindy were instruments of the Lord. Rev cried as he thought about his life. It had been all about the desire for power and control. Rev sighed; it was good to remember events, names and dates.

Rev saw his Bible on the nightstand. He placed his feet back on the wheelchair's footrest and, turning its wheels, rolled over to it. He brought his hands together to pray, "Lord, forgive me. I have sinned."

He cried softly as he picked up the Bible. It had been so long since he held the word of God in his hands. Tears of pain and joy flowed down his face. He lifted his face to heaven. *Our Father, which art in Heaven. Hallowed be Thy name. Thy kingdom come. Thy will be done in earth, as it is in Heaven. Give us this day, our daily bread. And forgive our debts, as we forgive our debtors.* Rev paused and wiped away more tears. He was so choked up he didn't realize he was crying out loud. *And lead us not into temptation, but deliver us from evil. For thine is the kingdom and the power, and the glory, forever and ever. Amen.*

His voice sounded strange to him, not having heard it in a long time. His words were slurred, but he didn't care. However, he wondered if his improved condition was only temporary, and if he would go back to the world of the living dead. *No,* he told himself. Faith, that's what he needed to show. Faith in God. God wouldn't have brought him this far to undo all that he had done. The healing was a miracle. God wanted him to do something—one last assignment.

When he heard Margaret talking to Alan in the hallway, he returned the Bible to the nightstand and rolled his wheelchair back to where she had left him. It wasn't time for Margaret, or anyone else, to know about God's miracle. They wouldn't understand. They wouldn't believe him if he told them that Amanda had healed him. Instead, he would have to *teach* the flock about the wonders of God.

CHAPTER TWENTY-ONE

In the early morning hours, the house was so quiet that Lindy could hear herself breathing. She glanced at her clock radio: it was 4:44. The last couple of days had unnerved her, and she wanted nothing more than to go and curl up in the bed with Paul, to feel his arms around her, but she knew that was out of the question. Years ago, she had slipped into his bed and put her head on his shoulder. He had gently removed her head, telling her it was not good for them to be physically close. Without further thought, Lindy had returned to her room, vowing never to make that mistake again.

Lindy checked the clock again; the hand had moved once. Unable to sleep, she finally got up and tiptoed down the stairs to the kitchen to make a cup of chamomile tea with honey. After drinking the warm, soothing liquid, Lindy returned to bed and her eyelids finally began to get heavy.

I never knew tea could make you feel so out of it, she thought, hearing a screeching noise in her ears that got louder and louder. All of a sudden, she realized she was looking down at her lifeless body from the ceiling in her room. Her consciousness existed outside her body. Lindy felt another tug and found herself drifting further away from her physical body. The speed in which her astral body traveled was unbelievable as she moved through a tunnel of darkness. She had no fear because she sensed four beings around her—one at her head, one at her feet, and one on each side of her.

The beings led her to a room full of brilliant light rays. Instinctively, she knew to lie on the table, which was in the center of the room. Her astral body felt weightless. Moments passed before she became aware that several beings were touching her on what she knew to be the acupuncture meridians of her body. Each point vibrated as if an electric current had passed through it. Lindy experienced the pulsating, heavy sensation in her hands again, as if she was in her physical body. Then, a flash, and she saw the face of the elderly lady she had bumped into earlier that day.

A loud noise pierced her eardrums. *It's Michael—he's crying.* She felt heavy and realized she was back in her body. Lindy sat straight up in the bed, the room was spinning. *I have to get to him*, she thought, jumping out of bed. She felt dizzy. *Steady, steady, Michael needs you.* She could hear him crying as she maneuvered her way down the steps. She found him halfway out of the bed, entangled in the covers. When Michael saw her, he stretched out his long, thin arms to her. Strength flowed back into her body, when she saw her son in such dire need.

Lindy picked Michael up and drew him close to her. Hugging him tightly, she whispered to him, "It's okay, baby, it's okay. Shh, shh, shh, I love you. I love you."

Lindy gently kissed him on the forehead. Her hand, pulsating with the blue-and-green light, moved up and down his spine, while she touched his forehead with her other hand like the beings had done to her. Several minutes later, Michael was sound asleep. Unaware of the colors emitting from Lindy's hands, Paul watched from the doorway as she calmed Michael.

Lindy, still not steady, leaned on Paul to help her back up the stairs. Instead of returning to her room, she lay down on the sofa in the room that connected the two bedrooms. Paul pulled up a chair next to her.

"No, impossible," she said out loud as she looked at the clock on the desk, which read 4:44 a.m. "That's impossible!"

Looking baffled, Paul asked her what was wrong. After she explained what she had experienced, Paul told her it appeared she had an OBE, or out-of-body experience.

"What did they do to you?" he asked.

"They were touching me all over, on the meridian points of the body."

"This is incredible! You are incredible! This is what I was talking about the other night when Betty was here. I expected you to do something like you did tonight."

"Paul, you of all people should know I don't control these things that happen to me. They control me, popping in and out of my life at their will—not mine."

"I know, but one day you will master them," he said with conviction. "Through our dreams and visions God communicates with us."

Lindy sat up and crossed her legs, her gown wrapping around her thighs. Paul diverted his gaze from her firm legs, fighting the urge to take her into his arms. Instead he asked, "Do you know what 4-4-4 means?"

"I'm not sure, but something to do with celestial time."

Paul went over to the bookshelf and removed a book on numerology. "Just what I thought," he said after scanning several pages in the book. "The numbers 4-4-4 correspond to the time the angels will awaken you. Didn't you say you felt the presence of four beings?"

"Yes," Lindy replied.

"It says here numbers are energy forms or vibrations that have hidden messages. The world was built according to sacred geometry, the divine science of God. The Freemasons refer to God as the Master Architect."

"But what does that have to do with me?"

"Four beings took you to Shambhala, the Golden City, and time froze at 4:44. There is a message for you here, Lindy."

"Can you decipher it?"

"I'll try, but I think you can do it better because of your gifts. I'll give the intellectual interpretation and you do the intuitive," he stated.

"Okay."

"The number four represents foundation, order, discipline. You need all of these to reach your goals. Four is the number of manifestation of a goal through perseverance and by following a process or steps. Every number has a positive and negative quality. The flip side of the traits above is that it can represent confusion, impatience, and instability. What are you feeling about the number? Remember, every number has a positive and negative quality and," he added, "remember to go with the first thing that comes into your mind, no matter how ridiculous it may seem."

Lindy closed her eyes for a second. She felt better but still disoriented. "I don't know what I want out of life anymore, Paul. I feel confused, like I'm in a box."

She opened her eyes and looked at him as if to say, *"You wanted to know."*

Where's all this psychological nonsense coming from? Paul wondered. He wanted her intuitive take, not her Freudian take. Looking a little bewildered, he tried a different approach. "Let's take the number four up another level. If you add four plus four plus four, you get 12, and then you reduce 12 by adding both numbers together. For example, one plus two equals three."

Paul looked at her to see if she was following him, then continued. "The number 12, which has a numerological root of one plus two equals three, relates to the creative process. The three is very significant, especially since it is your birth-path number. Your birthday—month, day, and year—actually comes out to 3, the number of the intuitive and of one who must learn how to express herself creatively." He turned to his wife again and asked, "Intuitively?"

Intuitively, I'll tell you what I think. I think we should jump in the bed and screw our heads off to make up for all those years we denied ourselves, she thought. Instead, she answered, "I'm not picking up too much. I think—but I am not sure—I vaguely heard the beings saying something about me expressing…" Lindy stopped talking abruptly. She was looking beyond Paul to the door.

"Paul," she screamed, "Michael is standing in the doorway."

Paul turned to see Michael, without his walker, standing in the doorway. *How did he come up the stairs and walk to the room?*

Unable to move, they stared stared at the child.

"How did he get up here?" Lindy asked, still in shock.

"I walked."

The parents exchanged looks. Michael had spoken clearly.

"You what?" they asked simultaneously.

"I said, 'I walked.' " He took several steps toward Lindy, as if to demonstrate.

"Oh, my God, you're walking! Paul, look! Michael's walking!" Lindy screamed.

She suddenly remembered the bluish-green light pulsating from her burning hands. She told Paul about going to the hospital to see her grandfather, meeting the elderly woman, and her hands. "Do you think the light had something to do with it?"

"Of course, healing or true miracles can happen instantaneously. It would be interesting to find out how your grandfather is doing."

"You really believe I had something to do with this?" She pointed to Michael, who was walking around the room and touching everything he could reach.

"You said your hands were on fire and you could see a blue-green light around them when you touched him. I don't know how it works, but that little old lady was more than what she appeared to be. What did she tell you?"

"She simply told me to believe in myself."

"That's it, Lindy!" Paul exclaimed excitedly. "The message is you have to believe in yourself. See, people born on the three life path have doubt, and they must overcome the doubt in order to do their life mission."

Lindy looked at Paul skeptically. He was a good numerologist, but she couldn't take credit for what had happened with her grandfather or Michael. God heals. If He used her, she was just the vessel for the healing to pass through. Silently, she whispered, "Thank you, God, however it happened."

"Do I have to go to school today?" Michael asked as Paul grabbed the boy and hugged him.

Paul looked at Lindy with a big grin on his face and said, "He can stay home today. We can't let him go back until we figure out how to explain what happened to him."

"You're right," Lindy agreed, sitting on the edge of the bed and looking at Michael standing next to Paul.

It was a miracle! She had been wanting this forever. Why then wasn't she ecstatic? Maybe because her medical training and knowledge told her this healing was not possible. Yet the child stood in front of her, walking back and forth.

Lindy pulled up Michael's pajama shirt, feeling along his spine. She told him to sit in the chair and then tapped each of his knees, which jerked as they were supposed to. She tickled his feet, and he laughed. He lifted his arms without problems.

"Can you bring him to my office today? I want to run some tests and take some X-rays."

"Why do you need X-rays?" Paul asked.

"I want to compare them to his previous ones and see what has changed."

"Lindy, you *are* an X-ray machine. You have an acute sense of when something is not right in the human body. Why not use your gifts?"

Lindy shrugged. "I have no way of knowing if I'm right about what I'm sensing. I don't want to take a chance; something else maybe going on. I need to check his shunt. I couldn't live with myself if something were to happen to him. I am a trained medical doctor, and I would feel more comfortable following medical procedures."

"Have you forgotten you are also a highly involved intuitive who can diagnose illnesses and heal them? Be who you are."

"That's easy for you to say. You weren't brought up as I was, to adhere to a strict Christian doctrine. It's in my blood. You would think after all this time I would have let it go, but there is a part of me that still holds on to the belief system. Maybe I am feeling guilty. At least Betty had the integrity to admit she was caught up in the illusions of two worlds, and how difficult it was to live in both. Me, I'm a spiritual sham." Lindy shocked not only Paul, but herself, with that admission. She had no idea where it came from.

CHAPTER TWENTY-TWO

In uptown Northwest, Rev lay in bed, wishing he could turn the light on so he could continue reading his Bible. But he didn't want to take the chance of Margaret discovering he could move. He had to wait until the time was right. He didn't want her to go snooping around the hospital and discover Amanda had returned.

Rev heard the doorknob click. Margaret crept inside and slipped into his bed. She felt safe at night in her father's bed. When she was younger, she would run and jump into his bed, pulling the sheets over her head. He would let her lie in the big bed for a little while, telling her over and over there were no evil spirits hiding in her room. She would insist that the spirits were there, but Rev wouldn't listen. He would simply pick her up and carry her back to her room.

Margaret curled up alongside Rev and put her head on his shoulder. "There, that's better," she whispered, rubbing her feet against his leg.

Rev didn't move, and he soon heard her snoring. The tears started again; he couldn't hold them back. *Where did I go wrong?* Rev stayed in that position a long time, the words of the Twenty-third Psalm echoing in his head:. *The Lord is my Shepherd; I shall not want. He maketh me to lie down in green pastures; He leadeth me beside the still waters....*

Lying still in the bed, Rev sensed the Holy Ghost had come upon him. He looked over at the clock; it was exactly 4:44 a.m. Another biblical verse popped into his head: *And a man's foes shall be they of his own household*, Matthew 10:36.

He began to pray silently. *Lord, I come before You this morning, and if I could, I would get down on my knees and bow before Your Mighty Presence. Lord, I tried my best to make up for her not having a mother. I taught her to put You first and to love and fear You. Lord, where did I go wrong? I ask for Your forgiveness——Forgive me my debts as I forgive others, and lead me not into temptation, but deliver me from evil.*

Rev sensed a strange feeling in his feet, then in his legs. The tingling sensation traveled up his body. He could only describe it as the Holy Ghost taking possession of him. *Lord*, he prayed, *give me the strength to make right what I have made wrong.*

He then heard the verse from Proverbs 31:10-13: *Who can find a diligent woman? For her price is far above rubies. The heart of her husband safely trusts in her, and her food supplies never diminish. She does him good and not evil all the days of her life.*

For the first time, Rev knew it was Margaret who needed the demons cast out of her. Margaret's head was heavy on his shoulder, but his heart was even heavier with sadness.

Margaret had to be struck down before she destroyed the lives of others. And he had to be the one to do it because he loved her, and it was all his fault. He had denied her the love she craved as a child. He had been bitter and angry because of what had gone wrong with him and Amanda, and had taken it out on her. *Lord, forgive me. Show me the way,* he prayed. Rev knew in his heart God was talking to him in the early hours of the morning, preparing him for whatever may come. He wasn't afraid.

Before falling asleep, Margaret's head numbing his shoulder, Rev heard the Holy Spirit send him one more message, Acts 3: 7-8: *And he took him by the right hand and lifted him up…And he, leaping up, stood and walked, and entered with them into the temple, walking and leaping and praising God.*

Rev smiled and closed his eyes. It was not long now before he would be with his beloved Amanda. She had come back for him.

CHAPTER TWENTY-THREE

Nick sat on the bed and removed the manila envelope he kept locked in his briefcase. He put its contents in chronological order on the bed. The newspaper article described an abandoned baby found in a dumpster on Howard's campus in December of 1967. Nick looked at the date on the letter Diana had sent him telling him the baby had died at birth—December 24, 1967. Then he looked at the date of the newspaper—December 18, 1967. Very close.

He lined up another piece of paper containing the information Lindy had given him about her son, Michael. She had found him at age five in a hospital ward for special children. That was during her internship, which, he calculated, would had been about five years after 1967. Diana said the baby was severely deformed. Lindy adopted a child who was severely deformed.

Nick kept going over all the details in case he missed something. He still didn't have proof Michael was his child. Maybe his mind was playing tricks on him. Why was he torturing himself?

His thoughts shifted to the night he almost died of malaria, and the Dogon shaman had brought him back. He hadn't wanted to come back, but she had told him he still had work to do. He had to be there for the child. At first, he had ignored what she told him.

When he returned to Paris, he embarked on a course of self-destruction, drinking excessively and sleeping around with too many women to count. But after another bout with malaria, which almost took his life, his doctor suggested he take some time off.

That's when he left for Malaga, Costa del Sol, one of Spain's most popular tourist provinces and a place he had always loved. He purchased a house on top of a mountain. Alone, except for the couple who took care of him and the house, he began to heal. It was then he felt the presence of the Healer and remembered his promise to her. He returned to Paris a year later to begin fulfilling that promise.

A soft knock on the door interrupted his reminiscing. Nick looked through the peephole, not expecting anyone that early in the morning. On the other side of the door stood Diana, wearing a white raincoat and holding a bottle of champagne. Nick quickly stuffed the pieces of paper back into the envelope and reluctantly opened the door.

"Good morning," she said as she entered, kissing him ever so lightly on the lips.

Amused at the boldness of this woman, Nick smiled and did a swooping motion with his hands. "Just come on in."

"Nicky, get a grip. I thought I would extend a peace offering since we didn't part on the best of terms the last time I was here. So I took a chance and stopped by." She stood in the center of the room, facing him.

Maybe it was a good thing she had stopped by. He needed more information to solve the mystery, and she just might have the answers.

"Ten minutes more, you would have missed me. I have to be at the museum for the arrival of some of the exhibit pieces today."

"What a shame. As I said, I thought I could make up for the last time," Diana responded seductively, unbuttoning the raincoat and letting it fall at her feet. She was clad in a halter bra and bikini panty, the red accenting her smooth brown skin. She was beautiful.

"Your husband let you go out like this?" he asked, smirking slightly.

Diana circled him, as if stalking an animal. "Since you asked, my husband has more important business to attend to than worry about what I'm doing. You leave him to me." She stopped in front of Nick and dropped to her knees.

Nick looked down at Diana as she unzipped his pants. Diana had a way of getting to him ever since they were young, growing up on those dirt farms in Alabama. They had a history together. Their families lived down the road from one another; they went to the same schools and church. She had even followed him to Howard University.

He wasn't in love with her and didn't want to hurt her again. He was here to make restitution, not cause more damage. Still, he felt himself getting aroused by her scent and touch as her warm hands pulled at his jockey shorts.

She gazed up at him, licking her lips. He grabbed her hair, pushed her head down, and promised himself this would be the last time.

Diana was a dangerous woman, Nick decided.

CHAPTER TWENTY-FOUR

Betty sat at her desk, working on the sermon she planned to deliver at the Friday night healing session. She had been at the church less than an hour when she heard Pops moving around in the hallway.

"Pops," she yelled, "come in here!"

Betty looked up to see an elderly woman peering in from outside the doorway. Surprised to see someone in the church this early, Betty got up and walked over to the woman.

"Did I frighten you, child?"

"No, no," Betty responded. "I'm just surprised to see someone here this early. I thought you were Pops, the custodian."

"My child, you look as if you are carrying the weight of the world on your shoulders. What is worrying you?"

Betty thought about the pending talk with Pops. It was bothering her, but not as much as the sermon she had to prepare for. How could she tell this old lady, who had probably come for the healing session, that she was contemplating discontinuing them?

Betty backed into her office and sat in one of the chairs in front of her desk. The elderly woman followed, and Betty was now able to take a hard look at her. She reminded her of someone. It was the eyes. Looking into the woman's eyes, she suddenly felt like a little girl caught with her hand in the cookie jar. She had to confess.

"I don't know if you know, but the media and others in this city are trying to stop the healing sessions, so I decided to end the sessions before they shut us down."

"What's behind all this, child?" the elderly woman asked, concerned.

"They want to know the identity of the Healer, and I can't tell them something that I don't know." The woman's eyes made Betty feel she could trust her.

The woman sat there for several moments without speaking. Then, she moved her cane in front of her and leaned on it.

"When I was young, I once met a man who told me that we create our own realities through our thoughts and emotions. We are responsible for everything in our world."

"I know our thoughts create our world, and I have tried to figure out what I am thinking to cause this kind of problem in my life. But where does God fit into this thought process?" Betty asked.

"God is the macrocosm, and man is microcosm. We are creators of our own small worlds that either allow or resist the flow of God into our lives. Search your heart and soul, child, and you will know why you are in the predicament that you are in."

Before Betty could respond, the elderly woman got up and waved her hand. "When we are at peace with ourselves in what we believe, then we can stand tall and face others from a place of strength. Well, child, I'll let you get back to work."

Betty watched as the woman walked out of her office. She looked down at the chair where the elderly woman had sat and saw a white handkerchief. Betty picked it up and rushed to the door, but the woman was nowhere in sight. Pops found Betty standing in the hallway looking perplexed.

"Good morning, Reverend Betty."

"Did you see an elderly woman leaving the building?"

"No, I have been cleaning out front and no one has come near the door. Are you all right?"

"Yeah, I'm fine, but I need to talk to you in my office."

Betty knew Pops could be charming one moment and ornery the next. It depended on whether he had one or two drinks in him. At sixty-eight, he was still a good-looking man, even though alcohol had taken its toll. She heard he was fooling around with a younger woman who was taking him for everything he owned, which wasn't much.

Betty returned to the seat behind her desk. Pops chose to remain standing.

Pops was a good janitor. She had taken him off the streets and had given him a chance. The question was, had he betrayed her for a bottle of scotch?

"I have to ask you this—did you sell me out?"

"What do you mean *sell you out*?" He put his hands on his protruding stomach and reared back.

"I need the truth, Pops. Did you talk to anyone about the Friday night healing sessions?" Her eyes hardened.

"Some newspaperwoman was snooping around here."

Betty knew it could only be Grace Perry.

"What did she ask you?"

"She asked me questions about the healing sessions."

"Be more specific."

"I was a bit under the weather. I don't remember the questions."

Betty knew his answer could only mean he was too drunk to recall the conversation that had taken place between him and Grace. Her instincts told her she had found the hole, and she knew what she had to do to stop the leak. If things weren't so critical, Betty would have scolded him and let it go, but she knew she couldn't let him get away with just a slap on the wrist.

"I have to let you go, Pops."

"What? What do you mean *let me go?*"

"I want you to pack up your stuff and leave immediately."

"Look, Reverend Betty, the woman only wanted to look around. I didn't see anything wrong with it. Everything was locked up."

"Point is you let her in. You know how I feel about the media, especially that reporter. Now, your services are no longer needed, so please leave."

"You'll be sorry!" Pops threatened, storming out.

Betty could hear him slamming drawers and doors as he cleared out his belongings. She was glad when the phone rang, sparing her his verbal abuse.

Paul was calling to inform her about Michael's miraculous healing and the meeting with the Awakeners at seven that evening. *Ruth had foretold that Michael had something special to accomplish this lifetime. Maybe she will be able to tell us more tonight.*

The phone was not on the hook a hot second before it rang again. It was Nick Lewis. He made polite conversation, asking her about the Professor and wondering if they were coming to his opening.

He had also called to ask her about the whereabouts of Cissy Carter, a name she hadn't heard in a long time. Betty was curious as to why Nick would be looking for Cissy, the same Cissy who, to take the heat off herself, had tried to get him buried under the jail for selling marijuana. Her ploy had backfired, and she was charged with possession with intent to distribute. Cissy was also known as a booster—selling stolen clothing to people who could afford them. Since Betty had been Cissy's attorney at one time, she had to be careful about what she said.

"Do you want to tell me what this is about, Nick?"

"Believe me, counselor," he joked, "I have no sinister intentions. I need to find someone, and I'm hoping she can help me locate the person."

"It was rumored she went to LA. I never heard any more from her. A little advice, Nick—Cissy isn't the kind of person you want to resurrect. Besides, you weren't one of her favorite people."

"I know, but I have no other choice. I need to find this person, and she is the only lead I have." Nick wanted to confide in her; instead, he ended the call, feeling it was best to leave certain things unrevealed.

Reflecting on what had transpired that morning, Betty picked up the letter she was going to send to the media and stared at it for a moment. Then she remembered what the elderly woman had told her about creating your own reality. That's when she knew exactly what she had to do with the letter.

CHAPTER TWENTY-FIVE

Grace Perry sat in her car. She was parked half a block from the house in Chevy Chase. She had made sure to be careful when she followed the good minister there. She watched as Betty got out of her Jaguar and sashayed up the walkway. A short time later, the golden couple showed up with their crippled child. Grace stared as they walked to the door, the kid skipping in front of them.

What the hell? I thought he was a cripple? Grace reached for her camera and snapped a picture of the trio. *I wish I could get closer to find out what's going on in that house.*

Earlier Pops had called Grace at the office to tell her about him getting fired and to ask for money. She agreed to meet him at a local restaurant/bar not far from the church in Georgetown. When she got there, he was nursing a scotch and water at the bar.

"What you got for me?" she asked, not wasting time on pleasantries.

"You still want the key to that special room?"

"I thought you said you didn't have one."

"Well, I lied. I was told to make two, and a good janitor always makes one extra because someone is always losing one."

"What's this going to cost me?"

"A couple of grand," he said, eyeing her Rolex watch.

Grace Perry slid off the stool. "Have a good life." She began to walk toward the door.

"Wait!" he hollered. "Five hundred."

She had reached the door and pushed it open a little. "Two hundred and fifty, and you have to give me something else." Grace looked back at the man downing his drink.

"Do you know about the house in Chevy Chase?"

Grace came back to the stool. "What about it?"

"They go there to the house. I know because I had to do some repair work for them. The house got all of these huge rocks and candles. No living room furniture. This one room got books everywhere and a big symbol on the wall. And they play the same music you hear when the Healer shows up."

"What symbol?" Her curiosity was now piqued.

Getting a pen from Grace, Pops moved the small white napkin from under his drink and drew the symbol on it, and then passed it to her. She stared at the strange symbol, but didn't recognize it. Grace stuffed the napkin into her purse.

Pops asked for another drink. Grace Perry sat down again. "What else do you know?"

"Those people are not right."

"Have you ever seen the Elder Healer?"

"Something weird about that, too. Never seen the Healer enter or leave the church. I have been trying to figure out when she comes in."

"Did you discover anything?" Grace Perry asked nonchalantly, not wanting to show her excitement.

"Back up to five hundred." He looked at her from over the top of his glass.

"Three hundred; I'm not the bank."

"You could have fooled me with all those fancy clothes and jewelry."

"Just tell me what you know, and I'll make it worth your while."

"One night I was tired and fell asleep at my desk after one of those Friday night healings." He didn't want to tell her he was drunk and couldn't move. "A noise woke me and I got up to see what it was. I was thinking one of the homeless had slipped into the building. I opened my door and the hallway was dark, but I could see someone near the Healer's door. I called out to the person. No answer. As I moved closer to the door, I saw this figure dressed exactly like the Healer, in an all-white robe with a hood. It took me a moment to realize that it was the Elder Healer. You're not going to believe this, but she turned and looked at me and her eyes threw off a light that almost blinded me. I had to throw up my hand to shield my eyes. When I looked again, she was gone." Pops looked at her out of the corner of his eye. He had her attention.

"Give me the key." Grace got down off the stool for the second time. He obviously had been drunk at the time—if it had even happened.

"You think I was drunk, huh? I admit I had a few that night, but as God is my witness, I saw what I saw." By now, he was getting a little indignant.

"The key." She held out her hand.

Pops took the silver key out of his pants pocket and handed it to her. Grace Perry then placed three one hundred dollar bills on the table. She was finished with him—the drunk.

Thinking back on what Pops had told her, Grace remembered her own experience with the blinding light. She took out her notebook and wrote the words *blinding light* and *Healer disappearing into thin air.*

What in the hell is going on here? she wondered.

CHAPTER TWENTY-SIX

White candles and rose quartz crystals were placed in the window sills. The room had a warm mystical glow about it. Two large amethyst crystals stood in each corner. Because Michael wouldn't sit down, the Awakeners were unable to meditate. He walked around them, poked their backs, and then let out a hearty laugh that was contagious. They were so enthralled with his ability to walk without assistance that the usual protocol didn't matter. The five of them sat in silence, watching the child's every move and hanging on his every word.

Finally, Ruth opened the meeting with a prayer of thankfulness for Michael's healing. Then she informed them that she would be leaving for India soon. She wanted to spend her remaining years there; Mark would accompany her. They would sell the house—unless Betty took it over to continue the work of the Awakeners.

Taken by surprise, Betty contemplated the responsibility of heading the Awakeners in D.C. What worried her most was the teaching of the doctrine. Who would do that? How could she teach anyone about the sacred doctrines when her behavior in the last weeks had shown her to be a doubting Thomas?

"Thank you, Ruth. I am surprised you think I am capable of leading the D.C. Center. I have my doubts about myself in the role of minister and teacher." Betty looked at her friends.

"Explain what you mean," Ruth said.

"I seesaw between good and bad. The role of a minister and spiritual teacher is one I am having difficulty achieving. I don't think good thoughts about people and situations all the time." Betty looked at the others for their reactions.

Silence.

"And another thing," Betty added, "I can't defend or represent the church as I want. I feel like a stepchild of the Awakeners because vital church information is withheld." Betty looked directly at Ruth and Mark. "Why can't I know, or all of us know, the identity of the Elder Healer? Why is there so much secrecy?"

To the group's astonishment, Michael said, "Because you're not ready." For the first time, he looked his age of ten. His speech was clear, without a slur.

Betty sat silent for a moment, unable to respond. Then she got up, kneeled before the boy, and looked into his eyes. "Say that again!"

The child gave her a blank look.

"Where is all this negativity and doubt coming from?" Paul said, looking at Betty and Lindy.

"That's easy for you to say, Paul," Betty responded. "You live in a cushioned environment of mystics and meditation that protects you from the real world of negativity and fear."

"Just because I live in this cushioned world, as you call it, doesn't mean I don't have to face the realities of this planet," Paul replied angrily. *Should I tell her about the doubt I have about my marriage after all these years?*

Ruth looked at Betty, then at Lindy and Paul. In her soft quivering voice, she said, "Fighting amongst ourselves is not the solution. The spirit of negativity is among us, and will destroy us if we allow it. Listen to what I have to tell you. We are aspirants on the path to spiritual realization. It is not enough to study our doctrines or spiritual principles in books. As aspirants, we have to live the truth. We will be given challenges to test us. The challenge you are facing is self-mastery of your lower emotions, such as doubt, jealousy, and anger. Do you understand what I mean?" Ruth continued, not waiting for a response.

"You have allowed negativity into your minds because you bought into the thoughts of others through the media, newspaper articles, and gossip. You have bought into it through your thinking. Having doubtful thoughts produces doubtful experiences.

"Michael's healing came as a sign to remind you of who you are, children of the light. Allow the power of God to flow through you, and then allow love to come forth. Love conquers fear. Each of you has to work through your fears, including all the negative emotions that swim in this vast ocean of conscious awareness. Your path as aspirants is to gain self-mastery of your logical and feeling bodies." Ruth motioned for them to move to the adjacent room, where they could sit at the table.

Reaching into the small wooden chest, which had the OM symbol on top of it, Ruth pulled out a blue satin drawstring bag. Inside were the Egyptian major arcana tarot cards that represent higher wisdom. Ruth used them for special occasions. The deck she drew from the blue bag was worn around the edges. In her small, fragile hands, the cards looked larger than they actually were. Ruth slowly shuffled them, trying not to let them fall.

"Michael, don't you want to go and rest?" Lindy asked her son. "It's been a long day for you."

"No, let him stay," Ruth suggested. "He needs to hear this. Subtle wisdom is revealed through these pictorial symbols. His subconscious will store the information until he needs it."

Ruth cut the cards into three separate piles and looked at Michael. He came around the table, stood next to her, and touched the cards.

Lindy looked at her son with amazement. This was incredible. Had he read Ruth's mind? Michael took his seat again.

Putting the cards back into one pile, she murmured, "Thank you, Divine Ones, for your wisdom and guidance in this matter. Before I read, let me remind you that the knowledge revealed in these cards suggests a connection to the esoteric wisdom of the Kabbalah, western mysticism. They tell about the spiritual and physical life of a soul."

Ruth started with Michael, who pulled the Emperor. Ruth studied the card for a few seconds before she spoke. "The Emperor—the key is power—will you wage war or peace within yourself? It will be the two that come after you that will determine the road you will take. "

Ruth turned to Betty to choose a card. At first, Betty hesitated. *Will Ruth talk about Stan?* She pulled. It was the devil. Betty did not flinch; instead, she stared at the card with uneasiness.

"You have put shackles or chains around your neck. You have imprisoned your mind, body, and spirit. You can free yourself at any time." Ruth never waited for the person to respond or ask questions; she just moved on to the next.

Paul selected a card and placed it on the table. It was the Hermit. *How appropriate,* he thought. He knew what it meant, but he wanted to hear Ruth's interpretation.

"Are you the teacher or are you seeking a teacher? Your heart is torn between the two. Desires bring suffering to man," was all she said.

Finally, Ruth turned to Lindy, who closed her eyes and reached for a card. She quickly turned it over and looked at the Lovers. A woman and man, nude, who stood beneath the outstretched arms of the angel Raphael, who gave them his blessing. The woman stood in front of the tree of knowledge, and the man in front of the twelve signs of the zodiac. The man is looking at the woman, but the woman is looking up at Raphael for inner guidance.

"You must look within your heart to find the answers you seek." Finished, Ruth placed the cards back inside the satin pouch.

Lindy's mind was racing, trying to absorb everything Ruth had said. *What did she mean by the two who will come after Michael?* It wasn't any use asking her about it, because Ruth never discussed her readings in depth. She believed the person must be the final interpreter of the oracle. It was always about self-perception.

CHAPTER TWENTY-SEVEN

Every seat in the church was taken. A long line formed outside the main entrance, stretching two blocks. Two D.C. police officers kept the traffic moving; it was bumper-to-bumper in front of the church and on the adjacent streets. The humidity was stifling, and the air conditioner was pumping. Nevertheless, people inside the church were fanning. Betty had water coolers strategically placed on the two sidewalks leading up to the church, not wanting anyone to have a heat stroke. Perspiration ran down her cleavage and under her armpits, but she ignored it, as she had ignored the reporters who tried to interview her when she arrived at the church.

Betty walked around the church to inspect the building. She had hired a temporary cleaning service, and the church was spotless. The crew had cleaned the wood panels and the stained-glass windows and had polished the floor. Betty returned to her office in time to hear the phone ring.

"I'm leaving early. Do you want to meet me?" Stan asked.

"Have you forgotten tonight is the first Friday of the month?"

"After everything you have been through, you are having the session?"

"Yes."

"I'm beginning to think you may need my professional services."

"Love heals," was all she said.

"What? I can see you are not yourself tonight. Baby, you're under too much pressure. What happened to the fun-loving woman that loved to play with Big Daddy?"

There was silence.

"Go play Mother Teresa to your flock, and when you get tired of sacrificing yourself, you know where I am."

She heard the phone click.

⟋⟍

Margaret locked herself in her office and headed for the rocking chair. It was special. She heard the voices more when she was sitting in the chair than at any other time. With her Bible in hand, Margaret walked around the chair a few times before sitting in it. She had sought out the voices only a few times. Usually, they made their presence known without any effort on her part. Today, she needed them more than ever.

Tonight, she was going into the devil's lair. She was going to clean house and destroy the work of Satan. She had even selected a new dark-blue silk suit for the occasion. It was important she looked the part of someone who could lead people.

They're going to steal it away from you. Margaret could barely hear the voice.

She bolted up. "Who? Tell me who?" she shouted.

They're all against you. Don't tell anyone what you're going to do tonight, or they will steal your glory, the voice whispered.

"No, no, this is my glory—my glory!" Margaret jumped out of the chair and the Bible fell to the floor. She quickly picked it up and kissed it. "Forgive me, Father. I didn't mean for your precious book to touch the dirty surface."

Alan stood outside his wife's office. He could hear her talking to herself. This wasn't the first time he had heard her one-sided conversations. Once, he had opened the door and found her waving her hands back and forth, talking to an empty chair. Margaret had pushed him out of the room and told him never to enter without knocking first. From then on, Margaret locked her office door when she was in there.

He knocked on the door several times before she answered. Alan looked at the woman who stood before him. Her usually neat hairdo was wild. Her glassy eyes were looking past him, rather than at him. When she finally focused on him, he wanted to run.

"What is it that you want?" she demanded, glaring at him.

"We need to talk. Can you come to my office? I left Rev by himself."

Margaret closed the door behind her and followed Alan down the stairs. Rev was sitting in front of the desk with his head down, a little saliva at the side of his mouth.

Alan hated to confront her. She acted as though he was stupid or beneath her when they talked, but this had to be done. The president of the board of trustees, Daniel Reilly, had called earlier, strongly urging him to keep Margaret under wraps tonight. He had heard she was going to try to preach. The president had warned him that if anything scandalous happened, the board would take extreme action. Alan was shaking when the conversation ended. He needed to remind her that she wasn't an ordained minister.

"Margaret, tonight let's keep everything nice and quiet." He was suddenly sorry he promised her that she could lead the group in prayer.

Margaret smiled. *They warned me.*

"I don't know why you're worried, Alan. I'm just going to do a prayer," she assured him, looking at her father. "Papa, blink twice for yes and once for no," she commanded, remembering what the doctor had told her about him being able to communicate through his eyes.

Rev sat there and deliberately forced saliva out of his mouth.

"Just what I thought. That doctor was lying."

"What are you talking about?" Alan asked.

"The doctor told me Papa could blink twice for yes and once for no. They're lying to me."

"Why are they lying to you, Margaret?"

"They want to take Papa away from me and use him for their experiments. I will never let that happen!" she bellowed in a voice Alan had never heard.

CHAPTER TWENTY-EIGHT

Nick left the museum early to go to the hospital to see Lindy. When he arrived at her office, she was making her hospital rounds. He persuaded the receptionist to let him into her office to leave some flowers. *Why didn't he see it before?* Right on her desk was a photograph of the child and one of the family. Nick looked at the man in the photograph. He knew that face. "Holy shit, it's the man who was on the plane." His Lindy was married to a pretty boy. Nick shook his head in disbelief.

He picked up the photograph of Michael. There was something about his eyes that reminded Nick of his own. Was this his son? Nick felt overwhelming sadness as he placed the photograph back on the desk. His heart ached. Was he the reason this child had suffered?

Nick sat in the hotel lounge drinking a rum and coke. Later, he was going to the Church of Melchizedek. He wanted to see the Elder Healer for himself. He was caught up in this mess because of her. *Make things right,* she had told him. She had not said it to him face-to-face, but it was what he remembered when he came back into consciousness. The villagers had told him he died, and the Elder Healer brought him back to life. Were they telling the truth? They had no reason to lie.

Nick ordered another drink.

How could he possibly make it right for this kid? The Healer told him the child had a special mission in the new millennium, which was still decades away. He could walk away from this now. No, there were so many questions he needed answered before he could walk away. Nick downed his drink and left the lounge. Scribbled on a piece of paper he held in his hand was the number for a private investigator.

CHAPTER TWENTY-NINE

Mt. Olive Baptist Church was empty. Rev. Alan Pierce counted about fifty people scattered in the pews. *Where are Deacon Coleman, trustee Reilly, and the rest of my people?* He held his head down as he walked to the pulpit to take his seat. This was a sure indication that he didn't have any clout with the members of the church. *Have they abandoned me?*

Margaret sat quietly in the first pew of the church. When he called on her to lead the prayer she stood in front of the pulpit. Speaking very softly, which was odd for her, she told the small group that Rev didn't feel too well and that she wouldn't be able to stay. She asked them to support Reverend Pierce as he led the congregation in prayer and pray for her father. "Let's show the world the power of prayer," were her parting words. Then she smiled at her husband and left.

Reverend Pierce was thrown by his wife's calm demeanor. He was even more thrown by the news that Rev was not feeling well. If anything, he thought, the old man had shown remarkable improvement over the last couple of days. His eyes were clearer, and he wasn't drooling or wetting himself as much.

Margaret hurried out of the sanctuary and rushed inside the house to her father's room. Rev was sitting where she had left him, dressed in one of his best suits. She rolled his wheelchair toward the back door of the house and helped him into the car.

"It's okay, Papa. We're going to get rid of the devil that has come into our town," she whispered to him as she drove.

Rev quietly wondered what his daughter was up to. He wanted so badly to ask her, but knew he couldn't, so he bit his tongue.

Margaret began talking out loud, but Rev knew it was not to him. "Yes, yes, I know. I know what to do. I'm the chosen one."

Chosen for what? Rev wondered. *Whatever it is, it's not good.*

Thirty minutes later, they were parked on a side street in Georgetown. Rev realized that they were a block or so away from the Church of Melchizedek.

It wasn't long before Rev saw his friend of many years coming down the street. Deacon Coleman reached the passenger side of the car and spoke to Margaret.

"They're just getting started. It's packed." He wanted to say, *as usual,* but they didn't need to know this wasn't his first time there. His gout had started up again and he wanted a healing. He hadn't gotten a chance to see the Elder Healer yet, but he wasn't giving up. He had let Margaret talk him into helping her bring Rev there. She told him it was for a healing, and if the Healer didn't heal him, she would expose her as an imposter.

Deacon Coleman knew better. He had witnessed enough healings to know the Elder Healer was far from being an imposter. The night of the meeting at Mt. Olive Baptist Church, he wanted to tell them he had attended to a few of the healing sessions. However, he feared their condemnation.

When they reached the front door of the church, a crowd was ahead of them. Deacon Coleman pushed Rev's wheelchair through the crowd, parting them like the Red Sea. They came to a halt at the door. It was closed. Margaret panicked. She couldn't come this far and not get in. She looked around; people were everywhere. Margaret was beginning to perspire. Seeing the look of desperation on her face, Deacon Coleman whispered to her that everything was taken care of, and they would get in. He then told the usher at the door he was bringing Dr. Lee's grandfather and slipped the young man a few dollar bills. Problem solved.

CHAPTER THIRTY

Reverend Betty Goldstein decided to open the healing sessions with a special presentation. If time permitted, she would read from the Bible, or the Bhagavad Gita, as she had been instructed to do on the healing night. Earlier that day, Betty agonized over how to tell them the truth. She wanted to tell them about Michael and the others who had been healed. After she talked to Michael and Paul, Betty did something she had not done in a long time. She prayed. Betty asked God for guidance, strength, clarity, and courage to stand up for what she believed. Finally, she decided to rely on the Spirit within her to speak through her.

As she approached the pulpit, the crowded church became quiet. Betty glanced at Lindy, Paul, and Michael, who were sitting in the first pew. Their presence gave her the reassurance she needed to say what she had planned.

Betty took a deep breath and looked down at the letter she had written.

"Many of you have been coming here for weeks to be healed. Some of you have received healings, or your family and friends have been blessed. As you know, there have been questions about the identity of the Elder Healer, and whether or not she has the appropriate medical credentials." Betty paused, looking around the room. Grace Perry sat in the first row on the opposite side of Lindy and Paul, and right in front of the door where the Elder Healer always made her entrance and exit. *Grace Perry has positioned herself well*, Betty thought. She was also surprised to see Nick Lewis standing in the back of the church. *Does Lindy know he's here?* She continued speaking.

"The Elder Healer asked to remain anonymous, because she doesn't want any publicity that might take away from the great and wonderful work done here. I have tried to honor the request, but I am being pressured to break that promise." Betty deliberately looked at Grace Perry. The crowd murmured their disapproval. Betty raised her hands to quiet them.

"I will not reveal her identity. What is important is that people are healed." The loud applause from the crowd gave Betty courage to continue. "As for inquiries about her medical credentials," Betty paused again. "I can tell you that the Elder Healer follows the footsteps of the Master Healer, Jesus Christ, healing by faith and the power within. Mental and spiritual healing is based on faith. Within you is a force that can heal you. It is equivalent to your belief that a pill can relieve your pain. The difference is that a pill may relieve your pain temporarily, but God heals you forever!"

People shouted out, "Amen!"

"Tonight, I want to talk a little more about the healing power that is within each of us and is a normal part of our human system. This healing power or force is the god within us, or the Cosmic Consciousness that knows all and is everywhere. Most of us were raised to be unaware of this healing power within us. We have been taught that to be healed, we must rely on forces outside of ourselves. A true healing takes place when we release resistance in the form of doubt, anger, and hate, and let God flow through us."

Betty spoke slowly. She wanted to make sure they understood, fearing the information would be above their comprehension. Many of the people who came to the healing sessions were not regular attendees at the church and might not be familiar with New Age concepts and terms. They simply came for a healing. Betty felt at this point she had nothing to lose. It was better to speak the truth than to keep hiding. They would either accept what she had to say or walk away.

All eyes were on her. Betty was so focused on what she was saying that she didn't see the three people maneuvering their way through the crowd to the pulpit. Just as she was about to speak about Michael's miraculous healing, she heard a woman scream, "Lies, lies, lies! These are all lies she is telling you, and using the name of Jesus in vain!"

Betty looked into the warped face of Margaret Johnson Lee Pierce, Lindy's mother. An elderly gentleman was pushing Lindy's grandfather, Rev, in a wheelchair right behind his daughter. They stopped midway up the aisle. Margaret raised her Bible and did a full 360-degree turn.

Before Betty could say anything, Margaret screamed, "Why are you here listening to these lies and distortions?" Margaret walked up and down the aisle, pointing the Bible at people. "God needs to strike down this place and all the sinners in here. If you can heal your body, then why aren't you healed?"

Margaret grabbed Rev's wheelchair from Deacon Coleman and pushed him closer to the pulpit.

"Look at my father, a man of God. If he could have healed himself, don't you think he would have by now? No, he's bound to this awful contraption." She pointed to the wheelchair. "Get out of this house of the devil! Run these heathens out of here!" Margaret's head was pounding and her eyes burned. She could hear the voices in her head, but they were incoherent. She looked around the church. Everyone was staring at her. People in the back row were standing, waiting to see what she would do or say next. Margaret inhaled and looked at Betty, who couldn't quite decide what to do.

"False prophets, sinners, liars, devil worshipers. If we had these healing powers, then why is the world in the state it's in? These healers are false prophets." She opened the Bible and read from Matthew 24:11: "And many false prophets will appear and will lead many people astray."

"Rise up and leave this place of shame and destruction. Ask God to forgive you for your debts," she yelled, continuing her tirade.

Margaret felt the back of her neck prickle as she watched her daughter walk forward and face her. Lindy was in a white dress. Her hair was loose, falling below her shoulders. She looked like a goddess. Lindy stretched her arms out as she looked past her mother to her grandfather. Margaret heard incoherent whispers coming from the audience. She turned and looked at her father.

Rev was getting out of the wheelchair, using the arms of the wheelchair for support. Then he stood up without holding on to anything. Deacon Coleman let out a small cry as he tried to reach for his old friend. Rev pushed the deacon's hand away. Margaret stood paralyzed. Rev took a step forward, then another, and another. He moved past his daughter with his hands stretched out. Lindy opened her hands to him.

Rev was reaching out for his beloved Amanda. She had come back. He had to get to her. He tried to say her name, "A—man—da," as he curled over and landed on the floor in front of Lindy.

Margaret ran to him. Mother and daughter knelt down together. Rev smiled and looked beyond them; his eyeballs went from the back of his head to the front. Margaret released a wail that shook every brick in the church. Stunned, Lindy reached out to touch her mother's hand. Margaret pushed Lindy away as she tried to pry Rev from her.

"Murderer, murderer," Margaret screamed at Lindy.

Deacon Coleman took hold of Margaret and pulled her away from Rev, but she fought to get back to her father. Two ushers helped him to get her to the back of the church. A tear ran down the side of the deacon's face. *God, what have I done?* He thought Rev would get a healing and mend things with Lindy. He had no idea this would happen.

Lindy looked at her grandfather as he lay peacefully with his head in her lap. She held him in her arms and rocked back and forth, as if she were rocking a baby to sleep. She heard someone screaming and crying, but it seemed so far away. Lindy felt someone kneeling next to her, urging her to get up. Paul was trying to get her to release Rev, but she wanted to hold him as long as she could. They had spent too many years apart. Why did it have to end like this? *He never met Michael,* was the last thought she had before relinquishing to Paul.

Nick made his way through the crowd, which surrounded the group on the floor.

He watched as a young boy circled Lindy. *Michael? This boy is walking. Why did Lindy tell me Michael was a cripple?*

"Damn," Nick said to himself. He looked around, and the Elder Healer was gone. He thought he had seen her briefly when the old man had tried to walk. But she disappeared, as she had in Mali.

Amid the confusion around Rev's fall, Grace Perry seized the opportunity to slip through the side door of the church that led to the basement. She had seen the door quickly open just after Rev had fallen. Grace hurried down the steps and saw that door to the special room was closed. She felt as though she was chasing a ghost. The Healer had a pretty good magic act of appearing and disappearing. She could have given Houdini some lessons.

Time dragged as Grace waited. Her plan was to confront the Elder Healer whenever she emerged from the room. The commotion on the upper level had died down. It was now quiet and eerie in the old church. She had positioned herself in a space under the steps, and doubted if anyone could see her since it was pitch dark. There wasn't even a light coming from under the door of the room. She pulled out her small flashlight and looked at her watch. Two hours had passed, and nothing.

Grace Perry finally decided to venture out of her hole. She cautiously moved toward the room, placing her ear to the door. It was quiet. *What the hell?* she thought.

Grace Perry turned the key in the lock and stepped into the room.

CHAPTER THIRTY-ONE

Lindy didn't want to leave her house. She had not gone to work since Rev died. She was in no condition to go, even if she had wanted to. Paul and the Awakeners tried to comfort her, but the grief was unbearable. She couldn't stop crying and blaming herself for Rev's fall.

She didn't have any desire or energy to do anything. She just wanted to lie in bed and hope the world would go away. The blinds were closed tightly because of the snooping reporters stalking her since the incident at the church. Lindy peeked out her bedroom window and didn't see any of them. They were probably at Rev's funeral. She prayed they wouldn't come back. Betty, experiencing the same harassment, told her to ignore them, and they would eventually go away.

She learned about the date and time of the funeral from reading the obituary section of the *Washington Star*. It didn't mention her, Paul, or Michael. It was as if they didn't exist.

Lindy reached over to her nightstand and picked up her appointment book. Inside was a white envelope with no return address or name. She pulled the letter out, knowing who had sent it even though it was unsigned.

It came in the mail a few days after Rev's passing. Lindy unfolded the letter. It was short and to the point, no heading, just hateful words.

Don't come to the funeral. You and your devil worshipers killed him. God will strike you and your kind dead.

Lindy read it over and over until tears clouded her eyes. *This can only be the work of my mother,* she thought. *My mother is denying me my last chance to pay respects to Papa.*

She wanted to go to the funeral, but Paul and Betty advised her not to, as her presence would create too much confusion. Lindy went over to the table with the three white candles and a photograph of Rev that

Paul had set up for her. She lit the candles, and then knelt and folded her hands in prayer. Lindy quieted her mind and wiped away her tears as she asked her grandfather to forgive her.

Some time had passed when she heard a voice say, *Why are you sad, child?*

"My grandfather died." The tears started again; it was so hard to say those words. "Who are you?"

I'm someone who loves your grandfather and you very much. Your grandfather is alive; that's what is important for you to know.

"I thought I believed in live after death until he died in my arms. It was so final. I tried to heal him at the hospital and it didn't work. I made things worse," Lindy cried out.

You're not responsible for him casting off the old shell.

"Why didn't the healing work?" Lindy asked, pressing for answers.

When a spirit or soul no longer wishes to focus its energy into a physical body, it withdraws itself and goes within. He had finished his mission. Therefore, for him, death was a healing. You brought happiness to him in his last hours. He was tired in that broken body.

"It hurts so much. All those years we were separated, and now this. There was so much I wanted to say to him, and most of all, I wanted to ask for his forgiveness."

He knows your heart.

"I feel so bad."

You are going through the cycle of feeling the loss of someone you think is gone from you forever. You know this is not true.

"I know, but my heart still aches for him."

The human part of you needs to go through this grief. Remember that prolonged grief will destroy you emotionally and result in sickness. I love you.

Minutes later, Lindy looked up as Paul was entering her room, carrying a lunch tray. *If only he was offering something more than food,* she thought wishfully. *I need someone to hold me.*

CHAPTER THIRTY-TWO

Rev. Alan Pierce had not seen that many people in the church since Rev retired. They squeezed into every available seat, lined the aisles, and jammed the lobby. The mayor, members of the city council, and members of Congress sat in the reserved pews. Even the President of the United States had sent a letter of condolence. Rev had done it again. They all came for his homecoming. Margaret, dressed in all black, sat in the front pew with Deacon Coleman and his wife.

Reverend Pierce, as did others in the church, wondered if Lindy would show up. He was glad to see that so far there was no sign of her. If Lindy came, he didn't know what Margaret might do. She was on the verge of hysteria. She kept repeating how they had killed her father. Days after Rev's death, he tried to reason with her, but his efforts were to no avail. Reverend Pierce tried to get her to use this time to forgive her daughter and make amends, but her only response was to accuse him of scheming with them.

Because dignitaries and friends wanted to say a few words about Rev, the service was longer than normal. Reverend Pierce reached for a glass of water and prayed it would be over soon.

When the last person finally walked toward the pulpit, Margaret jumped up from her seat, brushed by the person, and took his place on the pulpit. Reverend Pierce was dumbfounded, and the rest of the congregation stared at her in utter disbelief. Margaret used a white linen handkerchief to dab at her eyes. She took a second look at the vast sea of people watching her.

This is your chance to show them that you are the chosen one, she heard the familiar voice whisper.

"I could ask for mercy on those miserable sinners who did this to your pastor and my beloved Papa." She paused. By this time, Reverend

Pierce had sprung from his seat. He had to stop her before she got carried away. Margaret noticed him peripherally.

"Let her speak. That's his daughter!" someone yelled.

"You know me. I grew up in this church my Papa founded years ago in the basement of our small house with Deacon Coleman and a few others. He built this church up from a handful of souls to hundreds. Now he's gone." She wiped her eyes again.

"Many will say he was old and it was his time. Others will say he was sick and feeble. This morning I am here to set the record straight. He was old, and yes, he was sick. But Papa..." Margaret struggled to get the words out, "was not feeble. He was a man of God."

"Amen, amen," shouted the audience.

"Do you hear me?" she screeched. "I said he was a man of God, still leading the sheep and doing God's will."

"Amen, child, preach on," one of the deaconesses called out.

"He fought against Satan to save his flock. He, like Jesus, gave his life so we could be free." Margaret rocked her body back and forth. Some had stood and were waving their hands or programs in the air. She could hear the shouts of *Amen* over and over again.

"Satan and his forces tried to strike him down, but Papa stood up. He stood up by himself to face the devil. He gave himself to bring home God's sheep. God took him, and he is saved. He is saved! Thank God Almighty, my Papa has gone home to the Kingdom of the Lord!"

Reverend Pierce was in shock. Margaret was delivering Rev's eulogy. She had stolen his chance to bring an end to Rev's era and establish his own. Looking at the audience, he knew Margaret had captured them with her performance.

"They can't get to him or hurt him now!"

Get the Bible, she heard.

Margaret turned to Mark 3:28-30 and read, "But he that shall blaspheme against the Holy Ghost hath never forgiveness, but is in danger of eternal damnation." Before stepping down from the pulpit, she added, "Those that used the sword against Papa shall be in eternal damnation."

As the soloist began to sing "How Great Thou Art," Margaret threw herself across Rev's casket and started ripping adorning flowers off the coffin while trying to pry it open Those close to the front could hear her saying, "Papa, Papa, don't leave me."

Reverend Pierce quickly ran to the casket and tried to pull Margaret away. She screamed, cried, and wouldn't let go. With the help of Deacon Coleman and two of the church nurses, Reverend Pierce was able to get her back to her seat. While one nurse fanned her, the other opened the top buttons of her dress, took off her hat, and wiped her face with a damp cloth. The choir joined in with the soloist to sing the chorus:

Then sing my soul,
My Savior God to Thee
How great Thou art!
How great Thou art!

Margaret fought to get up, but strong hands held her down until she regained her composure. As he made his way back to the pulpit, Reverend Pierce looked into the disapproving face of trustee Reilly.

Rev. Alan Pierce moved the rest of the service along quickly, silently praying Margaret would not go into one of her spells at the burial site. He had had enough for one day.

CHAPTER THIRTY-THREE

Margaret was in Rev's old bedroom. Food littered the floor, and the smell was so bad that her husband refused to come in. Alan tried several times to get her to come out, but she wouldn't budge. She kept the door locked. He could hear her crying and screaming. The worst part was the cursing. He had never heard such foul language. *Was she possessed?* Alan was beside himself.

From the other side of Rev's bedroom door, he told Margaret about the meeting with the trustees and deacons and the meeting with the attorney for the reading of Rev's will, but she never responded; she simply threw something at the door.

Margaret was lying in a fetal position on the bed when she heard her husband's voice mumbling about some meeting and lawyers. She picked up one of her shoes and threw it at the door. She just wanted to be left alone. Papa was gone. There was no one to protect her now. The voice warned her that they were after her. They were jealous because God had chosen her to lead his people home to Mt. Olive Baptist Church.

The board and police need to be investigating what those devil worshipers did to Papa. They murdered him.

An autopsy report showed Rev had died of a heart attack. Lindy pushed him to get up and try to walk. It was too much for him. She had stood in the center aisle of the church in all white, as if she was a virgin or saint.

She tricked Papa into thinking she was his wife, Amanda. Margaret wiped her eyes with the back of her hand. *Why did Lindy have to look like Amanda?* Margaret took her fist and beat the pillow, screaming, "I hate them! I hate them, with their perfect noses and white skin! Look at all the grief they brought to Papa. Why, why couldn't he see that the woman who bore me was unholy and that Lindy is just like her?" Margaret continued to sob into the pillow. The throbbing of her head made her curl up into a ball.

Revenge, she heard the voice say. Margaret lifted her head up. *You are God's chosen one, and must stand in his place and take vengeance.*

Margaret immediately got up, opened the door, and went to look for her husband. She found Alan in his office working on his sermon for the coming Sunday. Margaret marched in and slammed her fist down on the desk.

"What will are you talking about, Alan?"

Startled, not only by the tone of her voice, but also by her appearance, Alan almost fell out of his chair. Margaret was filthy. She must not have taken a bath for days. She was pale and didn't have a stitch of clothing on.

"Don't you think you need to take a bath and get dressed?" he calmly asked her.

"Tell me about the will, damn you! Are you trying to cheat me out of my inheritance?" she shouted.

"Calm down, Margaret. No one is trying to do any such thing."

"Papa never told me about any will, and I handled all his finances and business. You are trying to deceive me. I want you out of my house! Do you hear me? Get out!"

"Margaret, no one is trying to do anything to you. You have been under a lot of stress lately. Go back upstairs before someone comes in and sees you."

"Tell me about the will, damn you! Then get the hell out of here!"

"Okay, okay. The Bittle and Bittle Law office called. Mr. Robert Bittle said he represents your father's estate and that he was holding a reading of Rev's will tomorrow morning."

"Bittle and Bittle? I swear if you are trying to trick me out of my inheritance, I'll help you to your grave," Margaret hissed at her husband as she walked out of the room.

Alan sat in the chair and loosened his tie. He felt hot. He poured a glass of water and drank it straight down. What was he going to do? Who could he get to help him? She had gone over the edge.

Hungry for the first time in days, Margaret went to the kitchen. In the refrigerator, she found pieces of fried chicken and potato salad. Feeling cold air from the refrigerator, she looked down at herself and realized she didn't have any clothes on. Margaret let out a whoop and danced about and then took out the chicken, potato salad, greens, and cornbread. She spread the food out on the kitchen table and sat there as if she was fully dressed.

The first order of business was to clean house. It was a mess. *Oh,* she thought, *I have to go and buy some clothes. I'm going right now and clean out my closet. Then I am going to move into Papa's room, until I get that man out of my house.*

Alan found the refrigerator door open and half the food on the table. Hearing loud noises coming from upstairs, he hurried to the second floor. There he found Margaret tossing clothes and shoes out of their bedroom closet and into the hallway. She was still naked, but now wore a pair of red heels.

CHAPTER THIRTY-FOUR

The following morning, Reverend Pierce was not surprised when Margaret showed up at his office ready to go to the reading of the will. She looked pale, but was exquisitely dressed. *Thank God*, he thought. *She has cleaned herself up.* Even her hair looked as if she had gone to the beauty salon.

Bittle and Bittle was an old, established family business in the northeast corridor of the city. When the Pierces arrived, Mr. Bittle wasted no time getting started. He told them there would be two readings of the will, with the second taking place in the afternoon.

Margaret looked at the attorney as if he had lost his mind. *Two readings? Who else would he be reading for? I'm the sole heir to my father's estate.*

"Who will be attending the afternoon reading?" she asked.

"Dr. Lindy Lee and her husband," he answered without looking up from the papers he was shuffling around.

Margaret, taken aback at the news that Rev might have left Lindy something in his will, bit her lip to hold back what she really wanted to say. Reverend Pierce, seeing blood on his wife's lip, offered her his handkerchief. Margaret jerked her head, and a drop of blood splattered on her nice new baby-blue jacket. Margaret excused herself and hurried to the restroom. She locked the door and leaned against the tile wall, which cooled her burning skin. She couldn't believe Papa had done this to her. He had included Lindy in his will.

Mr. Bittle must have persuaded him to do it. They tricked Papa and are trying to steal my inheritance. I'll contest the will; that's what I'll do.

Feeling better, Margaret returned to the office and eyed the two men, who looked like vultures to her.

Margaret sat and listened as the attorney read the will, which wasn't long. She got everything except the money from a second insurance policy.

Papa had a second insurance policy he hid from me?

She asked the attorney about the second policy, but he refused to give her any information about it. She couldn't help wondering if Lindy's amount was more than the $50,000 she received, but to find out, she would have to wait for the will to go through probate and become part of the public record.

Papa always did love Lindy more than me. How could he do this?

Margaret remained calm—until the attorney read that if she tried to contest the will, she might not get anything. Reverend Pierce had to drag his wife out of the office as she screamed and cursed the attorney out. She vowed to sue him, Lindy, and anyone else involved in stealing what was rightfully hers.

After the death of her father, Reverend Piece feared Margaret would never be a normal functioning adult again—as if she ever was. He had to get her help. But what if she refused?

CHAPTER THIRTY-FIVE

Betty was glad that Rev's funeral was over. Later in the day she and the Professor were keeping Michael while Lindy and Paul went to the reading of Rev's will. She hoped things would be quiet for awhile. She entered the church through the back door, using the new key. A temporary custodian discovered the door was unlocked after the Friday night healing session. He immediately called Betty, who came over to inspect the church. Everything was fine except for the door to the Elder Healer's room: it was partly open. Betty had not been in the room, which was always kept locked since the beginning of the healing sessions. The pedestal was gone. *Where was it?* she wondered. She decided not to call the police because she didn't want to go into a long explanation about the room and its use.

What worried her was that someone could get in and out of the church. *But who? Did Pops made an extra set of keys to the building?* she wondered. She had the locks changed.

The ringing of the phone startled her.

"Are you avoiding me?"

"I thought you were busy with your family," Betty retorted, referring to a previous conversation with Stan.

"You don't understand."

"Oh?"

"I didn't call to argue. I miss you, baby."

Betty's knees went weak. Her lips curled at the corners into a smile. "I needed you to be there for me."

"I *am* here for you, baby. I'm right outside the church. All of me. You should see the old boy standing at attention. Better still, you need to feel it."

"You're where?"

"At a restaurant not far from the church. Can I come by?"

"Yes!"

They didn't have to worry about anyone seeing them together, except maybe the custodian, but he was busy working upstairs. Stan was actually coming to the church. He hadn't been to the church since that first time. Betty checked her makeup, frowning at the outfit she had on. She liked to look sexy and classy when she was with him.

It didn't take him long to get there. The moment they were in her office, he kissed her hard on the mouth. He wouldn't let her come up for air, so she pushed against his chest.

"Sorry, baby, I just missed you so much." He kissed her again, gently this time. They backed up against her desk, and he started fumbling with her blouse. She tried to stop him; after all, they were in the house of God. But he was persistent. His hand moved up her back and unfastened her bra; her breasts dropped out of the cups. Stan unbuttoned her blouse and kissed each nipple. He circled each one with his tongue and began to pulling up her skirt. She couldn't stop him if she wanted to. With her skirt now above her hips, he used his free hand to brush her papers and bag off the desk.

"Not here in the church," she protested. Her words went unheeded as he entered her.

It was all over quickly. Stan looked smug as he pulled up and zipped his pants. Betty was going crazy looking for her panties. She finally found them under some of the papers he had shoved off the desk.

The bastard. He had gotten to me again, and in the church.

Stan walked over to her, lifted her face, and kissed her nose and lips. Then he sat in the chair facing the desk. Surprised that he didn't leave immediately, Betty decided to take back the word *bastard* and call him an abuser instead.

"I didn't want to tell you this until I had gone through with everything, but I asked Sandra for a divorce."

Betty stopped what she was doing and looked at him. "You what?"

"I asked her for a divorce."

"And?"

"We're working out the details."

"Details? What details?"

"Property. As an attorney, you should know it's not easy."

Ignoring his answer, Betty asked, "Have you moved out?" Her heart was racing.

"Not quite yet…"

She cut him off. "What does 'not quite yet' mean?"

"It means I'm not giving that bitch anything. She's not getting the house or any of my money. She thinks because she helped me get through medical school that I owe her my life and the shirt on my back. Well, she's wrong. If she wants a divorce, she needs to leave. She is not getting one cent from me."

So, he didn't ask her *for a divorce. She asked him.*

Sitting there, Stan looked old and mean. He was no longer the Billy Dee she imagined him to be. All she wanted right now was for him to leave.

"Leave, Stan! Get out now!"

"What?"

"Get out of here!"

"What is wrong with you bitches?" he grumbled, walking out the door. "You'll be running back to me when that old Jew you married can't get it up."

Betty locked the door behind him. How could she have stooped so low? Didn't she see what an ass he was? *No,* she told herself, *it wasn't all his fault.* She attracted him into her life because she went looking for love in all the wrong places. Hadn't she learned anything about life? She wasn't a spring chicken. It was time to grow up.

Remembering the tarot card she had selected, the devil and its meaning—self-imposed prison. *I'm taking these chains off, and it's time I figure out what's going on with my marriage and get my life back on track.*

170

CHAPTER THIRTY-SIX

Nick tried to reach Lindy several times at her office, but he always got the same response. She was out of the office on leave, and they did not know when she would be returning. He tried to charm the receptionist into giving him Lindy's address and phone number. But either he was losing his touch with women or this one was made of steel; he couldn't charm, coax, or beg her into giving out any information. The person who could give it to him probably would not, but maybe her husband would. Professor Goldstein owed him. Nick hadn't seen him in a long time, but they kept in touch by mail, and they would meet during the Professor's trips to Paris. Nick called him, and they arranged to meet for brunch at a French restaurant in Georgetown.

Nick was waiting when he arrived. He picked a table at the window so he could people watch; you never knew whom or what you might see in Georgetown. He spotted the Professor, walking with a cane, approaching the restaurant. He had aged. His once flaming-red hair had turned grey. Exchanging greetings in French, the two men embraced affectionately.

Near the end of the meal, Nick finally told him what he needed, and the Professor agreed to get it for him. He said he should have known the number by heart, but his memory had not been good lately. The Professor also told him that Betty and he were babysitting Michael later that day.

Nick thought it was ironic that years ago the Professor had advised him to push Diana to get an abortion, and now he might be the godfather of the child who had survived that foiled effort.

"What time do you plan to have him?" Nick asked nonchalantly.

"This afternoon when Lindy and her husband go to the reading of her grandfather's will."

"Professor, I would love to meet Michael and take some photos of him for Lindy. It might cheer her up."

"Good idea. Yes, I'll talk to Betty and…"

"No, let's leave the women out of this. It will be our surprise. I will take photos of you and him together. Can we meet back here around three? Is that a good time?"

The Professor agreed.

Nick prayed the old man wouldn't forget.

When Nick returned to the hotel several messages were waiting for him. A message from the private investigator said he had traced Cissy to California. She had disappeared, but a few folks owed him favors. He guaranteed Nick that he would have something substantial to give him in a few days.

The other three messages were from Diana, sounding possessive and demanding. He had let their relationship go too far. He had to break it off. No more sexual encounters with her. However, he wanted to remain friends. Nick decided to keep the peace by not bringing up the abortion again. There wasn't much more she could tell him, anyway. He was confident Diana believed the baby was badly deformed and died at birth. What would happen if she found out she had an eleven-year-old son being raised by the woman she despised?

CHAPTER THIRTY-SEVEN

Nick stood in front of the steps of the restaurant looking through the zoom lens of his camera. He spotted Professor's busy white hair and the little boy holding his hand as they walked down the steps of the hill behind the Georgetown Public Library. Nick started walking toward them. As he got closer, the Professor waved to him, then bent over and said something to the child. Michael grabbed the Professor's hand and tried to pull him back up the steps. The look on his face was sheer terror.

"Dark man wants to take Michael away from Mommy and Daddy," he kept screaming at the Professor.

Nick couldn't imagine what could have caused the child to look at him with such fright. He didn't want to frighten him further, so he stopped a few feet away.

The Professor assured Michael it was all right; Nick was a photographer and was going to take some pictures of him as a present for his mother. The boy stopped and took another look at Nick.

Nick smiled and offered to buy him an ice cream cone. "I'll never do that, Michael. I love your mom, and I wouldn't do anything to hurt her."

Michael finally calmed down, and they walked back to the restaurant with Michael holding the Professor's hand tightly. Nick brought a cherry vanilla ice cream cone for Michael, and then sat quietly watching the child eat. He couldn't help staring at the boy. Michael looked exactly like Nick's oldest brother. He had Nelson's eyes and light-brown-against-dark-chocolate skin. He also had Diana's wavy hair. Nick was now certain that he needed no further proof that Michael was his and Diana's child. Or was he letting his imagination run wild?

After the ice cream treat, Michael warmed up to him. Nick showed him how to use the camera, and Michael couldn't get enough of taking photo after photo. The time passed too quickly. The boy had stolen his heart, so he couldn't just let it end there. He had to see this child again, although he only said a few words the entire time they were together. Nick sensed the child had put up a wall between them. He didn't know the reason, but he planned to find out. Nick was also curious about the child's ability to walk. What had happened since he last talked to Lindy?

They were taking the last of the photos on the grounds of the library when Betty Goldstein walked up on them. Nick couldn't resist turning the camera on her and the look on her face was worth a million bucks. She looked first at Michael, then Nick. *She sees it, too,* he thought.

"Professor, where have you been? I was getting worried about the two of you." Michael ran and hugged Betty around the waist, almost knocking her over.

"Just an outing with Nick Lewis," the Professor mumbled.

"We had better get you home, young man. Your mom and dad are on their way," she said lightly, looking at Nick.

Nick stooped down to Michael's level and took the boy's hand in his. "You're a terrific kid, Michael, and I am glad I had the opportunity to meet you. I'll make sure your mom gets these photos. Okay, little man?"

"Okay, Nick. Can I show them to my dad, also?"

Betty saw the pain that crossed Nick's face.

"You can show them to anyone you want." Nick didn't want to let go. Betty reached down and took Michael's hand from Nick's. He watched the three as they walked down R Street, holding hands.

Betty didn't know how she was going to tell Lindy and Paul about Nick's visit with Michael. She decided it was best to be truthful with them. However, she would leave out the part that it was prearranged, and just tell them the Professor was taking a stroll with Michael and ran into Nick.

Tonight she would have a long talk with her husband. They had avoided the inevitable for a long time. Not talking had led to a break-down in communication between them. They had to decide what they were going to do. She knew his health was deteriorating, and he wanted to be around his family. What did she want?

CHAPTER THIRTY-EIGHT

Attorney Bittle hoped the daughter had more sense than the mother. In his years of law practice, he had never encountered anyone so disturbed. He couldn't believe the foul words that flowed from Margaret's mouth; and to think her father was a well-known minister.

As he waited for Lindy to arrive, he recalled the first time he met Rev. He was visiting his good friend William Coleman when Rev happened to stop by. They took a liking to each other instantly. Several times they met at Coleman's house, discussing their favorite topics: D.C. politics and the Redskins. Rev liked to debate, and they would go on for hours, with Mrs. Coleman serving them lunch or dinner. At times, the discussions lasted from one mealtime to the next. He went to hear Rev preach a few times and enjoyed the sermons, but he was Catholic and didn't plan to change.

Rev engaged Bittle to draw up his will, instructing him to include a clause stating that it could not be contested by either party. Bittle often wondered if Rev had a premonition about his incapacitation; just after he signed the will, he suffered a disabling stroke. A knock on the door brought him back to the present.

The young couple seemed serene on first sight. He hoped he was right. They were a handsome couple. The drab clothes she wore suggested the woman downplayed her beauty, but there was no mistaking she was a work of exquisite art.

They listened quietly as Bittle read the will. Lindy kept her eyes down until he read the part where Rev had left her $250,000 from his insurance policy.

"Could you repeat that last part?" She could hardly get the words out.

Bittle re-read the paragraph about the $250,000, bracing himself in case she reacted as her mother had. Instead, she cried.

Lindy asked if her grandfather had left her a letter or some other kind of written communication. There was nothing except the money. More tears. At first Bittle thought they were tears of joy, but when he looked in her face, he saw sadness. The money didn't excite her.

She asked if a letter could have been misplaced, and he reiterated that he had not received any correspondence.

Bittle read the no-contest clause, and assured them the will should proceed smoothly through probate. Because she didn't care about the money, Bittle decided she must be in shock.

They thanked him profusely and left the office as quietly as they had entered.

A strange family, he thought.

CHAPTER THIRTY-NINE

Lindy and Paul discussed her inheritance briefly, and then fell silent. She was still in shock. Rev had penned the will years after putting her out of the church. *Was this his way of saying he was sorry? Had he ever tried to contact her before his stroke?* She had tried to make contact a number of times, but her mother had always rejected her overtures. It was never Rev who rejected her.

They found parking not far from the Goldstein house. Lindy still had a key from when she lived there with Betty and the Professor. She loved the Georgetown area, where many freed slaves settled after the Civil War. Eventually, it was built up and became an area of wealth and culture in the District. She called out for Betty, but the house was quiet. They figured Michael had dragged Betty and the Professor out for a walk.

The house was filled with the aroma of freshly cooked food. Lindy went to the kitchen, while Paul went to the Professor's office to browse through his extensive collection of books. Lindy found baked chicken in the oven. Asparagus and rice were on top of the stove. These were Michael's favorites. A vegetarian dish for Paul was in the refrigerator.

The three came into the house looking content but tired. Lindy could see that the stress and strain of the last few weeks had taken a toll on Betty. She looked worried and worn out. The Professor's declining health was probably worrying her, also.

Michael was so excited he could hardly get the words out as he ran to Lindy. "Nick let me take photos, Mommy."

"What are you talking about, Michael? Nick?" Lindy looked at Betty and the Professor, bewildered.

"Harvey and Michael were out walking in Georgetown, and they accidentally ran into Nick Lewis," Betty explained. "He took some pictures of Michael and promised to get them to you." She then rushed off to set the table in the next room.

Did Nick just happen *to be in Georgetown, or was this meeting arranged by him and the Professor?*

Lindy shared the good news of Rev's generous gift, and Betty joked that Margaret was likely having a hissy fit. Lindy told them about the clause specifying that neither she nor Margaret could contest the will.

The men took Michael into the library to relax and talk after dinner, giving the women a chance to be alone as they cleaned the kitchen.

"Do you think it was a chance meeting?" Lindy asked.

"You want to know what I really think?"

"Of course I do."

"Nick Lewis is trying to get to you any way he can."

"What's that got to do with Michael?"

"He knows how attached you are to the boy. So he makes friends with the son to get to the mom."

"He can forget it!" Lindy said harshly.

"You protest too much, my dear," Betty looked at her and added, "It's still there, isn't it?"

"I don't know what you're talking about." Lindy busied herself putting away the china.

"You haven't got that man out of your system after all these years. You can fool yourself, but you can't fool me, and I don't think you are fooling Paul."

Lindy checked to make sure the men were still occupied in the library.

"I decided not to go to the reception for his exhibit."

"Why not?"

"It's just not right."

"What's not right?" Betty would not let her off the hook.

"Okay, Attorney Goldstein," Lindy joked, "I am not going to my ex-college boyfriend's exhibit. I don't owe him anything. In fact, he owes me for what he did to me."

"You haven't forgiven him yet?"

"I thought I had let that go."

"It looks as if you have more work to do in that area. Going to the exhibit might be beneficial for you."

"How's that?"

"Go looking like a million dollars on the arm of your handsome husband, so Nick and the world can see you have moved on."

"I don't know. Rev just passed."

"And?"

"I don't have anything to wear."

"No problem, Miss Rich Girl. We will go shopping and treat ourselves to new hairdos. After that, we'll get our nails done. There will be no ifs, ands, or buts about it."

"What was his reaction to Michael?" Lindy asked, changing the subject back to Nick.

"Love. Yes, when I think about it, love."

"How can you say that? He doesn't even know Michael."

"It was the expression on his face when he looked at Michael. He was glowing. I hate to tell you this, but they look so much alike. It's uncanny."

"I don't see how you can say that. It's difficult to know who Michael looks like because of his deformities."

"Maybe you have that problem, but I don't."

Lindy turned aside so Betty couldn't see the happiness on her face.

CHAPTER FORTY

Margaret was steaming. She was sure Lindy got to Rev and tricked him into making her a beneficiary. She was anxious to know the amount of money her daughter was getting. Was it the same as hers—$50,000? Did that scheming daughter of hers try to get the house, car, his checking and saving accounts, and personal possessions? Thank God Papa didn't let her completely pull the wool over his eyes. In a few weeks, she would know everything.

Margaret lingered on the bed in which she had lain beside her father many nights. She opened his closet, took out one of his jackets, and sniffed it. She could still smell his cologne and aftershave. Tears trickled down her face.

All her life, she just wanted him to love her—and let her preach. His final act showed what she always knew, that he loved Lindy more than he loved her. How could he have done this to her?

You've got to pull yourself together to fight them. Look how you've let them get what rightfully belongs to you, the voice warned her.

The voice was unceasing, and she so desperately wanted it to stop. Margaret didn't want to hear what she felt in her heart: that Satan had won.

Stop crying, stupid.

Of all the voices she heard, Margaret disliked this one the most because it cursed at her and called her names. She wished it would go away.

Margaret picked up Rev's favorite Bible and gently ran her hand over the front cover. He had willed it to Deacon Coleman, who was coming to pick it up the next day. "It belongs to me," she said aloud. "I must hide it and give him one of the other Bibles. He won't know the difference," she said, rationalizing what she must do to keep the

Holy Book. Margaret temporarily stopped her sniffling and actually felt better.

The voice was right. I have to get myself together, she thought. *If I am weak, the devil and his followers can attack me. I'll pack up Papa's belongings and finish moving my things in here. I'll be safe.*

Margaret spent the next several hours packing Rev's clothes in boxes and moving her clothes to her new bedroom closet. Boxes lined the hallway leading up to the attic, where she would store his clothes. She couldn't bear to give them away right now. She had refused Alan's request for several of the jackets. She couldn't bear to see him in Rev's clothes. He wasn't good enough for them.

The next morning, Alan found his wife in the kitchen, making breakfast as if nothing had happened. She fixed him a hearty breakfast of bacon, sausage, eggs, potatoes, biscuits and hot black coffee.

Although she still looked pale and withdrawn and had lost several pounds since the death of Rev, she seemed to have snapped out of her depression.

Margaret told him that she planned to sleep in Rev's room for a while, since she was up late at night and didn't want to disturb him. Alan looked at his wife; she sounded so sensible and logical. She almost had him fooled…until she revealed her plans for the day.

"I am going to see a lawyer and take legal action against those people who are responsible for killing my father and robbing me of my inheritance."

"You heard what Mr. Bittle said yesterday. If you contest the will, you will lose everything."

"What is there for me to lose? This house? I own half of it already. The little money he left me? She doesn't deserve to get anything. Somehow she fooled Papa. He wasn't in his right mind. Besides, if she and her kind are under the jail, they won't be able to use it, will they?" She smiled at him as she slapped food on his plate.

Having lost his appetite, Alan pushed away from the table. "Margaret, I'm going to ask you to wait before you do anything you regret."

"Wait for what?"

"Until after the meeting tonight. At least talk this over with the church leaders. Maybe they will help you." He was lying, but it got her attention.

"It would be nice if my own husband would support me for a change, and stop working against me. Sometimes I wonder why you married me."

I wonder, too, he thought.

As soon as Alan got the chance, he called Daniel Reilly and told him what to expect that evening, mentioning that he had something to give him.

The deacons and trustees were waiting for Margaret in the small sanctuary. She strolled in as if it was the middle of the day and no one had to go anywhere. Reilly was going over the finances and chose to ignore her entrance. If she wanted to play games, he was ready for her.

Daniel Reilly knew the day would come when the leadership of the church would be up for grabs. He had spent enough time and money to claim it. He wanted to be the power behind the pastor.

The old man finally kicked the bucket, and it was time for the new order to take over completely. Reverend Pierce was ideal in the role of minister; all the man wanted to do was preach and save souls, which was good. He had no interest in involving himself in the administration of church affairs.

Margaret Pierce was the problem; Daniel had bumped heads with her once before over accounting practices. He knew she had stolen money from the church when she was the treasurer, but he just couldn't prove it; she had been careful to leave no clue behind. After he became president of the trustee board, he had her removed from her position as church treasurer, which involved counting the donations in the collection plates and paying the bills.

Daniel was glad Reverend Pierce called to warn him about Margaret's ridiculous idea to accuse her daughter and other members of the Church of Melchizedek of murder. If anyone was responsible for the sudden demise of the old man, it was his own daughter. She shouldn't have taken him over there. He heard that Margaret gave a stellar performance, which was the talk of D.C. Reilly decided years ago the woman was mentally disturbed. He just couldn't understand why no one did anything about it. She definitely needed help, or to be put away.

Reverend Pierce assured Daniel that he had the leverage needed to convince his wife to drop her mad scheme to charge the other church with murder, but he wouldn't tell him what it was over the phone.

If only Reverend Pierce had the backbone to restrain his wife, they wouldn't have to deal with her behavior tonight. Reilly wanted to tell Pierce, *For God's sake, she's only a woman.* He had to rein in his own wife, Diana, who was spending a lot of time away from their home. He warned Diana that the investigation into his background included hers, too. Diana knew if she messed it up he would do the same to her career, and she would be washed up in D. C.

Reilly finally looked up and acknowledged Margaret, asking her to join them. She looked at the men gathered in the room and saw that Deacon Coleman, her only hope for support, was absent. She didn't believe what her husband said earlier about them helping her. Besides Reilly and a few other trustees, deacons Jones, Mitchell, King, Winston, and Hilliard were present. Margaret referred to them as the tyrants of the church. They either nodded a greeting or mumbled something vague.

Reilly got right to the reason for the meeting. The board wanted to know why she had taken Rev to the Church of Melchizedek. What happened at the church, and what was her role in it?

Margaret wanted to laugh. *My role in it?*

Looking directly at the men, Margaret calmly related the events of that night. She told them she was directed by God to go to that forbidden place and lead his lost sheep home. Rev was to serve as God's reminder to people of the Christian way of life. Taking care not to refer to her daughter by name, she went on to tell them that people there bewitched her father and made him believe he could walk, thus killing him.

Listening to her testimony, Reilly was stunned. He wanted to cut her off a number of times, but decided it was best to let her finish. After nearly thirty minutes, Margaret finally wound down her story.

"How did God tell you this?" Reilly asked.

Be careful, the voice said. *He's trying to trick you.*

"God speaks to us in many ways. Haven't you ever heard God, trustee Reilly?"

Reilly sat up straight in his chair. "Yes, um, but we want to know how God talks to you."

"Like he talked to Moses and Jesus." She looked at the men to see if they understood.

"You can't possibly think *those people* killed your father?" Deacon Hilliard asked.

"Think it? Ha! I know it."

"What proof do you have to support this?" interjected Deacon Jones.

"He's dead, and that's enough for me. He was well, considering his condition, when we entered that awful place."

"We are talking about tangible proof, something that can link them to or show they were responsible for your father's death. Did they put their hands on him? Give him anything? That's what we are talking about." Deacon Jones persisted.

"You gentlemen don't understand what we are dealing with. These are evil spirits that are able to control your mind if you are not strong."

"Your father, may his soul rest in peace, was one of the most God-fearing men alive. I can't believe if it was possible they could have gotten to Rev." Deacon Jones looked at the other men for agreement.

"The illness had weakened him, and they took advantage," Margaret said adamantly.

"What is it you plan to do?" Reilly asked her.

"My husband didn't tell you? I plan to go to the authorities with this information. I want that church, whatever it is called, shut down!"

"If you go to them with this preposterous story, they will laugh you out of the precinct. Mt. Olive cannot afford to have its name dragged through the mud," Reilly reminded her.

"I don't need you to support me. I will do it alone." Margaret was getting hot under the collar.

Reverend Pierce could see Margaret changing from calm to outrageous. He saw the attack coming, but didn't know how to warn the men.

"Your name is connected to this church, and the things you do reflect on us. Don't you understand what your role is here?" Reilly wasn't going to let her get the last word.

"I *am* the church. My father built this church from nothing, and I will carry on his legacy. Those who sinned against him must pay."

"You're not God. Have you forgotten what God said? 'Revenge is mine, said the Lord.' "

"You silly little man, you don't know who you are dealing with."

"Margaret," Reverend Pierce shouted. "Stop!" He couldn't let this go on any further. "Let me talk to you out in the hallway. Gentlemen, would you excuse us?" He grabbed Margaret by her elbow and led her out of the room, not saying a word until they were in his office.

"I'll make this quick. You have to get medical help. Reilly and the others are right. You can't accuse those people of anything. You don't have anything to base your accusations on." She tried to interrupt him, but for once, Pierce stood his ground. He had reached the end of his rope.

"It's not me who needs help. It's you," she shouted.

Reverend Pierce took out his keys and unlocked his desk drawer. He pulled out a manila envelope and handed it to her. Margaret pulled out the papers, which were copies of her second bank account and details of the money she had stolen from the church over the years.

"How did you get this?" She was in shock.

"That's not important. I have it, and if you don't agree to get help and stop this nonsense about going to the police, so help me God, I will use it against you."

Margaret began to weep. "I'm your wife. Why don't you work with me, instead of against me?" She looked at him with pleading eyes.

Ignoring her plea, Reverend Pierce took the papers from her and locked them back in the desk drawer. "I have made an appointment with Dr. Stan Higgs at Howard University for tomorrow at ten. If you don't keep the appointment, plan on going to jail. Now I am going to go down and tell the board this matter has been taken care of. Do I make myself clear?" He waited for her response.

She looked at her husband with pure hatred and nodded her understanding.

CHAPTER FORTY-ONE

Grace Perry loved to shop, especially when she felt pressured. She had a closet full of clothes with the tags still on them. She needed a larger closet; or maybe it was time to move again. Billy Ray had found her, and that wasn't good.

She was getting tired of this town and their cliques. Grace wished she could go back to California, where the weather was better and the people were beautiful and free. Here they were uptight and snobbish, and no matter how hard she tried, the right doors hadn't opened yet. Florida might be another possibility, or the French Rivera, since she still had some of Billy Ray's money stashed away. That gnawing feeling in the pit of her stomach was starting again. It was a signal that something was not right, and it was time for her to move on.

Her boss had been pressuring her lately to wind up the freak show, as he called it. He wanted the last article in the series on the Elder Healer. She promised him it would be worthy of a Pulitzer Prize. He said, "Yeah, that's what they all say." Grace knew she had to dig a little deeper to make it happen. So far, she had nothing that made sense.

She had waited in that dark, small space for a couple of hours, but the Elder Healer never left the room. Finally, she got up enough nerve to use the key. First, she knocked softly, but no response. Then she inserted the key. As she turned the knob her heart began beating off the charts. Grace pushed the door open to an empty room. Impossible. She saw her go into the room. Well, not really, she saw the door closing. Where could she have gone? Grace searched the room, but saw no hidden doors. A strange drawing on the back of the door caught her eye as she was leaving. Grace recognized it as the same symbol Pops tried to draw on the napkin. She pulled out her camera and took a shot of it.

The next day, she had the photos developed, but the negatives were blank. She questioned the clerk at the Kodak shop, and he repeatedly told her there was nothing on the negatives. She had been using that particular shop for a few years, and she never had a problem. Had her eyes played tricks on her? What could she tell her editor? *I waited hours in a dark basement for the Elder Healer to exit the room and she never did. She disappeared into thin air. I saw a strange symbol on the door and took a photo of it, got it developed, and the negatives were blank.* He would think she was crazy.

The story she wrote about Rev's demise superseded what she planned to write about the Elder Healer. She put in bits and pieces of information hinting at cult-like activities, but her editor toned it down. She didn't have anything to back it up. He told her he had gone along with the last articles, but now she needed more substantial information and not just speculation. They were a reputable newspaper, not a gossip rag. In other words, he was telling her to put up or shut up.

Grace still didn't know who the Elder Healer was. Reverend Betty was talking irrationally the night of the healing session. She made it sound as if the Elder Healer was a figment of the imagination. None of this made any sense to Grace, but she had one more lead she wanted to follow up.

Grace did not call the occupants beforehand to let them know she wanted to talk to them. She was now in front of the house in Chevy Chase, where she hoped she would find the Awakeners. She was taking a chance, but the element of surprise gave her an advantage. She learned that early in her investigative reporting in California.

The doorbell had a nice chime. She didn't have to wait long before an elderly woman opened the door. She had an inviting smile that took Grace by surprise.

"Come on in, dear. I have been expecting you." The woman motioned for Grace to follow her.

Expecting me? I didn't tell anyone I was coming here. In fact, I didn't know I was coming until a little while ago.

Grace followed the old woman to the patio. As she walked through the house, she took note of the interior—no furniture. She stopped abruptly for a second when she spotted, hanging over the fireplace, the symbol she had seen on the door in the room.

The woman, who had her back to Grace, turned and said, "It's the OM."

"OM?"

"A sacred symbol in the Hindu faith; it is the impersonal Absolute-Brahman-God." The woman saw the quizzical look on Grace's face. "OM is the primordial sound, the first breath of creation, the vibration that ensures existence."

They sat on the patio drinking a relaxing and soothing tea, which Grace later found out was from India. Called tulsi, the tea was known for its healing properties.

For once in her life, Grace Perry was at a loss for words. She didn't know where to start. She looked into the eyes of the woman and knew that the woman could read her thoughts and knew what she felt in her heart.

Her question brought Grace back to the present. "What is it that you want to know, child?"

"Who are the Awakeners, and are you one of them?" Grace looked at her suspiciously.

"The Awakeners are those who love and serve God with all their heart and soul," she answered serenely, sipping her tea.

"Pardon me? I mean what is their purpose? Where are they from?"

"They are God-driven, and they are from the same place you are from, child."

Grace looked at the old woman with disbelief. She still didn't know anything about the Awakeners, or about the woman she was interviewing. "Are you an Awakener?" she asked again.

"I guess you could say in another lifetime I was awakened." She smiled at Grace.

Grace frowned; she wasn't getting anywhere. She decided on a different approach. "Is the Elder Healer an Awakener?"

"At this time, no."

At last, an answer. "Do you know who the Elder Healer is?"

"Yes."

"Who is she?" Grace could hardly contain her excitement.

"Come closer, child, and let me whisper in your ear." Grace walked over to where the woman was sitting. *Why does she need to whisper in my ear? There is no one else out here.*

Grace stopped a few feet away from the woman. She felt dizzy and anxious, and everything seemed to be spinning. She had to get out of there; something was not right.

"There is nothing to fear. Come closer."

Grace looked into the violet eyes of the old woman. She saw her own past, present, and just as she was about to see the future, her eyes rolled back into her head. Grace grabbed the edge of the table to steady herself.

Has she drugged me? Oh, my God, she is a witch or psychic, whatever you call them. I have to get out of this house. Does she know about my plastic surgeries? I have to block my mind. That's it. I read if one of those people tries to control your mind, you block them by thinking of anything except what you don't want them to know. Let me leave now. Margaret was right; they are demonic. Our Father which art in Heaven...

Grace began to pray as she hurried to the front door. She didn't even look at the OM symbol. *It probably cast a spell on me when I first saw it,* she figured.

The woman was following her, saying, "Follow your gut, child." But Grace was trying hard to get out of there. She couldn't get out of the house fast enough. As she ran to her car, she looked back at the house and saw the woman standing in the doorway. Hours later, the old woman's parting words still stayed with her. *Follow your gut, child.*

CHAPTER FORTY-TWO

Betty lay in her king-size bed, thinking about Stan and all she had gone through with him. She decided he hated women, and that was why he treated her and his wife as he had. Not that she wanted to blame him exclusively; she had contributed to her unhappiness. But it was time for a change.

There were two important things she had to take care of immediately. She tried to talk to the Professor the evening before about their situation, but after a couple of glasses of wine, he had dozed off. This morning, she was no longer putting it off.

Harvey Goldstein was in one of his favorite places, the garden. While he was gone, Betty hired a gardener to look after it. The guy hadn't given it the love it needed, so the Professor was weeding and pruning when his wife appeared. She was holding two cups of coffee. It was seven in the morning.

Betty put the cups on the table and went over to where Harvey was working on the flowers.

"Aren't they beautiful?" he asked her.

"They missed you." Her voice was soft and caring.

"But that's not what you want to talk about, is it?" he reluctantly asked.

"Harvey, come sit at the table. I brought you another cup of coffee." Betty moved toward the table with the large umbrella. It was already eighty degrees, and the sun was bearing down on the patio.

Harvey put his gardening tools down and followed his wife to the table. He had been dreading this conversation for a long time, but always knew he would eventually have to face it.

Ignoring the look of dread on his face, Betty jumped right into what had been on her mind for some years now. "It's not working anymore, Harvey. Our marriage is over, and we need to realize that." She sighed heavily.

The Professor was quiet for a few moments. When he finally spoke, there was much anguish in his voice. "I know I haven't been much of a husband lately. I haven't shared everything with you about my trips back to the homeland. I have been going home for treatments."

Betty interrupted him. "Treatments? What are you talking about, Harvey?" She was alarmed.

"I know you think I have the beginning stages of Alzheimer's, but it is the medicine I am taking that has affected my memory. I have cancer of the lungs. I don't have long to live."

"Harvey, why didn't you tell me? I'm your wife," Betty said with distress. The wind had been knocked out of her. Betty felt the heat rising up from her breast to the top of her head. She should have waited until Harvey came inside the house. Together the hot flash and the heat of the sun were unbearable. The flashes were coming more frequently, especially when she was stressed.

"You had enough on you with the church. I didn't want to burden you with my problems." Betty could see the tears in his eyes.

"Burden me? We could ask the Elder Healer to help you! Why didn't you seek her help?"

"That has always been your passion, Betty. I have never interfered with that part of your life. I am not religious."

"This is not about religion, Harvey. It's bigger than religion. It's about truth and the healing laws of God." Betty couldn't believe how much she sounded like Ruth. "The Elder Healer helps to facilitate the already God-given power of a person to heal him or herself."

"One has to believe that's possible, and I don't believe." He frowned.

"Harvey, look at me. I could request a special healing session for you. Won't you please try?" Betty pleaded with him, but didn't tell him that she didn't know how to get in touch with the Elder Healer. She would leave that to Ruth.

"No, listen to me. It's just too late for anything."

"Don't give up! Look at Michael; he's a miracle. I'll call Ruth and we'll set up something immediately. If the Elder Healer can't do it, then Lindy will. Do this for me, Harvey."

Harvey saw the concern and love in his wife's face. He would do it for her, but he knew it was too late.

"For you, yes."

Betty felt trapped. She wanted to tell him she wanted out of the marriage; instead, he was telling her he was dying. The Professor had always been there for her. She couldn't possibly leave him now. She needed to be there for him, whether she liked it or not. Betty stood over her husband and put her arm around his shoulder. He was thinner than usual. Why didn't she notice this before? She kissed him on his bald spot.

"I'll call Ruth and Lindy to make arrangements for tonight. We don't want to wait another day," she said before hurrying off to the kitchen.

She didn't want him to see her crying. She didn't know if she was crying for her husband or herself. Ruth had been right about the devil card when she said, "You have put shackles or chains around your neck. You have imprisoned your mind, body, and spirit. You can free yourself at any time."

At last she knew what she wanted in life; she would visit Ruth and discuss taking over the Awakeners and starting a more formal esoteric school. She was aware the media and people like Margaret Pierce weren't educated about what the Elder Healer was trying to do. They didn't understand about energy healing or about what and how to work with the spiritual laws. It was time to educate them, and the idea of teaching esoteric wisdom gave her the passion she had been missing in life recently.

Betty decided to spend her time meditating, praying, and reading to define the purpose of her life. She had chosen *Seth Speaks* by Jane Roberts to read first. The book made her think of what the Healer had been doing in the church, and of Lindy and Michael's psychic gifts.

Seth was an entity from another dimension that spoke through the body of a spirit medium, Jane Roberts. The book described such things as what happens after death, how to contact those who have passed over, and past lives. Most important, it covered the stages of human consciousness and the path to self-healing.

Ruth had been telling them this for years. Instead, they continued to choose fear, and fear creates disharmony, illness, and a host of other unpleasant roadblocks in life. She wished Ruth was not leaving, because she would be the best teacher for the school considering all she had taught Paul, Lindy, her, and a host of others.

First, she had to take care of the Professor. He needed her now, but she would not let her needs go unfulfilled. She was the creator of her world, and she could now create what she wanted in her life.

CHAPTER FORTY-THREE

After what she had been through with Rev, Lindy couldn't believe Betty was asking her to do a healing for the Professor if the Elder Healer didn't show up. She had decided to stick to her traditional medical practice, even though in a vision the Elder Healer had told her she was not responsible for what happened to Rev. She just needed more time to heal herself and integrate her allopathic training with her healing gifts. Lindy decided to approach her gift scientifically.

After years of seeing the colors, she had devised her own chart of what they meant. The chart wasn't inclusive; it just listed the basic colors and derivations. Next to some of the colors, she had written specific illnesses that she had observed in patients after seeing them repeatedly. The colors usually pointed to an area of the body that needed healing. The night they dined with Betty and the Professor, she noticed dark, muddy, reddish orange around his lungs and black near his head.

The colors and traditional medical diagnoses always matched, so Lindy felt pretty comfortable with her ability to see colors. What bothered her was the healing method, because she didn't understand how it worked. Lindy knew her logical mind would not accept the healing gift. Even with the healing of Michael, she needed more. Who was going to teach her?

CHAPTER FORTY-FOUR

Grace Perry was happy to see some movement in the Chevy Chase house. Her gut told her right when it told her to watch the house. She laughed, because the old woman told her to follow her gut, and that's exactly what she was doing. Grace waited in her car. She didn't want to miss anything, but it was still too light outside to position herself at the side window of the house. She had about another twenty or thirty minutes before it would be dark.

To kill time, Grace decided to flip through a fashion magazine. She saw the perfect dress for the Nick Lewis affair, which was coming up on Friday. Tomorrow she would go to Lord and Taylor's and get the dress, not that she didn't have plenty of evening clothes to wear. But it was something about the dress. She had to have it. *Follow your gut*, she said, mocking the old woman.

She started to feel uneasy. If she didn't produce, the editor was going to ride her back forever. He would never let her forget how much time and money he let her put into the Elder Healer story if she came up empty-handed. Grace wasn't the praying type, but she prayed tonight that something would turn in her favor. If not, it was time to find another city. She wanted to go somewhere Billy Ray couldn't just reach out and call her. Yes, overseas sounded good. Money was not a problem. Grace had been thinking of settling down, finding a husband, and maybe having children, since her biological clock was counting down.

Dusk began to fall over the city. Grace slouched down in the car. She was tempted to leave until she saw Harvey and Betty Goldstein arrive, and a few minutes later Lindy and her husband. She eased out of the car and made her way down the street. There was something about the old woman she couldn't shake. Grace wanted to talk to her again, but fear of what the woman might say or do made her settle for peering through a side window.

=====

Harvey Goldstein was lying on a massage table with a white sheet draped over his body. From what Grace could see, a large clear rock, with several points jutting out, had been placed directly under the center of the table. Several other crystals were near the top of his head, on his forehead, throat, heart, stomach, and right above his groin. It was difficult to see the faces of the people because the only light came from white candles. She had to get closer to see and hear what was going on.

Grace could feel her adrenalin pumping. The scent of a big story was exhilarating. She checked the back door; it was locked. The neighbors' dog barked, and she decided to return to her window perch. Seeking to avoid rousing the dog again, she took the long way around, passing in front of the house.

Grace didn't know whether to call it luck, or God watching over her, but she noticed the front door was cracked open. *People in these affluent neighborhoods wonder why they are always getting robbed. They invite the perpetrators in by leaving windows and doors opened or unlocked.*

Grace took off her shoes, placed them on the porch, and quietly slipped through the front door. Holding her breath, she stood in the hallway. Grace positioned herself so she could look in the mirror on the wall and watch everything going on in the room without being seen. Her recorder was on.

The sound of *AUM* filled the room. The group, all eyes closed, stood around Harvey Goldstein, chanting. Grace began to relax. The chanting had a hypnotic effect on the people in the room, as well as on her. She felt a breath of air pass her. Grace looked back at the door. It was still cracked, but no air was coming from it. There was no humming of an air conditioner, as they were using ceiling fans. Ruth motioned for the others to take seats. She stood at the head of the table and looked down at Harvey. She took her right hand and placed it over his third eye and held it there for a few seconds. Then she sat facing the group.

"What did you do to him?" Betty asked, looking at her intensely.

"He's in a deep rest; nothing to worry about. His body needs to rest to heal itself. He'll be fine." Ruth said. "I know you came here for the Professor's healing session, but we must do something else first." She paused to catch her breath. "You have been asking for some time about the Elder Healer. In light of what has recently happened," she nodded at Lindy, "it's time. As I told you before, I could not give you the information you wanted because I was bound by a vow. The Elder Healer now wishes to speak to you directly."

The group looked around the room, but they didn't see anyone.

Grace put her hands together. She couldn't believe her luck. At last, she would get to see this mysterious person.

They waited, but no one stepped out of the dark corners of the room. Then they looked at Ruth. Her head had fallen onto her chest, and she was breathing rapidly. She then lifted her head and began to speak in a strong voice with an accent.

"Good evening, my friends and family."

Dumbstruck, the group did not readily respond.

Betty spoke first. "She is channeling. Ruth has let the Elder Healer use her body. "

"In my last incarnation, I was known as Amanda Johnson."

Lindy cried out, "What? You're my grandmother, Amanda?"

"Yes, my child, I am your grandmother. Ruth, my dear friend of many years, has graciously relinquished her body to me. She is weak, and will not be able to allow me to talk for long. I would have come forth earlier, but I had to wait until Ruth was strong enough for me to take over without doing her any harm. Let me speak, and later, if you have any questions, you can ask Ruth. First Betty has something to share with you."

IT'S NOT OVER YET

The Elder Healer looked at Betty with such intensity that she instantly received the thought and knew what she had to do. *How did she know what I have been studying?*

Pleased she had been recognized, Betty quickly told the group about the Seth book and channeling.

CHAPTER FORTY-FIVE

Grace Perry didn't know whether to jump for joy or scream in frustration. Who was going to believe this craziness? She checked the tape recorder, which was still running, as Ruth—no, Amanda Johnson started her story.

"I am not dead, just vibrating at a different rate, and in a place that matches my vibrations. Death is a shift of consciousness, and your spirit lives forever. I have reached a level in my spiritual evolution that allows me to travel between dimensions. I know this may be hard for you to accept and believe, but I am not here to convince you of my existence. I am here to complete unfinished business from my last incarnation as Amanda Johnson, and that involves each of you.

"This outer garment is what I used to live in this third-dimensional plane as Amanda Johnson. I have used and discarded many of these outer shells to experience this planet, and so have you. You are caught up in the visible, so I had to lower my vibratory energy to manifest in this world again as Amanda Johnson.

"You met me in the hospital, Lindy, as the old lady who bumped into you. As much as I wanted to introduce myself to you as your grandmother, I knew it would be too much of a shock for you. To the extent that you allow me, I work with you through your dreams and visions to help you understand the gift of healing that runs through your spiritual DNA system, and I will continue to work with you from the higher planes.

"I chose to come into this incarnation at the time when women were persecuted, and those with the gift of esoteric wisdom were scorned. I reincarnated to fulfill my karmic debts. My family, race, gender, and lessons were determined before birth. Once a soul enters the atmosphere and time zone of this dimensional plane, it gradually forgets where it came from and what it is supposed to do. However, the knowledge is inside of us to discover for ourselves. Thus, my journey begins.

"After Perlie's father and the other men of the church threw me out of the house, I ran as fast as I could, with only the clothes on my back, to the people I had come to love—the missionaries known as the Order of the Awakeners. They hid me in the attic of their home, fearful that my father-in-law might send someone to do me harm. I stayed there for several weeks, until a ship came to take us to London.

"Once I set foot on the ship, I became the niece of a white woman. I passed for white. I ate with them and was afforded the same respect as any rich white woman. The missionaries agreed it would be easier for everyone. I was torn. All my life, most folks who didn't know me thought I was white and treated me as such.

"We stayed in London for several months. The first couple of weeks, I stayed close to the house. I cried for my husband and baby; if only I could have brought her with me. I wrote Perlie several letters, but never heard from him. I vowed to one day return and claim what was mine. I could not escape the pain and hurt in my heart.

"Then I met my sadhu, spiritual teacher, and my life changed. He told me things happen in life for a reason, and that we create our own reality. At first, I could not believe this. How could I create a life filled with so much sorrow and not be with the two people I loved the most in the world, my husband and daughter?

"Each day I had to meditate at sunrise. My teacher taught me to let go of my thoughts and focus solely on the space between my eyes. It was difficult because I could not control my thoughts. They were horrible. I wanted to kill the man whom I had defied, my father-in-law. He cast me out of the world and away from the people I knew. I thought of every conceivable way of destroying his life as he had destroyed mine.

"I was soon meditating twice a day, then all day. The destructive thoughts became fewer, and one day, they disappeared altogether. The pain and anguish did not go away as quickly. It was years before I did not feel the pain when I thought of my husband and daughter.

"My sadhu left for Tibet, but promised he would be in contact with me soon. Several weeks later, as I was doing my daily sunrise meditation, he appeared before me, even though I knew he was in Tibet. He told me that I must join him there, for I had proven through my discipline that I was ready for the next stage of my studies. He told me not to be afraid, because I was divinely protected. Later that day, I found out everything had been arranged for me to leave for Tibet the very next morning.

"How frightened I was to travel to such an isolated place in the world. My destiny was in a place called Lhasa, the Forbidden City. The captain of the ship told me it was not an easy place for a woman. I soon found out the terrain made traveling hazardous. There were many high mountains with snow-capped peaks, and labyrinths of lush valleys. It was breathtaking. I lived in Tibet with my sadhu for many years, studying Tibetan Buddhism as well as esoteric Buddhism. You see, Tibet is the seat of esoteric schools. It is said among the Tibetans that the area is where many spiritual adepts or highly evolved spirits are able to vibrate in the visible as well as in the invisible worlds. I became a master of Sanskrit and metaphysical laws.

"I had always been clairvoyant, but it was in Tibet that I underwent the studies of the manipulation of energy, both in this world and in other worlds. I learned how to make things materialize and disappear. My sadhu told me that my gift lay in healing, and it was time for me to go to the mother country, Africa. First, I would have to stop in India. He would not be accompanying me. I would be on my own for the first time in many years.

"The stop in India lasted several years. He had given me the name of the guru I was supposed to find and study under. I was saddened to leave my teacher and friend of many years, but I knew my destiny was not there. It was in India that I met Ruth. We were the only two white women in this small village. I am referring to the color of our skin, but

I had ceased thinking of myself as white, black, or any color, for that matter. I knew I was a soul, and colorless.

"I lived in an ashram and studied Hinduism. I read the Upanishads and Bhagavad-Gita. But it was in India that I started to learn about healing arts. At last, I had found my destiny, or so I thought. I learned about herbs, oils, and spiritual mind-healing. I left the ashram to live and work in a mission to serve the healing needs of children and the elderly. I remained there for many years. While meditating one night, my sadhu came to me again and told me it was time to leave for Africa. As before, the funds and all the arrangements had been made for me, and I left the next day.

"It was in Africa that I finally let go of my identity as Amanda and became the Elder Healer. I sent a letter and clothes to my husband to close the door to that part of my life forever. I lived among the Dogon tribe of Mali as their healer. I was home, never to see America again. So I thought.

"I was old, but didn't know how old because I never took notice of my age. One day, several children came to me and told me a man was dying in a village not far from where I lived. I got my pouch of herbs and went to him. They had placed him in the sacred cave. He was feverish and hallucinating. He had malaria. I gave him the herbs, but death was calling him. I had to find his spirit and bring it back, or he would die. To do this, I had to find something that meant a great deal to him. He kept talking about a woman.

"I put myself in a trance and searched for his spirit in the under-world. I found him in a place of darkness, agonizing about the hurt he had inflicted on himself and others. He had made choices in his life that had taken him down paths that created more karma than dharma, the effort to eliminate karma by surrendering to divine will. I knew if he was to return to the middle world, he had to hope there was still a chance for him to change.

"I envisioned the love he had for the woman and projected it into his consciousness. He began to dream of her, and it is through his dreams that I discovered the woman was of my DNA and soul group.

It was through the story of this young man's love for this woman that awakened deep in me the love and desire I still had for Perlie. It was hidden in my deep subconscious mind. For years, I had wondered why I could not move on to the next step in my spiritual evolution. Now I knew.

"I could not leave without my twin flame. His soul was lost in the realm of materiality. I could not interfere with his free will. He could choose to stay in his body, or to leave with me. He had completed his mission, and had decided to leave."

Her voice became faint as Ruth stirred.

"No, come back!" Lindy cried out. "I have so much to ask you."

"Not now, child, Ruth is weak and tired. I must leave her body," she said as her voice faded out.

The room was quiet and no one moved.

Lindy tried not to show any emotions, but her face had turned red. She remembered her vision of being in the cave with Nick and her grandmother. She wouldn't look at Paul, keeping her attention on Ruth. Lindy thought how it was the story of Jesus and Mary Magdalene all over again. As twin flames her grandfather and grandmother had learned the spiritual lesson that their love should have remained unconditional, no matter what was occurring in the outer world.

Lindy wondered again who her twin flame was—Paul or Nick?

CHAPTER FORTY-SIX

Grace Perry struggled with whether she should stay or leave. She had enough to write a book. She was glad she had it on tape. This way, that chauvinistic editor of hers could hear it for himself. But would he print it?

___

Ruth could hardly stand up. She was weak after letting the Elder Healer use her body. Still, she had promised Betty that she would help the Professor.

"The Elder Healer will assist us with the healing of the Professor. She will be working on the ethereal plane where the cause of his illness originated. I had planned for her to continue working through me, but I am too weak to carry on." Ruth tried to get out of the chair. She had to sit again.

"Why can't the Elder Healer come forth as Amanda Johnson?" Betty asked anxiously, remembering the elderly lady who had come to her office. She was sure that the woman was the Elder Healer.

"Her mission has finished on this plane. She will no longer materialize here, but will continue to work with us from the other side. That is why she had to speak through me," Ruth replied.

"What are we going to do?"

Ruth looked at Lindy and said, "You will be the channel she will work through, and with your own natural abilities you will help the Professor."

Lindy looked at Ruth and the others with fear in her eyes. "I can't."

"It's not that you can't do it, it is, are you willing to try, child?" Ruth asked her.

J.J. MICHAEL

Betty walked over and put her arms around Lindy. "Try," was all she said.

Paul nodded encouragement and mouthed the word, "Try."

"Ok, I'll try," Lindy said.

"Let us call on the Elder Healer, all those cosmic beings, and the Professor's guides to create a sacred healing space by chanting the OM."

On cue, the group chanted the sacred sound for three to four minutes. Ruth raised her hand for them to stop.

"Lindy, hold your left hand over the Professor's face and begin to move it slowly down his body. As thoughts come to you, speak out, ask questions, and the answers will come."

Following Ruth's instructions, Lindy moved her hand down the Professor's body. She paused at certain areas of the body before continuing.

Lindy spoke, and her voice changed as she looked more self-assured. She stood up straight, and her eyes took on a faraway look. *"He has an overabundance of red energy in his lungs, causing the cells of this area to suffer and spread to the brain."*

Betty flinched.

"The entity has been harboring deep hurt and carrying hatred against others and himself that he is having difficulty releasing," she continued.

"What is the remedy for this entity?" Lindy asked in her normal voice.

Grace was fascinated by how Lindy would go from her own voice to one different and stronger. It sounded as if two people were talking. Lindy was acting the same way the old woman had acted earlier that evening when she was the Elder Healer.

"The entity must change his thoughts. He brings this resentment over from past lives. He must forgive himself, others, and release the past. There is a need for the entity to love himself."

"Change his thoughts? Can you provide more clarification on this point?" Lindy asked.

207

"*Yes. There is no such thing as a diseased cell. It is an illusion. It is a belief in such that creates a diseased cell. One may choose at any time to create a healthy cell with the power of one's thought.*"

"You're saying the entity can heal himself through healthy thinking?"

"*The entity, through his thought pattern, is choosing to build either a negative, fear thought pattern; or a positive, love thought pattern. Again, the entity can choose one of the above to determine what he creates for the body. Years of thinking negative thoughts and harboring negative feelings create unhealthiness.*"

"Is there something else we can do?"

"*You cannot create his world. Only he can do that. But you can help him tremendously by seeing him as a perfect soul of God. Jesus spoke with authority when he healed because he knew and understood the principles that govern this universe—especially the Law of Mind.*"

"Please explain?"

"*You must not have any doubt in yourself or in the treatment you will give. What you hold in your inner consciousness is important. Your thoughts will eventually affect the entity's thoughts. Your job is to uphold in your mind the truth that the entity is a perfect manifestation of God. You know that the thought you hold will eradicate the destructive thought of the manifestation of illness.*"

The others sat with their eyes closed as they listened to the Healer speaking through Lindy.

"*This is all that is necessary. But, because of man's limited belief system, you need a demonstration or technique. The most powerful healing is the power of the mind, but you may restore energy to what you consider a damaged cell by letting the energy pass through your body to heal, always keeping in mind that the entity is the perfect manifestation of God. AUM Peace.*"

Lindy stood on the right side of the Professor, and using both of her hands, with her fingers spread out, she moved down the Professor's body. When she reached his lungs, she acted as if she had something in her hands which she threw at the flame of one of the candles. She did this several times, then returned to his head, placed her hands on his face, and moved down each side of his body. Again, she paused at a particular area of his body for a while. Then she would move on to the next section. This went on for an hour. Her final act was to go over the body, making circular motions with her hands.

Lindy then touched the Professor gently on the shoulder. He opened his eyes and looked around the room. She cautioned him to take his time getting up. Ruth took a gold chalice filled with water off the four-foot white pedestal that was placed in the rear of the room. She smiled at Betty as she handed the chalice to the Professor.

At this point, Grace left. As she did, a cool breeze swept through the room. Everyone looked toward the front door, but Ruth told them it was nothing to worry about. It was just an undesirable wind that would soon be gone.

Grace was exhausted and stiff from being in the same position for so long. She was grateful the healing session had come to an end. She kissed the tape and tucked it into her bra, having already decided how she would use the information. She would tone down some of the nonsense to make it more reflective of what she knew people wanted to read.

Who would challenge her? What are they going to say? That they talked to someone from the dead?

"Crazy people," she chuckled.

CHAPTER FORTY-SEVEN

Too excited to sleep, Lindy decided to run a warm bath to relax. She submerged herself in the hot water all the way up to her neck. The bubbles covered her body, and she closed her eyes, thinking about everything that had happened that night.

Would her grandmother speak through her again? Lindy wanted to know how her grandmother materialized and disappeared. She had so many unanswered questions. Her thoughts soon drifted to Nick. The young man her grandmother talked about had to be him. He was in Africa, and she was the woman he dreamt about, or maybe it was someone else. *No, it's me.* She smiled inwardly. Lindy remembered her grandmother saying she and the young woman had the same DNA.

She hadn't seen Nick since the night Rev passed. For a fleeting moment, she had spotted him standing in the back of the room. The thought of him made her body shiver. *No,* she told herself. *Get him out of your mind. You're married to Paul.* The thickness of Nick's lips flashed through her mind. They were so sensual. Lindy knew where her thoughts were headed, but then she heard the phone ring. Wrapping a towel around her wet body, she hurried to answer the phone.

It was Betty; she couldn't sleep either. She poured her heart out about the Professor's health problems and what the future held for them. Lindy listened attentively before responding.

"Reverend," she teased, "you need to have faith. The challenge for him, or anyone who is ill, is to align his consciousness with love and perfection, and then to see himself as healthy regardless of outer appearance."

"That is easier said than done. Life lessons are hard. First we have to know what the lesson is and then we are tested on the lesson, to see if we have mastered it. This is a hard one for me," she said, weeping quietly.

"You're under a lot of stress dealing with church issues and now the Professor's health," Lindy responded.

"It's pity-party time. But I know what I have to do."

"What?" Lindy asked.

"I have to go to Israel with him. I met Harvey in Israel. At that time, I was very sick, and Israel became my haven from home. Harvey was there for me, and now I need to be there for him!"

"Then tell him. He needs to hear it from you now."

"When I get off this phone, that's exactly what I'm going to do. I just have to decide about the church and the healing sessions. Do you want to take over?"

"I'm not a minister, and I have never wanted to preach."

"It's in your blood."

"Healing is my calling."

"Then when I return, let's open a school to wake up the sleeping souls out there."

"School?"

"Yes, with a healing center just for you. Think about it. You can be who you really are."

"A healer? After everything I have been through—Michael's healing, my grandfather's healing and the Elder Healer channeling healing energy through me—I still lack the courage to step out on faith and just heal."

"One day you will!"

"You sound like my old friend. I'm glad that you are back," Lindy exclaimed.

"It's good to be back," Betty sighed.

The two women talked way into the night about their hopes and dreams for the future. They went to sleep feeling lighter than they had in years.

CHAPTER FORTY-EIGHT

Nick missed a call from the private investigator he hired to track down Cissy, the booster. He called the PI back but missed him; they were playing phone tag. He couldn't worry about it right now; his big event was the next night and he was busy with last-minute arrangements. He had to get a haircut and pick up his tuxedo, as well.

Diana had stopped by earlier that morning for their usual bedroom tryst and he had deliberately let her knock and knock, praying the maid wouldn't let her in. He was serious about what he wanted in his life, and she wasn't it.

He looked at the photos propped on the dresser. They were another reason he didn't want to let her in. He would have to explain to her about Michael or put the photos away—and he was not ready to do either. He picked up the photo he had blown up for the exhibit. It was the best because there was so much love in it. Michael looked angelic but mischievous, in an odd sort of way. It was his surprise for Lindy, who he hoped and prayed would come tomorrow night. If she didn't show, then he had another job for the private investigator—find his woman!

The phone rang, and Nick hesitated before answering, assuming it was Diana calling from the lobby. It could also be the PI, so he had to take the chance. He breathed a sigh of relief when he heard the husky voice on the other end.

"Mr. Lewis?"

"Yes, this is Nick Lewis."

"This is Keith Schuster, the PI you hired."

"Yes, I missed your call this morning. Did you find her?"

"She's still in D.C."

"What? Where?" Nick was excited.

"Hope you are sitting, Mr. Lewis, because this may shock you."

Nick didn't know what to expect. The PI told him how he had tracked Cissy to Billy Ray, who was in prison but didn't mind spilling his guts about how Cissy set him up, stole his money, and ran away to D.C. The PI promised to send his report by airmail right away.

The phone rang again. Thinking it was the PI calling back, he answered. It was Diana.

"Where were you? I knocked and knocked on the door this morning," she was irritated.

"Probably in the shower."

"I'm here now, I'll be right up."

"No!" he blurted out, but she had already hung up.

He couldn't believe what the PI told him. Cissy, the booster, was Grace Perry. He was right about her when he first saw her. His gut instinct had told him she had plastic surgery. Her surgeon had done a good job. Cissy had fooled everyone in D.C. and terrorized people, especially Lindy. Her reign of terror was about to end; he would see to that. When he got a hold of her, she was going to wish she had never returned. He owed her one from the time she tried to pin a drug rap on him. Diana's knock at the door broke his train of thought.

When he opened the door, she rushed into his arms. Diana smelled good, and looked even better. This woman was the devil herself. He loosened her arms from around his neck and stepped back.

"Can't today, baby. I've got to get over to the museum. I have too many things on my mind and too many things to do."

"Oh, okay, I understand. Anything I can help you with?"

"No, no. Thanks anyway." He gave her a quick peck on the lips.

"Sure you don't have time for a quickie?" She brushed up against him before he could move aside.

"Like I said, baby, I got to go," Nick said, edging her toward the door. It was then that Michael's photo caught Diana's eye.

"Wow, who is this child?" she asked, picking up the photo.

Your son, he wanted to say. He was sure of it, but he couldn't say it to her without definite proof.

"His name is Michael. This is one of the many photos you will see tomorrow night in larger-than-life size."

"The photo is superb. His eyes capture you. Is he African?" she asked.

"No, he's not. I couldn't resist taking the shot." Nick took the photo from her. She was mesmerized by it, and he was certain the photo would have the same effect on anyone seeing it.

What would Lindy say?

CHAPTER FORTY-NINE

Grace awoke at three in the morning, her favorite time to write. This article was special because she had to make people believe this eerie cult exists. Grace sat at her IBM typewriter, anxious to get started. She had listened to the tape several times last night before retiring. The more she listened to it, the more she believed the Awakeners were skilled in trickery and magic and were able to make people think they were healed by a godly creature that no one can see. She had the name of the Elder Healer, and also had an admission that the woman had faked her death. The tape was the most important backup source for her editor; it was concrete proof.

She worked diligently for hours. The floor was littered with balls of paper as she discarded one approach and then another to the story. Tired and frustrated, she pulled the last sheet out of the typewriter and put it with the other papers on her desk. It was six a.m.; the sun was rising.

Grace lay down to rest for a short while. She closed her eyes and smelled victory. It wouldn't be long now. Everyone would be kissing her ass or trying to get next to her.

Eleven years ago, she left D.C. under a dark cloud. She had reinvented herself, courtesy of Billy Ray, a cowboy from Galveston, Texas, who ran the biggest prostitution and drug ring in L.A. He catered to the rich and famous; anything they needed, he got. Their secret cravings were safe with him. Grace had been in the city only a short time when she met him at a club that looked more like a Texas bar. She was sitting alone when he asked her to dance.

He told her up front she was ugly, but that it was a problem he could fix. She didn't know whether to be angry that he had called her ugly or happy that something could be done about it. People get new identities all the time, so why not her? Billy Ray arranged for her to have plastic surgery, and it took several operations to completely change her facial features.

Grace, for the first time in her life, let a man dictate to her. Billy Ray had her best interest at heart, even when he told her to lose twenty plus pounds. Her lightened skin was what she loved best about the changes. She checked herself in the mirror every chance she got, and couldn't believe how light she had become. Who would recognize her now?

Billy Ray was a pimp who had a sixth sense about women. He was high the night he asked her to dance, but could sense something different about her. Grace was strong and streetwise, and now she was beautiful. She was his invention, but she wasn't going to prostitute for him. He told her often that he owned her just as he owned the rest of his whores. He owned her even more because she was his creation. He was pleased with her, except for one thing—Grace liked to steal.

He would give her a fist-full of money to buy anything she wanted on Rodeo Drive, and what would she do? Steal. Billy Ray didn't need the heat if she was caught stealing. He had built his business based on street ethics, and stealing was not part of what he was about. Billy Ray didn't like thieves because it was against what he stood for. So he gave her an ultimatum. Stop stealing or he would stop her. Grace knew when to mess with him and when not to. Billy Ray had a mean streak, especially when he was drunk.

If he had a rough night, he would start with the name-calling as soon as he hit the door. His favorite names for her were 'ugly hick' or 'black bitch from D.C.' He loved to tell the same story over and over, how he had found the ugly duckling and turned her into a beautiful swan. Grace swore one day he would be sorry for those words. They would argue all night and then make love. Grace loved Billy Ray, and he loved her.

She got the name Grace Perry from an actress in a porn movie she saw at Billy Ray's place. She liked the sound of the name because it had a movie-star ring to it.

Billy Ray got her the papers to match the name. She had a new birth certificate, Social Security number, driver's license, and library card. Determined to make something of herself, she then enrolled in college. She moved into Billy Ray's pad in the Hollywood Hills, but still kept her own place in Crenshaw. He could never get her to give it up.

For the first time in her life, Grace was happy. Billy Ray had class and associated with the right people. He was proud of her accomplishments and showed her off to everyone. She couldn't believe her luck.

After finishing college, Grace got a job with a tabloid newspaper and learned the art of investigative reporting. She loved the thrill of spying on people and discovering their dirty secrets. Billy Ray hated the idea of her working, because he was the breadwinner and wanted her home. It didn't seem right to him that his woman would be in the streets all hours of the night pursuing some sleazy story. Billy Ray planned to go legitimate after he saved enough money.

To his dismay, Grace wouldn't stop stealing. He wasn't used to a woman not doing as he told her. Billy Ray thought about beating some sense into her, as was his custom with his whores. But it was a thought quickly discarded, as he had spent too much money on her face and body to mess with it. He was just going to put his foot down, and maybe a push or two would get her to come around. But in teaching Grace a lesson or two, Billy Ray went a little too far. She ended up in the hospital with a bloody nose that needed additional plastic surgery. Despite his remorseful tears, Grace knew what she had to do. Even though she loved Billy Ray, she was too pretty now to let some cowboy mess her over. Billy Ray was arrested for possession of cocaine when a kilo was found in his car.

With Billy Ray safely in jail, Grace said good-bye to L.A., moved back to D. C., and took the job at the *Washington Star*. The Feds took the house and cars, and she cleaned out Billy Ray's hiding places of all the cash he had left. She was glad to get away without getting involved in his mess. Grace promised Billy Ray that she would come and visit. He waited and waited, but Grace was gone, and so was his money. Billy

Ray was sure she had orchestrated his downfall. He swore that Grace had not seen the last of him.

Grace looked at the clock; it was 10:15 a.m. She must have dozed off. She put the article in her briefcase, planning to drop it off at her office later in the day. Feeling rejuvenated, Grace decided to treat herself to the dress she saw in the fashion magazine.

Grace looked through the collection of wigs she wore for special occasions and selected a long, dark brown wig with bangs. It totally changed her appearance, especially when she added the large Dior sunglasses. She wanted to look sophisticated and rich.

Twenty-five minutes later, Grace sat in her car, baffled by its failure to start. That old woman had put some kind of hex on her. She hadn't felt like herself since she had gone to that house. First, she spilled juice on her dress and had to change it, and then she couldn't find her keys; now the car was stalling. What in the hell was going on? Part of her just wanted to go and drop off the article, while the other part wanted to go and get the dress, even though she had plenty of choices in her closet.

Grace tried the car again; it started. *My gut is telling me to get out of this town.* Grace glanced at the magazine in the passenger seat. Deciding it was a sign, as she pulled out of the garage, turned right, and headed for the shopping district.

Lord and Taylor's was not far from her apartment. Grace loved the way the store symbolized old money and class. *I belong,* she thought, moving along the aisles. She went to evening wear, and it didn't take her long to spot the off-shoulder black Valentino dress she coveted. Grace held the dress against her and looked in the three-way mirror, shaking her head and frowning as if she didn't like it.

Grace looked around and saw no one nearby, so she took the dress off the hanger and quickly stuffed it into the large underwear she was wearing. Acting as if she had all the time in the world, Grace continued walking through the store. She bought a pair of shoes and a purse to go with the dress. She didn't want to look suspicious. It was a dangerous game, but she was addicted to the thrill. Billy Ray used to tell her that she was a kleptomaniac, that stealing was as much a part of her as eating. She couldn't help herself.

Grace casually made her way to the door. From the corner of her eye, she saw a fine young white man looking at women's bathing suits. As Grace proceeded toward the door, she thought it was odd to see a man buying a woman's bathing suit. She thought she heard the old woman's voice saying, *"Trust your gut."* She stepped outside the door.

"May I ask you to step back inside the store, madam?" the young white man politely asked her.

Grace snarled at him. She had to act fast, or her worst nightmare would come true.

"I don't understand. Let me go or I'll call the police. Help, help," she screamed. People stopped to gawk at the young white man escorting the well-dressed black woman back into the store.

"Store security, madam. We need to search you and ask you some questions." A man in uniform joined them.

The thrill was over, and she felt nothing but fear. Grace was taken by the two officers to the security office of the department store. They asked her for basic information about herself, which she refused to give them. Two female officers searched her bag and then made her strip, finding the dress. Grace was standing in front of the two officers naked, humiliated, and scared for the first time in her life. The worst humiliation came when D.C.'s finest came to take her to the police station. She was now sure the old woman had put a hex on her.

Grace was fingerprinted, photographed, and booked. She was finally released on her own recognizance. The *Washington Star* reporter covering the crime beat dropped his pen when he heard one of the paper's own had been picked up for shoplifting. He couldn't get to a phone fast enough to call his editor. All hell broke loose.

CHAPTER FIFTY

Nick went to the *Washington Star* to look for Grace. He had no idea what he was walking into. When he mentioned her name, he observed how people became tight-lipped. No one would give him any information about her whereabouts. Nick hung around the building until he saw a group of the clerks going to lunch. He followed them to a nearby deli and sat as close as he could without arousing suspicion. Grace was the subject of the conversation. When one of the women left the group early, Nick followed and caught up with her halfway down the block. Money talks, and in no time, he had Grace's address and phone number.

Nick made his way across town. It was late and he still had a million things to do. But by this time tomorrow the news would be out, and it would be difficult to get to her. Her secret was no longer a secret. Nick found a parking space directly across from Grace's building. He exchanged money with the doorman to get into the building and for a tip-off. Now all he had to do was wait for Ms. Cissy Carter, aka Grace Perry, to maker her entrance. He was using precious time he needed for the exhibit. He called his hardworking assistant and told her to expect him later in the evening.

At first, Nick didn't recognize the woman who entered into the building. She had long brown hair and wore large sunglasses. She came through the door with her head down. The doorman said very loudly, "Good afternoon, Ms. Perry." The woman mumbled something and headed for the elevator. She never saw Nick coming. He followed into the elevator, and it wasn't until they got to her floor that Grace became aware of his presence.

"Hello, Cissy," he said mockingly.

Grace turned and looked up at the tall stranger. Her jaw dropped. "Nick Lewis, get out of my way."

Nick's large frame blocked the opening to the elevator. "Not until you tell me what I want to know."

"What the hell are you talking about?" she hissed back at him.

"What happened to that medical student?"

"What student?"

"You know—the one who did abortions back in the day?"

"That's what you want to know?"

Nick pretended he didn't know about all the other stuff going on. "Yeah, that's all I want to know. Where is he now?"

"That fool is strung out on drugs. Last I heard he was supplying Howard students with whatever they needed."

"How do you contact him?"

She wanted to ask him what this was all about, but she had too many problems of her own right now. "He hangs out at Meridian Park. Now will you let me go?" The elevator was jumping as the door tried to close.

"What's he called, and what does he look like?"

"Butch, for all the butchering of women he did." Nick's body tightened when he heard the words. She then gave him a general description of Butch.

Nick pulled off Grace's sunglasses and looked into her puffy eyes. "If I find out you lied to me, Cissy, I will hunt you down. And if you think you have trouble now, you haven't seen trouble."

Grace grabbed her glasses and quickly walked away. She needed more than a lawyer. She had to find someone who could remove the hex the old woman had put on her.

CHAPTER FIFTY-ONE

Nick hurried to Meridian Park. It was once beautiful and known for its historical significance, but it had turned into a haven for drug addicts. Nick was returning to his old stomping grounds dressed in a five-hundred-dollar suit, sporting a Rolex watch and wearing Gucci shoes. He looked out of place in the park, and the regulars knew it. He wouldn't be mistaken for an undercover cop. They probably thought he was there to score.

A couple of guys approached him, flashing their hands to show him the small bags of white stuff. He ignored them and made his way through the park. Just when he thought he had to wait, a guy fitting the description Cissy gave him entered the park from the west side. Nick didn't want to act too anxious or spook the man, so he took his time walking along the east end, finally crossing the park to where Butch was standing.

Nick knew he had to be careful approaching the group. Then lady luck stepped in. As Nick got closer, he recognized one of the guys. He used to live right under Nick's old apartment. Nick eased his way to the group and called out the man's name. When he turned and faced him, Nick couldn't believe what he saw; his old friend was a junkie. At first, the guy didn't recognize Nick, but then he remembered. He introduced him to the others and when he called one "Butch," Nick knew he had found his man. Nick stood there talking with the group as if it was the most natural thing to do. He felt blessed that he had not ended up like these guys. He wished there was something he could do to help them.

When Butch left the group to make a quick exchange with a young woman, Nick used the opportunity to be alone with him.

"You still taking care of little girls who get into trouble?" he whispered to Butch.

"What are you talking about, man?" Butch had been watching the well-dressed man for a while, wanting to get a hold of the Rolex watch on Nick's wrist.

"I was the boyfriend of one of your old clients."

"Oh, yeah? I don't remember you. You must have me mistaken for someone else."

"It's you. Cissy turned me on to you."

Her name stopped him in his tracks. "What happened to that black bitch?"

You'll find out soon enough, Nick thought. "For now, I need to find out what happened in '67. You helped out my woman back then."

"And?" Butch was getting a little weary of the stranger.

"In 1967, you delivered a young woman's baby." Nick described Diana. "The baby was severely deformed." Butch's expression changed. "What happened to the baby is all I want to know, bro. No hassle, man, just info."

"It's dead."

Nick felt his heart sink.

"That sucker looked like something from outer space. I told her to let it go. It was small, dark, and the head was pointed."

Nick cut him off. "What did you do with it?"

"You sure you not some type of law officer?"

"No." Nick wanted to stomp him and dump *him* in the trash. But, he blamed himself. How could he have trusted him with Diana?

"What's in it for me?"

"What do you mean?" He wanted to add, *you piece of shit*.

"You want to know what I did with it, right? I figure you want to know awful bad, then how about that watch?"

Nick began to walk away.

"Okay, okay," Butch yelled. "Come on, bro, help me out. Give me a few dollars then," he begged.

Nick reached in his pocket and pulled out a twenty.

"That's all?" Butch asked snatching the money. "I put the squirmy little piece in the dumpster," he added.

Stunned, Nick moved closer to Butch. "You said squirmy. Was it alive?"

"Like I said, man," Butch replied, starting to sweat, "I told her to let it go. It was a mess. It wouldn't have lived long. When I went back later, they had emptied the dumpster."

Nick wanted to beat the life out of him, but he knew the drugs would do it for him. Now he only had contempt for himself. He was the one who had put these awful events into motion.

"What's all this to you, anyway?" Butch asked, stuffing the twenty into his pocket.

Nick turned his back on Butch and walked out of the park. Michael was his son, and that's all he could think of.

CHAPTER FIFTY-TWO

Grace sat in her living room in the dark with the phone off the hook. Throughout the evening there were several knocks on her door, but she ignored them. The reporters were hounding her. She was now the game. Refusing to turn on the evening news, Grace knew how they would spin the story. She had done it so many times herself. She continued to sit there in anguish and regret. The story of a lifetime was still in her purse. She had tried to get her editor to at least consider the story. He laughed at her. She could hear the elation in his voice when he told her she was on leave pending the court hearing and for her to clean out her desk. The next morning a short article appeared in the *Washington Star* about Grace's alleged shoplifting incident. Grace Perry was the talk of D.C. If she wasn't already a household name, she became one.

Betty received a call from the *Star's* editor. He was going to publish an article about the church's exceptional healing services. This was his way of asking for pardon for any undue stress that Grace, not the *Star*, of course, might had caused her and the church members.

Betty called Paul, Lindy and the other Awakeners about Grace's unfortunate fate. They all agreed that Grace had only attracted into her life what she had created——bad press.

Reverend Pierce and the members of Mt. Olive Baptist Church stated that they would keep Miss Perry in their prayers. Margaret worried whether or not Grace, no, Cissy, would bring up old business. In any case, she had decided that she would deny that she had ever bought any stolen clothes from Cissy.

CHAPTER FIFTY-THREE

Lindy didn't recognize the woman in the mirror staring back at her. She had spent the day with Betty, getting a makeover for Nick's affair. Her hair had been cut and lightened; she was blonde. She had seesawed between cutting her hair and leaving it long, so Betty had gone under the scissors first. After seeing what a good job the hairstylist had done with Betty's hair, Lindy gave in.

Betty had picked out the strapless, long-fitting green dress for Lindy, which detailed every curve of her body. Lindy turned around slowly, looking at the cut of the dress. She felt a little apprehensive wearing something that was not only a snug fit, but was also cut low in the front. The silver stiletto shoes made her appear at least two inches taller. She hoped she didn't tower over Paul. Her face glowed with a perfect blending of green eye shadow, tan blush, and red lipstick. She looked sexy. Was it enough to make her husband take notice?

The drab, covered-up doctor was gone, replaced by a beautiful, sophisticated woman. Lindy leaned over closer to the mirror and saw the small lines around her eyes. Not long now, she thought. People with less melanin in their skin show signs of aging earlier than those with a greater amount. Tonight, though, she was a fairy princess and wouldn't worry about anything. Lindy dabbed Opium on her wrist and neck, then she went to look for her husband. She couldn't wait to see how he looked in his tuxedo.

Lindy found Paul in Michael's room, tucking him in bed. He turned when he saw her, and his eyes told her everything. But her focus was on why Paul wasn't dressed in his tuxedo and was putting Michael to bed.

"What are you doing? Where is Marianne?" she asked.

"I sent her home. Michael is not feeling well."

"No." Lindy was crushed.

Lindy placed her hand on Michael's forehead; it was hot. She was disappointed because the shopping, primping, and excitement were for naught. They were not going, and she would not see Nick.

Paul looked at his exquisite wife. Any man would be proud to have her on his arm. The dress was cut low in the front and showed off her beautifully-formed cleavage. He could tell by her reaction that she really wanted to go. Her face had gone from pure delight to abject disappointment.

He touched her arm. "I want you to go tonight and enjoy yourself."

"No, we'll both stay with him." They never left Michael when he was sick, especially if he had a fever.

Lindy sat on Michael's bed and began to give him a quick physical examination. She didn't find anything that warranted taking him to the hospital. He was only running a low-grade fever, but with Michael's medical history, they were always careful.

"I want you to go. There is no reason for both of us to stay here," Paul insisted.

"You know I don't like to leave him when he's sick." Lindy gazed at the peacefully sleeping child.

"It's okay, Lindy. You deserve to enjoy yourself for a change."

"I wanted you to go with me," she pleaded.

"Parties aren't my favorite pastime. I would rather meditate."

"I know. Michael's illness is your way out. I just don't want to be alone at the affair."

"Betty and the Professor will be there. They will meet you." He led her out of Michael's bedroom. She called Betty and the Professor but didn't get an answer. She was relieved that they had already left.

A few minutes later, Lindy stepped out into the night air. The weather was balmy and a full moon shone brightly on the streets. She was ambivalent about going to the opening without Paul. She couldn't trust herself alone with Nick. As she drove toward the museum, she thought about how her life had twisted and turned. She still couldn't get it back on track. She was still on leave from the hospital, and Michael still hadn't returned to school. However, thanks to Rev's gift, her unpaid leave was not a financial burden.

Lindy handed the keys to the young car attendant, who couldn't take his eyes off her. Checking her purse for the invitation, she made her way to the entrance. Lindy was not prepared for the crowd inside the museum. She had missed the opening ceremony and the presenting of Nick's award. She wished she could have been there. Lindy spotted the mayor and city council members, as well as officials from Howard and the museum.

Lindy opened her program to the page with Nick's picture. He looked striking, but it was his statement that moved her.

I have traveled throughout Sub-Saharan Africa and to remote corners of the continent to reveal the plight of children who had lost one or both parents to poverty, war or disease. I endured many hardships to put this exhibit together; however, it was worth every effort to bring to the world's attention the dreadful living conditions of African children. I hope that the photographs will raise the awareness of the need for aid. I dedicate this exhibit to the shaman, or elder healer, of the Dogon tribe, who saved my life and set me on a journey of spiritual attainment.

Lindy re-read the statement and thought about how much Nick had spiritually matured. She looked for Betty and the Professor as she absently moved from one wall exhibit to the next. The photographs were spellbinding. As she looked at them Lindy realized that Nick had captured not only the children's struggles, but he had also revealed what was in their souls—apprehension and hope. The children's faces told it all; there was no need for words. Lindy could tell by the facial expressions of the guests that they, too, were touched by the photos.

Her heart missed a beat when someone gripped her arm. It was the Professor.

Betty looked stunning in her black off-the-shoulder Oscar de la Renta gown. The Professor was in good spirits, and Lindy nudged Betty to find out what was going on.

"I told him I was going to Israel with him, and I would stay as long as he wanted me to." Betty smiled.

"It worked, because he is beaming."

"Where's Paul? Trying to find two glasses of water?" Betty teased.

"Michael's not feeling well, and you know Paul, he decided to stay with him. For once, I was willing to let Marianne keep him."

"You are saying your husband didn't want to come?"

"Exactly. He left me to the wolves."

"Well, get ready, because the big bad wolf is coming directly at you."

Lindy turned to see Nick a few feet away. She caught her breath; he looked twice as good in person. Nick leaned over and kissed her on the cheek. "When I didn't see you at the ceremony, I thought you weren't coming."

"Hello, Nick," was all she could get out.

"You look like a million dollars." He put a hand on each of her shoulders.

To escape the heat from his touch, Lindy moved away to give her wine glass to the waiter.

Nick admired Betty's outfit, and shook hands with the Professor. He then asked them to follow him to one of the interior rooms.

A crowd had gathered around a single photograph on the wall. Nick took Lindy's hand and pulled her through the crowd until they stood before the largest of the photographs. Her Michael looked back at her; he was breathtaking. She could hear the comments of the people around her. *What a work of art. Who is this child? Look at his eyes. He's an old soul for sure. He's beautiful.*

Her head was swimming, and she couldn't take her eyes off Michael's photograph. She didn't know whether to be angry or happy that Nick had captured what she saw every day in her son—his inner beauty.

"When the exhibit ends, this photograph is my gift to you," Nick whispered in her ear.

Lindy looked back at Betty and the Professor and saw how they, too, were enthralled by the photograph.

"Come with me. I have something else to share with you." She knew he wasn't going to take no for an answer. He led her back to the main entrance, which took some time because people kept coming up to congratulate him.

—

Diana watched Nick and Lindy leave the museum through the main door. She wanted to follow them, but she was glued to her husband, who would not let her out of his sight. He had even waited for her outside the ladies' room. She wondered what was wrong with him tonight.

She had not had a chance to be alone with Nick, not even for a second. He greeted her and Daniel when they first arrived, treating her like an old college friend and not a lover, which she understood he had to do to keep up appearances. After all, she was there with her husband. Nick was just being respectful. *Come to think of it, where is Lindy's husband?* She watched Nick parading Lindy around as if she were his wife. It was obvious to see he still loved her.

"Are you okay?" Daniel asked her.

"Yes, but I think I might need some air." She started walking toward the door Nick and Lindy had gone through, but Daniel took her by the arm.

"There's a chill out there, and it will not be good for you." He smiled at her.

It's hot as hell out there. What's he talking about? He knows. Daniel knows about Nick and me. How? The federal investigators doing the background check had to tell him. He is silently letting me know not to make waves because of his new appointment as Director of Presidential Personnel. This administration is family-oriented.

As if reading her mind, Daniel reached over and stroked her arm. Turning away from the door leading to Nick, Diana returned her husband's smile. She gently touched her diamond pendant, on which he had spent a fortune. Diana figured the diamond was at least two carats. Daniel had given it to her earlier to celebrate his achievement, or *their* achievement, as he called it. It was a gift to keep her tied to him.

She had come so close to getting the man she always loved. Diana was pretty sure Nick had feelings for her, too. She was ready to give up everything for him. But seeing the way he had looked at Lindy sent a pain through her heart. It hurt so badly she wanted to scream. She was in a daze as Daniel led her from one group of photos to another. They stopped in front of the photograph of the child with the incredible eyes she had seen in Nick's hotel room. The intense and bottomless eyes of the child called out to her. She just didn't know what he was trying to tell her. Clenching her fists, she held back the tears.

CHAPTER FIFTY-FOUR

They walked a few feet from the main entrance of the museum to the gate of the Enid Haupt Garden. Once inside the garden Nick pulled her to him and kissed her deeply. She pushed him away.

"Why didn't you return my calls? I know you got the messages I left for you at the hospital."

"You forget, Nick, I am a married woman," she rebuked him.

"Only on paper. You're my wife in the eyes of God."

"You mustn't say things like that."

"Why not? I am speaking my truth. I am too old not to say what I feel."

"You're right about that! We are not college kids anymore. We can't let this go any further." Lindy backed away from him and almost tripped on her gown. Nick caught her and the next thing she knew, his tongue was inside her mouth. This time, her body responded to his.

Then he stopped cold and began leading her across the lawn of the museum.

"Where are we going? Don't you have to go back inside?"

"The ceremony is over. The organizers can handle it now. Don't ask any more questions. Just follow." They stopped in front of a black limousine parked at the entrance of the museum. Nick said something to the chauffeur, and they got into the back seat.

Before she could say anything, Nick was kissing her again. She was glad that an opaque glass separated them from the driver. Nick's hands moved up and down her body. Deep down Lindy knew she should stop him, but she wanted him as much as he wanted her. She didn't even notice when the limousine stopped in front of Nick's hotel. He got out and reached for her hand. She had a choice. She could close the door and demand that the driver take her back to the museum, or she could go through the rabbit hole as Alice did.

Had Betty suspected something like this might happen? She had urged Lindy to buy the black bra and bikini panties, not that Nick had taken time to look at them. He peeled every stitch of clothing off her in seconds. There was no holding him back. Lindy felt him kiss her neck and ears, and then he moved down her body, finding the spot that gave her the greatest pleasure. Nick entered her at the throes of her ecstasy. It was then that she let go. She wanted to savor the moment forever, wishing time would stop. She wasn't in her bathtub, but in Nick's bed.

"Nick, Nick!" she called out his name as she continued to come in pure joy. He was experiencing the same intensity of pleasure as he thrust back and forth, kissing her deeply with each thrust. Their fingers interlocked as they came together. Nick lay on top of her, not moving. She didn't want him to move. The only way she could describe that moment and the ones that followed was 'unbelievable'.

Later he ordered tea and cake for her and coffee for himself. They sat on the bed naked, eating and opening up to each other. Nick told her about Africa and how he had almost died of malaria, but the Elder Healer had saved him. He described how he was delirious and didn't know if she really existed. When he was in Spain, he felt her presence, but again he thought he was hallucinating. Lindy told him about the Awakeners and what her grandmother had told them about her life through Ruth.

"It was real then. I wasn't hallucinating?"

"No, my darling." She touched his face. "She is real." Lindy told him the story her grandmother had told them about him.

He told her how he had promised to make amends for his behavior toward Diana and her, and to find out about the child, because the boy had a special mission.

"You knew it was a boy?"

"Yes, a baby boy thrown into a dumpster behind the dorm at Howard University." He waited for the words to register. Lindy put down the cake and looked at him.

He described how he had tracked down Cissy and discovered she was Grace Perry, the reporter for the *Washington Star*. Information from Grace, or Cissy, led him to the medical student, who had performed the botched abortion and later delivered the deformed baby. He was also the one who tossed the baby into the dumpster.

"Lindy, I believe that the baby is Michael."

Lindy had started to dress. "What you are saying is that my son, Michael, is your blood son?"

"It's a fact, Lindy."

"She put him in a dumpster. What kind of person is she?" Lindy leaned down to strap on her shoes; Nick put on his shorts and stood in front of her.

"Don't blame Diana. She thought he was dead. It wasn't her fault."

"Does she know?" Lindy asked, feeling as though her world had crashed.

"No, she doesn't."

"Do you plan to tell her…if this is true?"

"What do you mean *if* it is true?"

"You only have the word of an addict. This could destroy people's lives." Lindy, standing with one shoe on, looked defensive.

"I don't want to hurt anyone, especially not you or Diana," he replied, putting on his pants and shirt.

"Then what are you planning to do with the information?"

"I don't know, Lindy. All I know is that the Elder Healer told me that he was alive and had a special purpose in this lifetime that would change the course of destiny."

"And you, how do you fit into this?" She must have lost her senses to have gone to bed with him. *This man is trying to take my son away for Diana, the woman he loves.*

Nick stumbled as he tried to find the words to tell her what he wanted. "It's not what you are thinking, Lindy. I love you, and I love

Michael. I would never do anything to hurt either of you. I want you and Michael. I don't know what I'm supposed to do about his special mission, but my gut tells me that I am to be a part of his life." He stood in her way. "For once in your life, trust me!"

Tears began to flow down her face. She felt his warm body against her and wanted to stay there forever. Instead, she slipped out of his embrace and moved toward the door. Nick stepped in front of her, blocking her exit.

"What you are asking is impossible. We shouldn't have done what we did tonight. Other people could get hurt."

"Nothing is impossible. I don't want to hurt anyone else, but I will not give you up this time."

"Please move out of my way. It's late, and I have to go." She brushed past him. "This was a mistake. How many times do I have to tell you that I am married? Believe it or not, I love my husband."

Those words stung him. "I don't buy your '*this was a mistake*' crap for one moment. Don't desecrate this, Lindy. Look me in the eye and tell me that you don't love me, and I will walk out of your life forever."

She couldn't lie to herself, or to him. She did love Paul, but it was different—spiritual. They hadn't consummated their marriage. It needed to be done.

Nick kept talking. "Where was he tonight?"

"Michael wasn't feeling well, and Paul decided to stay with him." Lindy reached for the doorknob.

"I don't want you to leave like this. You asked me what I want. Give me a chance to get to know Michael and spend some time with you. Don't answer now, just think about it."

She closed the door.

CHAPTER FIFTY-FIVE

The limousine driver dropped Lindy off at her car. She was oblivious to the rain that had started. She drove home without paying attention to where she was, or what was happening on the street. She had one thing on her mind—Nick and Diana may be Michael's biological parents.

Lindy pulled into her block and parked. The street was dark and deserted, but she had gotten used to coming home late when she worked shift hours at the hospital during her internship and residency. Should she tell Paul? How would he handle it? Then she realized there was no concrete proof. Paul and Betty would ask her for proof. All Nick could tell her was what some drugged-out former medical-school student had told him. Nevertheless, in her heart, she knew it was true. She began to cry. Suppose Diana wanted to take him away. Lindy decided she would use every cent she had to keep Michael; he was her son.

It was pouring when she stepped out of the car. The rain felt good against her skin as it mixed in with the tears, which she couldn't stop no matter how hard she tried. It was not just about Michael; it was also about being with Nick. Never could she allow that to happen again. She had violated her marriage vows, and part of her didn't care. She wanted to lie there forever in his big, strong arms.

Lindy fumbled in her purse for her keys. The makeup and tears were blurring her vision when Paul opened the door. He had been watching for her at the window. His first thought was she had been in a car accident. Paul reached out for Lindy and pulled her into his arms. He followed her to her bedroom. She was soaked but, as far as he could tell, not hurt. Paul got several towels from the bathroom and proceeded to dry her, beginning with her hair.

Without speaking, Lindy motioned for Paul to step back. She unzipped her dress, unfastened her bra, and took off her panties. She let everything fall to the floor where she was standing, and Paul was unable to take his eyes off her. This was the first time, in all their years of marriage, he had seen his wife completely naked. Through the years, he had caught glimpses of her in the shower or walking around in her room, but never up close.

"I'll wait in the other room until you get dressed," he said, turning to walk out of the room.

Lindy reached out and grasped his arm. "No, look at me, Paul. I'm your wife. Look at me," she begged as she moved closer to him.

Her scent and her nakedness began to arouse him.

Lindy took his hand and moved it to her breasts. Her nipples were hard again. She envisioned Nick and started to breathe heavier. She let go of his hand and reached for the buttons on his shirt. Paul just stood there as Lindy undressed him.

Lindy caressed her husband's body and began kissing him gently on the lips, neck, nipples, and then she was on her knees. She felt his hardness and brought him pleasure unlike he had felt before. He lifted her up and carried her to the bed. Lindy straddled him, but it was Nick's body she saw. With each thrust, she wanted to call out Nick's name. She dug into his chest with her nails until he cried out with pain and pleasure. Then she collapsed in his arms.

Shivering, Paul pulled the sheet over them. She was asleep. He lay there for a while. It was difficult to move with her still partly on top of him.

She's in love with him, Paul thought. She had called out Nick's name. He didn't think she was aware of it because she was so immersed in wherever she had gone. He felt empty.

The sound of Michael screaming made him move Lindy over and reach for his pants to go see what had disturbed the child. The scream also awakened Lindy, who joined her husband. Neither one said anything to the other about what had happened.

Michael was burning up with fever and drenched in sweat. There was an infection somewhere, because his temperature was 102 degrees. Lindy quickly scanned his body, and saw that his shunt was blocked. She gently touched the soft spot of his head; it was bulging, a sign of cranial pressure. There was nothing she could do but take him to the emergency room. It was times like these she wished she had the ability to instantly heal him, but she still didn't have the confidence to even try. Lindy preferred to play it safe and take him to the hospital for the necessary tests. She had to let them tell her his shunt was blocked. She couldn't walk into the hospital and say, *I intuitively looked at his shunt and it's blocked.* They would take her license away.

Paul and Lindy stood on each side of Michael's bed and held his hands while waiting for the neurologist. Michael was lethargic, and the white part of his eyes showed above the pupil—what the neurologists called sun-setting.

The neurologist ordered a series of X-rays for Michael. The tests showed just what Lindy thought—a blocked shunt. Michael needed his first revision. He'd had the shunt since birth, which was a pretty good stretch considering how much he had grown in the last few years. As a pediatrician, Lindy knew children with shunts often needed frequent revisions. When he was small, she would pump the little button on the back of his head to keep the fluid flowing.

They assigned Michael a private room and scheduled his operation for later that day. The pediatric neurosurgeon had a full schedule, and it was only because of Lindy that they even managed to fit Michael in.

With Lindy refusing to leave the hospital, Paul went home later that day and brought her a change of clothing.

CHAPTER FIFTY-SIX

Michael was out of the operating room and in the intensive care unit when his fever returned. The neurosurgeon told Lindy that if he didn't respond to the medicine, they might have to try another revision. It was possible he was allergic to the type of material the shunt was made of. They just weren't sure. The doctor also said Michael might need a blood transfusion, and it would be advisable for her and her husband to donate blood beforehand. It was then Lindy told the doctor about the adoption. She had assumed he had at least read Michael's history, since she herself always read everything regarding her patients. He asked if she knew any of Michael's blood relatives. Lindy hesitated before saying no.

She watched Michael's condition worsen. His blood pressure was unstable and his fever wasn't breaking. The neurosurgeon planned to operate on him again that night. Drained and tired, Lindy knew she could no longer put off what she dreaded.

She told Paul and Betty what Nick had told her about Michael's birth, and that she wanted to ask Nick to donate blood. As she expected, both felt Nick didn't have any concrete proof that Michael was his son. To settle the matter, Betty suggested that a paternity test be done at the same time he donated blood. Paul agreed.

Lindy left the room to call Nick. She didn't feel comfortable talking to him in front of Paul, especially since she considered herself truly, really married for the first time. Nick was not in his room, so she tracked him down at the museum. He was beside himself when she told him about Michael's condition and that she needed him to donate blood. She then asked him to take a paternity test. He agreed, and promised to come to the hospital immediately.

Lindy met Nick in the hospital lobby. He had never seen her so distressed. She was wriggling her fingers, and looked as if she hadn't slept in days. He wanted to take her in his arms to comfort her, but her body language told him to back off, so he maintained a safe distance. Lindy led Nick to the lab, where the doctor had left the order for both tests. Afterwards, he wanted to see Michael.

Paul was sitting next to the bed when Lindy and Nick entered. Betty had gone to check on the Professor. Lindy formally introduced the two men, who shook hands.

"We meet again." Nick said, extending his hand to Paul.

"Yes, we do, and I hope the ride won't be as bumpy." Paul shook Nick's hand.

"You two have met?" Lindy glared at them.

"On the plane coming home," both men responded at the same time.

Nick turned his attention to Michael, bent down, and kissed him on the forehead. He spoke to him in French. As Nick kissed him again, Paul walked out of the room.

"What did you say to him?" she asked Nick.

"I told my son that I love him and want him to get well so I can take him to see the wonders of the world. Is something wrong with that?"

"Paul, my husband, speaks fluent French."

Lindy knew Paul was devastated to hear another man—and not just any man, but her former lover—call Michael his son. She wanted to go to him, but her fear of leaving Michael wouldn't let her.

"I know." Nick said, shrugging helplessly.

Lindy couldn't let it go.

"Nick, you asked me to think about letting you be a part of my life and Michael's. It's not going to work. You just can't waltz in here after all these years and lay claim to us. I can't hurt Paul," she cried.

"This isn't the time to talk about that. The only thing that matters is Michael getting well. I will respect you and your marriage."

"If you really care for me, leave."

"You know how I feel about you. You just can't call me to give blood and then dismiss me, Ms. Lindy, as if I don't count."

Lindy hated it when he used that tone of voice. She wanted to scream.

"Michael had nightmares about a dark man coming to take him away from Paul and me. I guess he was right," she said, looking drained.

"That's why he was frightened of me when we first met. I would never do anything to hurt you or him. Trust me."

"I did. Eleven years ago."

Paul returned with some food for her, which she had no appetite for. The doctor found them sitting in the room, their eyes fixed on the child. He sensed something was wrong, but if it didn't affect his patient, he was not getting involved.

Lindy introduced Nick to the doctor, who told them he had some good news and some bad news. Nick wanted to hear the bad news first. The doctor said he would not be able to use Nick's blood if the need arose because Nick had malaria. The good news, at least to one person standing in the room, was that the test had a probability of ninety-nine percent certainty that Nick was Michael's natural father. At a loss for words, Lindy walked over to Paul. He put his arm around her as they looked at Nick, who was trying not to show how happy he was. The doctor asked him about Michael's biological mother.

Nick called Diana's office and asked her to come to Children's Hospital. He wanted to share something with her, and not over the phone. Diana hesitated, and then said she would meet him there in twenty minutes.

On the drive over, Diana pondered what Nick had to tell her. His voice sounded strange. *What could he possibly want to share with me at Children's Hospital? Has he gone out of his mind and found some poor child he thinks is ours? The baby died.*

She guessed it had something to do with what happened years ago. Well, she was tired of it, but agreed to go, especially if he would finally stop bringing up the past. She planned to get ugly with him, because he had gone off with that half-white woman. She was going to let him have it good.

Nick waited for Diana in the lobby. She stepped off the escalator, perfectly dressed in a pale-gold suit with matching shoes, and was putting her sunglasses into her Gucci handbag. She was wearing the diamond earrings and pendant Daniel had given her the night Nick's exhibit opened. She had promised him never to see Nick again, and here she was already breaking her word. All Nick had to do was beckon her with his little finger, and she would come running.

Nick told her they were going back down to her car to talk. Diana was tired of this cloak-and-dagger mess. *What is wrong with this man?*

They got into her two-seater Mercedes, and Nick began with his experience in Africa, ending with his taking the paternity test and finding out Michael was his son.

Diana sat there, never saying a word. He stopped and looked at her for a response of some kind.

"Get out."

"What?"

"You heard me. Get out. I don't have any son. You made me get rid of the baby years ago. Now you are trying to ruin my life and marriage by telling me that I have an eleven-year-old son. No, sir, that is impossible."

"Come with me upstairs and see him."

"On top of it, if it is true, he is being raised by that crazy half-white woman. No!" she screamed, and started to hit him with her fists.

Nick knew women, and was glad he had decided to tell her in the car and not upstairs. Nick slapped her twice, and Diana froze. She then grabbed the steering wheel and began to cry.

"Please, just give the blood. It might save his life. You don't have to see him or Lindy if you don't want. But whether you like it or not, Michael is our son. He didn't die in the dumpster."

The mention of the dumpster made her cry even harder. "What does he look like?" she asked between sobs.

"You saw his picture in my room and at the exhibit."

"The boy with the piercing eyes?" She looked at Nick, suddenly realizing that what she couldn't accomplish eleven years ago had come to fruition after all. They had a son, and Nick was crazy about him.

"Yeah, that's him."

"I want to see him, but I don't want that woman in the room. If she wants me to give blood, then she has to let me see him only with you."

"I'll see if she will agree. In the meantime, you can wait in the waiting room of the lab."

Nick had gone from one raging woman to another. Lindy refused. She didn't want Diana near her son. It took Paul to convince her to let Diana see Michael for a few moments. He told her there was nothing Diana could legally do to get him back; she would be considered an unfit mother for leaving him in the dumpster. She needed to get something to eat anyway, so he would take her to the cafeteria.

The two couples passed each other in the hallway. Nick escorted Diana into Michael's room, and the two stood over the child that each had abandoned. Diana looked at the child's swollen head. His forehead was protruding, giving his face an odd shape. His body was small and underdeveloped for a boy his age. Michael looked nothing like the picture she had seen earlier that week; instead, he was pitiful. Nick was holding his hand and kissing it, but she could not bring herself to make any gestures toward him. She didn't feel anything. She expected him to look at least halfway normal, but he was broken, and she wasn't the one to fix him. He had the right mother, but she would never let that woman know it.

Diana turned to Nick and told him that she was ready to leave. She had spent fewer than fifteen minutes with Michael, and Nick saw a side of Diana's personality he didn't know existed. She had done her part in giving the blood, so he walked her to her car. *What has happened to her?*

IT'S NOT OVER YET

"My husband has been appointed to the presidential team. Before he starts his new position, we are leaving for a two-week cruise. I plan, as I told you before, to put the past behind me. My baby died. Bye, Nick."

Diana shut the car door before he could say anything. Looking back at him through her rearview mirror, Diana wondered if it was really over. She would always love Nick, but Daniel had promised her that one day she would be the first lady of D.C.

CHAPTER FIFTY-SEVEN

Lindy sat on the wooden park bench, watching Michael run and play with the other children. In four months, he showed remarkable growth due to the new shunt. The third one was inserted without complications; before his surgery, she had used her healing gift on him. She had stepped out on faith. He still had a way to go to catch up with children his age, but Lindy knew deep inside that eventually he would be where he belonged.

It's funny how life is always changing like the seasons, Lindy thought. At the beginning of summer, she would have never thought so many momentous events would have changed her life forever. The passing of Rev was one of the hardest things she had to go through. Even now, the pain of not having a chance to make amends surfaced to haunt her. The pain was gradually getting better, especially when she focused on what the Elder Healer had taught her about death and Rev's generous gift to her.

She had already put the funds to work by helping Betty build a school and healing center for esoteric wisdom, which would be the first of its kind in the metropolitan area. She and Betty had taken several trips to Virginia Beach, before Betty's departure to Israel, to study the organizational structure of the Edgar Cayce Association for Research and Enlightenment (A.R.E.). They decided that in addition to the classrooms, they would also have a meditation room, bookstore, and, of course, the healing room. Betty would be the CEO, and Lindy the resident physician. She had resigned from Howard University Hospital, which meant another burden off her shoulders.

Lindy reached into her handbag and pulled out three envelopes. They had arrived together, but from three different parts of the world. She opened the one from Israel first. It was from Betty, and it informed her of the passing of the Professor. He had died at home with his family and her at his side. Betty wanted her to know that since their healing night, both she and the Professor had reached a state of peace. In all their years of marriage, they had never experienced such bliss together. He went to the other side with a smile on his face.

She wrote, "*So you see, my dear friend, a healing can come in many ways. My beloved Harvey wanted to go, and the healing helped to make his transition much smoother than if he was full of remorse and anger. I believe that is what the Elder Healer meant to about the transition of your grandfather. Allowing the loving energy of God to flow through you to Rev helped him also to forgive and love. I'll be back in a few weeks, after I settle Harvey's affairs. I know and feel in my heart that starting the school is the right thing to do. No more secrecy or hiding. It's time for us to be who we are.*"

Lindy folded the letter and placed it back inside the envelope. She closed her eyes for a few moments and silently focused on the Professor, sending him love and asking Archangel Michael to assist him as he moved to the light.

Lindy tore open the second letter without any thought. It was probably the last one she would receive from Paul for a long time. He was in Nepal on a spiritual quest.

Paul never touched her again after the night they made love. Instead of becoming closer, they had drifted further apart emotionally, physically, and mentally. What held them together was their love for each other and their strong spiritual belief system. The faraway look in his eyes and his restlessness told her everything. Lindy returned home one evening to find Paul sitting in the living room chair in total darkness. Startled, Lindy didn't know what had happened. He asked her to sit down opposite him, saying he had something to discuss with her that had been weighing on his mind. He took her face in his hands and looked into her eyes. She could still hear his words.

"Lindy, I love you and Michael with all my heart." He paused. "I have been living a lie for many years now, trying to be here for you and Michael, but only being here in the physical body and not in spirit."

Lindy tried to interrupt him, to tell him she knew, but he put a finger to her lips to silence her.

"All my life, I have just wanted to pursue the path of the guru, with no attachments. I tried to live in both worlds, but as you know, I was unsuccessful. I can't be a husband to you. The night that we," he could hardly say the words, "made love was the most beautiful thing I have ever done, but I don't know how to explain it. I felt I betrayed who I am—just a simple spirit wanting to serve God. Hearing your grandmother's story was a wake-up call for me. All I ever wanted in life was to follow the path of the Masters as she did." Paul let her face go. He decided it was best not to tell her that he yearned for his childhood friend, Dhar.

"I know, Paul. I have selfishly held on to you all these years, knowing in my heart that you wanted to be free."

"I am leaving for Nepal. I don't know whether or when I will be back." He studied her closely, looking for any hint of remorse.

Lindy wondered if she should tell him her secret then, or wait. After reflecting a few moments, she decided to wait, because it would only make him stay.

"You must go. I love you. You have already given up so much of your life to me and Michael. You have been a good husband and father, and now it's time for both of us to walk different paths."

Paul gathered her in his arms. There was no animosity between them; they were friends for life.

Lindy didn't tell him about her pregnancy until he was on his way to Nepal. She handed him a letter just before he boarded the plane. In it, she begged him to follow his dream and insisted that she was happy. Once he was in Nepal, Paul wrote her back immediately. Feeling as if he was deserting her, Paul offered to return to D. C. In her reply, Lindy told him she wanted to be with Nick. Just as he must follow his soul, she wrote, she had to follow her heart.

What she didn't tell Paul or Nick about the pregnancy was that she didn't know—or care—who the twins' father was. They were her babies.

Soon after Lindy discovered she was pregnant, she dreamt she saw her grandmother, the Elder Healer, holding a girl named Gabriela and a boy named Raphael. Michael was standing next to them, and above the scene in gold were the words HOLY TRINITY. Her grandmother told her that she was the vehicle and nurturer for these special souls, Paul their teacher, and Nick their protector.

Before opening the third letter, Lindy rubbed her belly. She was already big, probably because she was carrying twins. The third letter was short. All it said was, 'I'll be home for Christmas. Love you madly, Nick."

Nick had returned to Europe to finish out the exhibit. She had told him that she and Michael needed time to adjust to living without Paul. He had promised he wouldn't push. He told her that he didn't understand about soul mates or twin flames, that the only way he could explain it was that he was her man now and forever, and he wasn't ever going anywhere.

Lindy got up off the bench. Whenever she thought about those words, she would get all hot inside. Nick was coming home to her, Michael, and the twins.

Home was now the house that she once lived in as a truth student in the Order of Melchizedek. Lindy had purchased the house in Chevy Chase. She needed a larger house, and this one was perfect because it held so many memories for her. Ruth and Mark had kept it in good condition, so she only had to do a few minor repairs.

"Come on, baby. It's time to go home," Lindy called to Michael.

"I'm no baby. I'm Michael." The boy smiled at her.

"You're right." Lindy looked at her miracle child and said, "God is good."

Without batting an eye, he ran ahead of her and shouted back, "All the time, Mom, all the time."

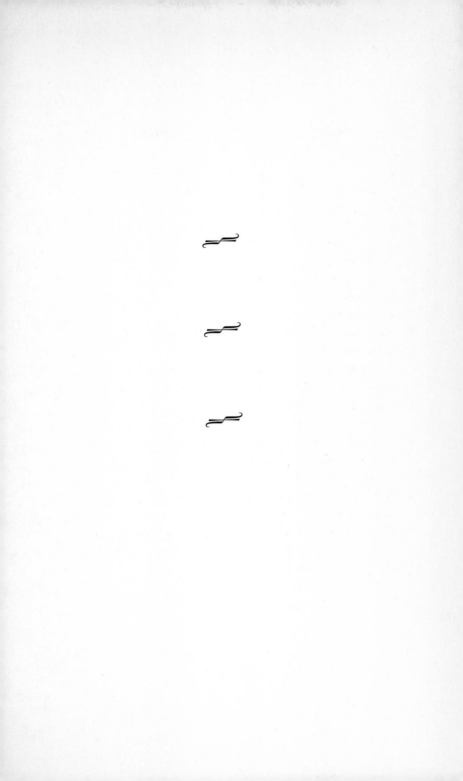

ABOUT THE AUTHOR

J.J. Michael is a lifelong student and teacher of Metaphysics and healing principles. She is the founder of *Pathtotruth.com* and publisher of Path2truth.com, an ezine that promotes spiritual awareness, self-development and world peace. Ms. Michael is the author of *Path to Truth: A Spiritual Guide to Higher Consciousness*, iUniverse.com 2000 and *Life is Never as It Seems*, published by Genesis Press, Inc. in 2005. Ms. Michael has appeared on the local Virginia Cable Television and has been featured on National Public Radio (NPR). A renowned numerologist, Ms. Michael has appeared in CNN's segment, "A Wrinkle in Time." Her formal education includes a B.A. from Howard University and a M.L.S. from the University of Maryland. Ms. Michael is currently working on her third novel, *Deception*. For more information, visit: **www.jjmichael.org** or email her at **jj@jjmichael.org**.

IT'S NOT OVER YET

2007 Publication Schedule

January

Corporate Seduction
A.C. Arthur
ISBN-13: 978-1-58571-238-0
ISBN-10: 1-58571-238-8
$9.95

A Taste of Temptation
Reneé Alexis
ISBN-13: 978-1-58571-207-6
ISBN-10: 1-58571-207-8
$9.95

February

The Perfect Frame
Beverly Clark
ISBN-13: 978-1-58571-240-3
ISBN-10: 1-58571-240-X
$9.95

Ebony Angel
Deatri King-Bey
ISBN-13: 978-1-58571-239-7
ISBN-10: 1-58571-239-6
$9.95

March

Sweet Sensations
Gwendolyn Bolton
ISBN-13: 978-1-58571-206-9
ISBN-10: 1-58571-206-X
$9.95

Crush
Crystal Hubbard
ISBN-13: 978-1-58571-243-4
ISBN-10: 1-58571-243-4
$9.95

April

Secret Thunder
Annetta P. Lee
ISBN-13: 978-1-58571-204-5
ISBN-10: 1-58571-204-3
$9.95

Blood Seduction
J.M. Jeffries
ISBN-13: 978-1-58571-237-3
ISBN-10: 1-58571-237-X
$9.95

May

Lies Too Long
Pamela Ridley
ISBN-13: 978-1-58571-246-5
ISBN-10: 1-58571-246-9
$13.95

Two Sides to Every Story
Dyanne Davis
ISBN-13: 978-1-58571-248-9
ISBN-10: 1-58571-248-5
$9.95

June

One of These Days
Michele Sudler
ISBN-13: 978-1-58571-249-6
ISBN-10: 1-58571-249-3
$9.95

Who's That Lady?
Andrea Jackson
ISBN-13: 978-1-58571-190-1
ISBN-10: 1-58571-190-X
$9.95

2007 Publication Schedule (continued)

July

Heart of the Phoenix
A.C. Arthur
ISBN-13: 978-1-58571-242-7
ISBN-10: 1-58571-242-6
$9.95

Do Over
Celya Bowers
ISBN-13: 978-1-58571-241-0
ISBN-10: 1-58571-241-8
$9.95

It's Not Over Yet
J.J. Michael
ISBN-13: 978-1-58571-245-8
ISBN-10: 1-58571-245-0
$9.95

August

The Fires Within
Beverly Clark
ISBN-13: 978-1-58571-244-1
ISBN-10: 1-58571-244-2
$9.95

Stolen Kisses
Dominiqua Douglas
ISBN-13: 978-1-58571-247-2
ISBN-10: 1-58571-247-7
$9.95

September

Small Whispers
Annetta P. Lee
ISBN-13: 978-158571-251-9
ISBN-10: 1-58571-251-5
$6.99

Always You
Crystal Hubbard
ISBN-13: 978-158571-252-6
ISBN-10: 1-58571-252-3
$6.99

October

Not His Type
Chamein Canton
ISBN-13: 978-158571-253-3
ISBN-10: 1-58571-253-1
$6.99

Many Shades of Gray
Dyanne Davis
ISBN-13: 978-158571-254-0
ISBN-10: 1-58571-254-X
$6.99

November

When I'm With You
LaConnie Taylor-Jones
ISBN-13: 978-158571-250-2
ISBN-10: 1-58571-250-7
$6.99

The Mission
Pamela Leigh Starr
ISBN-13: 978-158571-255-7
ISBN-10: 1-58571-255-8
$6.99

December

One in A Million
Barbara Keaton
ISBN-13: 978-158571-257-1
ISBN-10: 1-58571-257-4
$6.99

The Foursome
Celya Bowers
ISBN-13: 978-158571-256-4
ISBN-10: 1-58571-256-6
$6.99

Other Genesis Press, Inc. Titles

A Dangerous Deception	J.M. Jeffries	$8.95
A Dangerous Love	J.M. Jeffries	$8.95
A Dangerous Obsession	J.M. Jeffries	$8.95
A Dangerous Woman	J.M. Jeffries	$9.95
A Dead Man Speaks	Lisa Jones Johnson	$12.95
A Drummer's Beat to Mend	Kei Swanson	$9.95
A Happy Life	Charlotte Harris	$9.95
A Heart's Awakening	Veronica Parker	$9.95
A Lark on the Wing	Phyliss Hamilton	$9.95
A Love of Her Own	Cheris F. Hodges	$9.95
A Love to Cherish	Beverly Clark	$8.95
A Lover's Legacy	Veronica Parker	$9.95
A Pefect Place to Pray	I.L. Goodwin	$12.95
A Risk of Rain	Dar Tomlinson	$8.95
A Twist of Fate	Beverly Clark	$8.95
A Will to Love	Angie Daniels	$9.95
Acquisitions	Kimberley White	$8.95
Across	Carol Payne	$12.95
After the Vows	Leslie Esdaile	$10.95
(Summer Anthology)	T.T. Henderson	
	Jacqueline Thomas	
Again My Love	Kayla Perrin	$10.95
Against the Wind	Gwynne Forster	$8.95
All I Ask	Barbara Keaton	$8.95
Ambrosia	T.T. Henderson	$8.95
An Unfinished Love Affair	Barbara Keaton	$8.95
And Then Came You	Dorothy Elizabeth Love	$8.95
Angel's Paradise	Janice Angelique	$9.95
At Last	Lisa G. Riley	$8.95
Best of Friends	Natalie Dunbar	$8.95
Between Tears	Pamela Ridley	$12.95
Beyond the Rapture	Beverly Clark	$9.95
Blaze	Barbara Keaton	$9.95

Other Genesis Press, Inc. Titles (continued)

Blood Lust	J. M. Jeffries	$9.95
Bodyguard	Andrea Jackson	$9.95
Boss of Me	Diana Nyad	$8.95
Bound by Love	Beverly Clark	$8.95
Breeze	Robin Hampton Allen	$10.95
Broken	Dar Tomlinson	$24.95
The Business of Love	Cheris Hodges	$9.95
By Design	Barbara Keaton	$8.95
Cajun Heat	Charlene Berry	$8.95
Careless Whispers	Rochelle Alers	$8.95
Cats & Other Tales	Marilyn Wagner	$8.95
Caught in a Trap	Andre Michelle	$8.95
Caught Up In the Rapture	Lisa G. Riley	$9.95
Cautious Heart	Cheris F Hodges	$8.95
Caught Up	Deatri King Bey	$12.95
Chances	Pamela Leigh Starr	$8.95
Cherish the Flame	Beverly Clark	$8.95
Class Reunion	Irma Jenkins/John Brown	$12.95
Code Name: Diva	J.M. Jeffries	$9.95
Conquering Dr. Wexler's Heart	Kimberley White	$9.95
Cricket's Serenade	Carolita Blythe	$12.95
Crossing Paths, Tempting Memories	Dorothy Elizabeth Love	$9.95
Cupid	Barbara Keaton	$9.95
Cypress Whisperings	Phyllis Hamilton	$8.95
Dark Embrace	Crystal Wilson Harris	$8.95
Dark Storm Rising	Chinelu Moore	$10.95
Daughter of the Wind	Joan Xian	$8.95
Deadly Sacrifice	Jack Kean	$22.95
Designer Passion	Dar Tomlinson	$8.95
Dreamtective	Liz Swados	$5.95
Ebony Butterfly II	Delilah Dawson	$14.95
Ebony Eyes	Kei Swanson	$9.95

Other Genesis Press, Inc. Titles (continued)

Echoes of Yesterday	Beverly Clark	$9.95
Eden's Garden	Elizabeth Rose	$8.95
Enchanted Desire	Wanda Y. Thomas	$9.95
Everlastin' Love	Gay G. Gunn	$8.95
Everlasting Moments	Dorothy Elizabeth Love	$8.95
Everything and More	Sinclair Lebeau	$8.95
Everything but Love	Natalie Dunbar	$8.95
Eve's Prescription	Edwina Martin Arnold	$8.95
Falling	Natalie Dunbar	$9.95
Fate	Pamela Leigh Starr	$8.95
Finding Isabella	A.J. Garrotto	$8.95
Forbidden Quest	Dar Tomlinson	$10.95
Forever Love	Wanda Thomas	$8.95
From the Ashes	Kathleen Suzanne	$8.95
	Jeanne Sumerix	
Gentle Yearning	Rochelle Alers	$10.95
Glory of Love	Sinclair LeBeau	$10.95
Go Gentle into that Good Night	Malcom Boyd	$12.95
Goldengroove	Mary Beth Craft	$16.95
Groove, Bang, and Jive	Steve Cannon	$8.99
Hand in Glove	Andrea Jackson	$9.95
Hard to Love	Kimberley White	$9.95
Hart & Soul	Angie Daniels	$8.95
Havana Sunrise	Kymberly Hunt	$9.95
Heartbeat	Stephanie Bedwell-Grime	$8.95
Hearts Remember	M. Loui Quezada	$8.95
Hidden Memories	Robin Allen	$10.95
Higher Ground	Leah Latimer	$19.95
Hitler, the War, and the Pope	Ronald Rychiak	$26.95
How to Write a Romance	Kathryn Falk	$18.95
I Married a Reclining Chair	Lisa M. Fuhs	$8.95
I'm Gonna Make You Love Me	Gwyneth Bolton	$9.95
Indigo After Dark Vol. I	Nia Dixon/Angelique	$10.95

Other Genesis Press, Inc. Titles (continued)

Indigo After Dark Vol. II	Dolores Bundy/Cole Riley	$10.95
Indigo After Dark Vol. III	Montana Blue/Coco Morena	$10.95
Indigo After Dark Vol. IV	Cassandra Colt/	$14.95
	Diana Richeaux	
Indigo After Dark Vol. V	Delilah Dawson	$14.95
Icie	Pamela Leigh Starr	$8.95
I'll Be Your Shelter	Giselle Carmichael	$8.95
I'll Paint a Sun	A.J. Garrotto	$9.95
Illusions	Pamela Leigh Starr	$8.95
Indiscretions	Donna Hill	$8.95
Intentional Mistakes	Michele Sudler	$9.95
Interlude	Donna Hill	$8.95
Intimate Intentions	Angie Daniels	$8.95
Ironic	Pamela Leigh Starr	$9.95
Jolie's Surrender	Edwina Martin-Arnold	$8.95
Kiss or Keep	Debra Phillips	$8.95
Lace	Giselle Carmichael	$9.95
Last Train to Memphis	Elsa Cook	$12.95
Lasting Valor	Ken Olsen	$24.95
Let's Get It On	Dyanne Davis	$9.95
Let Us Prey	Hunter Lundy	$25.95
Life Is Never As It Seems	J.J. Michael	$12.95
Lighter Shade of Brown	Vicki Andrews	$8.95
Love Always	Mildred E. Riley	$10.95
Love Doesn't Come Easy	Charlyne Dickerson	$8.95
Love in High Gear	Charlotte Roy	$9.95
Love Lasts Forever	Dominiqua Douglas	$9.95
Love Me Carefully	A.C. Arthur	$9.95
Love Unveiled	Gloria Greene	$10.95
Love's Deception	Charlene Berry	$10.95
Love's Destiny	M. Loui Quezada	$8.95
Mae's Promise	Melody Walcott	$8.95
Magnolia Sunset	Giselle Carmichael	$8.95

Other Genesis Press, Inc. Titles (continued)

Matters of Life and Death	Lesego Malepe, Ph.D.	$15.95
Meant to Be	Jeanne Sumerix	$8.95
Midnight Clear	Leslie Esdaile	$10.95
(Anthology)	Gwynne Forster	
	Carmen Green	
	Monica Jackson	
Midnight Magic	Gwynne Forster	$8.95
Midnight Peril	Vicki Andrews	$10.95
Misconceptions	Pamela Leigh Starr	$9.95
Misty Blue	Dyanne Davis	$9.95
Montgomery's Children	Richard Perry	$14.95
My Buffalo Soldier	Barbara B. K. Reeves	$8.95
Naked Soul	Gwynne Forster	$8.95
Next to Last Chance	Louisa Dixon	$24.95
Nights Over Egypt	Barbara Keaton	$9.95
No Apologies	Seressia Glass	$8.95
No Commitment Required	Seressia Glass	$8.95
No Ordinary Love	Angela Weaver	$9.95
No Regrets	Mildred E. Riley	$8.95
Notes When Summer Ends	Beverly Lauderdale	$12.95
Nowhere to Run	Gay G. Gunn	$10.95
O Bed! O Breakfast!	Rob Kuehnle	$14.95
Object of His Desire	A. C. Arthur	$8.95
Office Policy	A. C. Arthur	$9.95
Once in a Blue Moon	Dorianne Cole	$9.95
One Day at a Time	Bella McFarland	$8.95
Only You	Crystal Hubbard	$9.95
Outside Chance	Louisa Dixon	$24.95
Passion	T.T. Henderson	$10.95
Passion's Blood	Cherif Fortin	$22.95
Passion's Journey	Wanda Thomas	$8.95
Past Promises	Jahmel West	$8.95
Path of Fire	T.T. Henderson	$8.95

Other Genesis Press, Inc. Titles (continued)

Path of Thorns	Annetta P. Lee	$9.95
Peace Be Still	Colette Haywood	$12.95
Picture Perfect	Reon Carter	$8.95
Playing for Keeps	Stephanie Salinas	$8.95
Pride & Joi	Gay G. Gunn	$8.95
Promises to Keep	Alicia Wiggins	$8.95
Quiet Storm	Donna Hill	$10.95
Reckless Surrender	Rochelle Alers	$6.95
Red Polka Dot in a World of Plaid	Varian Johnson	$12.95
Rehoboth Road	Anita Ballard-Jones	$12.95
Reluctant Captive	Joyce Jackson	$8.95
Rendezvous with Fate	Jeanne Sumerix	$8.95
Revelations	Cheris F. Hodges	$8.95
Rise of the Phoenix	Kenneth Whetstone	$12.95
Rivers of the Soul	Leslie Esdaile	$8.95
Rock Star	Rosyln Hardy Holcomb	$9.95
Rocky Mountain Romance	Kathleen Suzanne	$8.95
Rooms of the Heart	Donna Hill	$8.95
Rough on Rats and Tough on Cats	Chris Parker	$12.95
Scent of Rain	Annetta P. Lee	$9.95
Second Chances at Love	Cheris Hodges	$9.95
Secret Library Vol. 1	Nina Sheridan	$18.95
Secret Library Vol. 2	Cassandra Colt	$8.95
Shades of Brown	Denise Becker	$8.95
Shades of Desire	Monica White	$8.95
Shadows in the Moonlight	Jeanne Sumerix	$8.95
Sin	Crystal Rhodes	$8.95
Sin and Surrender	J.M. Jeffries	$9.95
Sinful Intentions	Crystal Rhodes	$12.95
So Amazing	Sinclair LeBeau	$8.95
Somebody's Someone	Sinclair LeBeau	$8.95

Other Genesis Press, Inc. Titles (continued)

Someone to Love	Alicia Wiggins	$8.95
Song in the Park	Martin Brant	$15.95
Soul Eyes	Wayne L. Wilson	$12.95
Soul to Soul	Donna Hill	$8.95
Southern Comfort	J.M. Jeffries	$8.95
Still the Storm	Sharon Robinson	$8.95
Still Waters Run Deep	Leslie Esdaile	$8.95
Stories to Excite You	Anna Forrest/Divine	$14.95
Subtle Secrets	Wanda Y. Thomas	$8.95
Suddenly You	Crystal Hubbard	$9.95
Sweet Repercussions	Kimberley White	$9.95
Sweet Tomorrows	Kimberly White	$8.95
Taken by You	Dorothy Elizabeth Love	$9.95
Tattooed Tears	T. T. Henderson	$8.95
The Color Line	Lizzette Grayson Carter	$9.95
The Color of Trouble	Dyanne Davis	$8.95
The Disappearance of Allison Jones	Kayla Perrin	$5.95
The Honey Dipper's Legacy	Pannell-Allen	$14.95
The Joker's Love Tune	Sidney Rickman	$15.95
The Little Pretender	Barbara Cartland	$10.95
The Love We Had	Natalie Dunbar	$8.95
The Man Who Could Fly	Bob & Milana Beamon	$18.95
The Missing Link	Charlyne Dickerson	$8.95
The Price of Love	Sinclair LeBeau	$8.95
The Smoking Life	Ilene Barth	$29.95
The Words of the Pitcher	Kei Swanson	$8.95
Three Wishes	Seressia Glass	$8.95
Through the Fire	Seressia Glass	$9.95
Ties That Bind	Kathleen Suzanne	$8.95
Tiger Woods	Libby Hughes	$5.95
Time is of the Essence	Angie Daniels	$9.95
Timeless Devotion	Bella McFarland	$9.95
Tomorrow's Promise	Leslie Esdaile	$8.95

Truly Inseparable	Wanda Y. Thomas	$8.95
Unbreak My Heart	Dar Tomlinson	$8.95
Uncommon Prayer	Kenneth Swanson	$9.95
Unconditional	A.C. Arthur	$9.95
Unconditional Love	Alicia Wiggins	$8.95
Under the Cherry Moon	Christal Jordan-Mims	$12.95
Unearthing Passions	Elaine Sims	$9.95
Until Death Do Us Part	Susan Paul	$8.95
Vows of Passion	Bella McFarland	$9.95
Wedding Gown	Dyanne Davis	$8.95
What's Under Benjamin's Bed	Sandra Schaffer	$8.95
When Dreams Float	Dorothy Elizabeth Love	$8.95
Whispers in the Night	Dorothy Elizabeth Love	$8.95
Whispers in the Sand	LaFlorya Gauthier	$10.95
Wild Ravens	Altonya Washington	$9.95
Yesterday Is Gone	Beverly Clark	$10.95
Yesterday's Dreams, Tomorrow's Promises	Reon Laudat	$8.95
Your Precious Love	Sinclair LeBeau	$8.95

Order Form

Mail to: Genesis Press, Inc.
P.O. Box 101
Columbus, MS 39703

Name _____
Address _____
City/State _____ Zip _____
Telephone _____

Ship to (if different from above)
Name _____
Address _____
City/State _____ Zip _____
Telephone _____

Credit Card Information
Credit Card # _____ ☐ Visa ☐ Mastercard
Expiration Date (mm/yy) _____ ☐ AmEx ☐ Discover

Qty.	Author	Title	Price	Total

Use this order
form, or call
1-888-INDIGO-1

Total for books _____
Shipping and handling:
 $5 first two books,
 $1 each additional book _____
Total S & H _____
Total amount enclosed _____
Mississippi residents add 7% sales tax